JOYRIDERS

JOYRIDERS

STORIES

GREG SCHUTZ

UNIVERSITY OF MASSACHUSETTS PRESS

Amherst and Boston

ISBN 978-1-62534-855-5 (paper)

Designed by Sally Nichols
Set in Adobe Freight Text Pro
Printed and bound by Books International, Inc.

Cover design by adam b. bohannon
Cover art by Nancy Friedland, *Roadtripping in My Mind,* © 2023.
Courtesy of the artist.

Library of Congress Cataloging-in-Publication Data

Names: Schutz, Greg, 1983– author.
Title: Joyriders : stories / Greg Schutz.
Description: Amherst : University of Massachusetts Press, 2025. | Series:
Juniper Prize for Fiction | Identifiers: LCCN 2024033087 (print) | LCCN
2024033088 (ebook) | ISBN
9781625348555 (paperback) | ISBN 9781685751302 (ebook) | ISBN
9781685751319 (epub)
Subjects: LCGFT: Short stories.
Classification: LCC PS3619.C4775 J69 2025 (print) | LCC PS3619.C4775
(ebook) | DDC 813/.6—dc23/eng/20240723
LC record available at https://lccn.loc.gov/2024033087
LC ebook record available at https://lccn.loc.gov/2024033088

British Library Cataloguing-in-Publication Data
A catalog record for this book is available from the British Library.

These stories have appeared in the following publications,
sometimes in slightly different form:
Alaska Quarterly Review: "Breeders' Cup"
American Short Fiction: "A High School Production of *Titus Andronicus,*"
winner of the American Short(er) Fiction Prize
Carolina Quarterly: "The Sweet Nothings"
Colorado Review: "To Wound, to Tear, to Pull to Pieces"
Fractured Lit: "Pelican"
The Masters Review Volume X: "A String of Lapis Beads"
New Stories from the Midwest: "You Are the Greatest Lake"
Ploughshares: "Joyriders"
Story: "The Little Flashes"
Sycamore Review: "You Are the Greatest Lake"
Third Coast: "Ten Thousand Years"
Willow Springs: "Not for Nothing"

CONTENTS

JOYRIDERS

When I come to the right place, I believe I'll paint a door on it and walk right through.
— *Sandra Lim, "The Vanishing World"*

IF I NEEDED YOU

Doing eighty, maybe ninety, between walls of dry corn, the Trans Am swerves, catches the shoulder, and flips. The girls in the backseat are both seventeen. They don't know each other well. The boys up front are friends, recent graduates of the local high school. One works on his family's dairy farm; the other's a commuter student at UW-Oshkosh.

Aloft, nobody screams. Nobody makes a sound. They don't even close their eyes.

Connie's the one who crawls from the wreck, the only one who can. Does she have any pain, a paramedic asks, shouting to be heard over the roaring in her ears. Yes, she tells him, her thigh. In moments she's being cut from her jeans. But they find no injury, only a spider of bruises left by the girl beside her gripping down as their headlights crazed into the sky.

She can't remember much, she tells the deputy who asks, tells her parents and her friends. It's true: Connie can't remember the Trans Am stalking the parking lot, halftime, homecoming, the spattering rumble through its glasspack muffler. She can't remember the boy who's dead now hanging out of the passenger window and calling to her, not by name but like she knew all his needs. She can't remember getting in, or the other girl getting in, too, or the look that passed between them: knowing they'd been called, knowing they'd answered, shocked by their own assent. She can't remember her happiness or the exhilaration of escape.

She remembers something astringent passed back in a plastic cup. She remembers the boy at the wheel howling lyrics at the moon. She can still hear the engine's roar. She closes her eyes in bed, and acceleration sinks her into the seat again, waking her with a start. But she hardly remembers the girl beside her, silent as a ghost.

Weeks pass before the other girl, Trish, returns to school. Once, Trish wore her hair in a dishwater drape to the small of her back—from one of those families for whom a woman's hair is God's glory, Connie supposes; apparent, too, in the way she used to skulk the halls with her Trapper Keeper, fluorescent horses on the front, clutched to hide her breasts. In the hospital, though, they stapled her scalp, shaving her head to a soldierly fuzz. She looks older now, her face full of bones, her eyes overlarge.

Those eyes are watching Connie. In the halls, in the cafeteria, in the parking lot after school, she looks up to see the other girl look quickly away. *It was the biggest mistake of my life but also, the one I will learn the most from,* Connie's written in her college application essay, with the gratifying sense she might compact the night down into something small, hard, and unchanging, its meaning contained in the palm of her hand. So it feels unfair to be pursued like this, haunted. She learns Trish's locker number, slips a note into it one morning. *stay away from me you freak.* Her bruises have long since faded.

One dead, two injured, one unscathed. In a community where such things do, after all, happen from time to time, this symmetry encourages a sense of closure. In Madison, Connie gives her Chi-O sisters no clue about what happened. And even though it becomes a story she sometimes tells later, in pharmacy school, at parties, cross-legged atop someone's Formica breakfast bar beside the jug wine, depending on who's listening, on whom she wants to hear it, especially the part with the paramedic, which features her pantsless and invulnerable, she never says somebody died.

Dan, who was driving, has pins inserted into his shattered ankle. He sets off metal detectors on his way to and from his honeymoon in Mary Esther, Florida, where his wife's great-uncle holds a timeshare, and he doesn't fly again after that. The farm is his: its acreage and debts, its 130 Holsteins, its share in the cooperative that operates the local grain elevators. He chairs the cooperative in time—church deacon, lodge trustee of the Elks. But he never forgets the steering wheel slithering through his hands.

On the night the cooperative, overleveraged, files for bankruptcy, he takes the Takamine twelve-string his younger son, off to college, has left behind and carries it out to the milk room. Amid the humid chug of condensers, he picks through the few songs his fingers still recall, titles like fragments of some long-ago fight—"Your Cheatin' Heart," "I Ain't Never," "If I Needed You"—and shocks the stanchioned cattle with the sweet, high voice of his youth.

As her father's long decline grows steep, Trish begins coming home on the weekends, driving up from Milwaukee to give her mother and sister a break. She fears for them. Besides the silences from which he stirs only via his own unpredictable volition, the old man has two moods left: amazement and fear. Both are dangerous. There's still strength in his withered limbs.

He no longer remembers the long years they spent at odds, how he so often said she was breaking his heart, the coolness between them since. She holds his spotted hands until he forgets they're being held. He wanders the house, looking for something, refusing to settle or settling wherever—at any window, in any corner, emptied—and calls her by her mother's or sister's names. But one afternoon, as she reads to him from the Bible, those old invitations to ceaseless love that once meant the world to her—*They forsook all,* she reads, *and followed him*—he barks a laugh and shakes his head. "What?" she asks, but he won't say. He only stares, his features slowly darkening with alarm.

Trish is suddenly reminded of how she used to stare at that other girl, whose name escapes her, all those years ago, thinking she needed someone to share the terror and joy of having learned a life was a thing that could change.

JOYRIDERS

Because nights on the third shift stretch longer than they should, and because sleeping through the day has been giving him nightmares, Jimmy Barnes buys coffee at the truck stop on Sugar Hill Road. He circles the place once before parking. In the big lot out back, tractor-trailers sit aligned, sleeping cabs dark. Between two of the trucks, a figure steps aside, out of the wash of his headlights. Barnes doesn't stop. He's not sure what he's looking for, not sure he'd know trouble if he found it.

Heads swivel when he enters the diner. At a booth by the window, a man chews a corner of his steel-wool mustache. The woman with him eyes the revolver on Barnes's hip, her fleshy face sober as a bulldog's. The kid at the register adjusts the paper hat atop his head. A rind of sweat darkens the folded brim.

"Evening, Officer."

"Deputy," Barnes corrects him. The kid stiffens as if scolded.

When Barnes walks out of the diner, thermos refilled, there's no conversation at his back, just a few stray clinks of silverware, the television muttering to itself like an unhappy drunk. He shouldn't have said anything. Third shift's like that, he's discovered: the world emptied out like an old movie set, the remaining bit actors sleepy and sullen, their parts already played. They have nothing to offer but suspicion.

As he rounds the building to where his Crown Vic is parked by the coin-op air gun, a white pickup with a squalling fanbelt swerves into the lot and skids to a halt at the pumps. A boy springs out, says something to a passenger still inside.

Barnes sets his thermos on the roof of his car.

"In a hurry?" he calls, approaching.

The boy pumping gas looks to be a few years younger than Barnes, maybe still in high school. A narrow chin and pointed nose give his face a sniffing, ferrety look. Seeing Barnes, he forces a grin, tucking his chin like he's trying to swallow something. Cords stiffen in his neck.

"Sorry, Officer. Guess maybe I swung in a little fast, huh?"

"Guess maybe you did. Got somewhere to be, this late?"

The boy glances into the truck. "No, sir, not really."

The girl in the passenger seat is lost inside a sweatshirt the color of blank newspaper. It must belong to the boy. When she sees Barnes looking, she pretends to be fascinated by the price of diesel on the sign. Barnes steps around the rear of the pickup: local plates. In the bed, atop a scrim of old straw, is a pair of wadded blankets, the kind folks wrap around furniture during a move, the kind horny high school kids might spread in the woods for a little padding.

The mustached man and the bulldog woman are watching from the diner. Oxy, Barnes supposes. Or fentanyl, or crystal, or sex: there's a steady trade in these things, in this part of the world, in places like this, at night. Barnes has begun carrying a naloxone kit in his cruiser, but tonight, the night in question, is still back before the worst of it—years ago, now—back when Barnes can still say to himself it can't get any worse, back when he still sometimes believes it. This will be as bad as it gets, he promises. This will be the worst year of his life.

Of course, they could just as easily be an old married couple, those folks inside, watching him now.

The pump clunks off. The boy drags the toe of his sneaker: bashful, frozen, a rodent caught on the centerline by oncoming high beams.

"Go on, then," Barnes says. "You kids just be careful tonight."

A few minutes later, Barnes pulls to the shoulder. Coffee is running down his rear window. For a moment it takes the shape of a hand, fingers reaching, before melting away.

He kicks the door open. The thermos is gone, probably dented in a ditch somewhere. He clicks on his Maglite and combs the roadside weeds. Barnes, Jimmy Barnes thinks, considering himself as if from afar—a skinny young man caught in the cone of deep shadow behind his flashlight, his shoes rapidly losing their shine in the muddy grass—is a fool.

It's because he's tired. Sometimes he wakes in the middle of the afternoon to the applause of talk shows through the duplex wall and, outside the window, the thunder of lawnmowers. In his nightmares, he's always searching for something he needs to find but cannot; waking, he wanders the duplex, still wondering what he's looking for. His life, he supposes. He wanted this job so much, worked so hard to get it. Outside, lawnmowers make perfect swipes across the grass. Watching their patterns, his head soft with sleep, Jimmy Barnes grows sure he's been missing something during his night patrols, something obscene lingering just out of sight. Now he thinks of the boy and girl, the white pickup that pulled from the truck stop, crossed Sugar Hill Road, and climbed the ramp to I-40.

Why take the interstate if you're just looking for a place to spread some blankets?

He runs the plates. The flash of letters and numbers is still with him; he has a memory for images like that.

Registered to Earl Clevis, sixty-two, of Montford Cove Road.

Barnes presses thumbs to his eyes. Clevis could be an uncle, an old father, a young grandfather, a family friend. But more likely he has no idea his pickup's gone. The kids stole it.

Sounding dizzied, as though he were the one just jerked from sleep and not the other way around, Del Carroll calls to say his horse has been shot. Doc Jeffries listens through the rush of his own pulse. The buzzing phone pinned him to the bed—impossible not to immediately fear the worst. He has to remind himself his daughter is still down the hall in her bedroom, safe.

"Say it again, Del: a shooting?"

Del Carroll pants into the phone. "Jesus, Doc, right in the chest."

"You're going to want to stay calm," Doc says, hoping he sounds calm enough himself. "Start at the start. Tell me what happened."

"All I know, Doc, is he's shot and he's bleeding. What am I supposed to do?"

By now, Doc's sitting on the edge of the bed, rolling boot socks up his calves before stepping into yesterday's jeans. His name's Arthur, but no one calls him that. After a few years together, even his wife only ever called him Doc. His daughter Dani opens her door a second after Doc opens his. Her voice is sleepy, vaguely accusatory: "Your phone rang."

"Go back to sleep," Doc says.

"No way." She follows him downstairs and stands at the door to the kitchen while he scoops coffee into a filter. "I get to know who it was."

Spoiling, as ever, for a fight. Like her mother, Dani has a habit of leaning forward as if to invite a blow, chin jutting like a prow. The resemblance undoes him.

"I have to run over to Del Carroll's. Might be a while."

"I don't know where that is."

Only after he's started the coffeemaker does Doc realize he used four scoops, four cups of water. Months after the fact and still he's making the same mistake. The coffeemaker burbles, brewing coffee for two.

"It's past Sugar Hill, honey. Out by Montford Cove."

"No," she says, "I don't know where that is."

"I'll have my phone. You can call if you need me."

Dani makes a face. "I won't *need* you. That's not the point."

So he gives her the address, as if the numbers are what she needs. Marooned with his daughter in this house at the end of a dead-end road, he never knows what to offer her. If he's being honest, she was always more Susan's domain than his—at least since adolescence. Fifteen now, Dani's a mystery, secretive and strange. She hoards her life from him. How was school today? *Fine.* Did you have fun at volleyball practice? *Yeah, sure, it was fine.* Yet she still needs to know where he's going. She makes a show of punching the address into her own phone, which she tucks into the waistband of the cotton shorts she sleeps in as if it's information she needs to keep close.

"What's at Del Carroll's?"

"Someone shot his horse."

"Yuck," she says without force.

"School tomorrow. You should be in bed."

"Well, your phone woke me up."

He caps his travel mug, leaving the pot half full. He'll need more in the morning, he knows. *No exit wound,* Del told him. He'll have to dig for the bullet.

"Who shoots a horse?" Dani asks.

"Honey, I don't know."

"It's just a question."

"Promise me you'll go back to bed."

"Can't," she says with the thin smile that once was Susan's.

Susan and Doc chose this house for its seclusion. You could sit on the front porch all day, gazing out at the staked reflectors where their driveway met the gravel turnaround at the end of the road, without seeing a single car. Doc wants to feel safe now, leaving Dani alone. But he pictures how the old farmhouse will look from the road—the kitchen window's lonely glow, his daughter a shadow smoked onto the glass—and nothing about the image makes him feel safe.

It's natural for her to keep things from him. Doc understands that. For example, he recently found Kools snugged down the pencil sleeves in the front pouch of her backpack. Harmless enough, he thought, and tried bringing it up gently: "Honey, I wish you wouldn't smoke."

There was a fight. With Dani, these days, there's often a fight. "If you ever go through my things again," she said, tasting every word, savoring the opportunity he'd given her to say such a thing, "I'll throw myself out the window. I'll just roll down the roof and die."

It made Doc think of Susan—about whom, three months prior, he'd received a call in the middle of the night: a voice telling him about an accident, a smashed-in car, a body he needed to identify.

In a trailer court up Montford Cove Road, Barnes pilots his Crown Vic past row after row of shoebox shapes, dozens of windows dark as lead. Some of the homes sit atop blocks. One still sits atop the flatbed it'd been brought in on, and though weeds twine the wheels, it looks ready to depart at a moment's notice.

The address for the white pickup leads to a single-wide hidden in a stand of scrub pines and poplars. Instead of a front step, there's an overturned milk crate. Earl Clevis answers the door in underwear and socks, bloated and pale as a dead carp.

"You own a white Sierra?"

Clevis leans out the door and spies his empty driveway. "Oh, hell's bells."

At the center of the narrow, sour-smelling living room sits a child's playpen. Inside, little brown chicks trip and flutter through a scruff of wood shavings and straw. Clevis flops down on the sofa, cheesy gut spilling over his lap. "Quail," he says over the chirping. "Got to raise them indoors until they're old enough to roost, else you're just feeding the foxes."

One of the chicks makes a run at the wall of the playpen and bounces off the netting, landing on its back with its twiggy feet kicking at air. Clevis reaches down and scoops the chick up, righting it. His gentleness surprises Barnes. The chick stares up at Clevis's giant hand, stupidly blinking its oildrop eyes.

"You sell them?"

Clevis snorts. "Course not."

Barnes balances a clipboard on his knee, ballpoint scratching out details. The truck was unlocked, keys on the dash. "Done it that way for years and never was a problem," Clevis adds, bristling at a reprimand Barnes hasn't voiced.

Barnes presses on. "Anything of value inside?"

Some gas money, maybe, in the glovebox. And also—Clevis shrugs as if this were an afterthought, and the self-consciousness of the gesture warns Barnes he's not going to like what he's about to hear—there was a rifle. A bolt-action Marlin .22 that Clevis uses for popping foxes and stoats. It would've been lying across the bench seat, barrel clicking up against a full magazine, when the kids found it.

"A loaded rifle," Barnes says.

Clevis scowls. "Man's allowed to keep his gun anywhere he pleases."

Sleepy, missing his spilled coffee, Barnes feels much the same as he does after waking from a nightmare of searching to a room opaque with sunlight. Could've been under the seat, he thinks, or between the back of the seat and the wall of the cab. Or right there in the bed of the pickup, beneath those wadded blankets. In the playpen, chicks gape at one another in dazed astonishment.

Clevis doesn't know his neighbors. "Wouldn't recognize nobody's teenagers even if I *did* see them," he says. His frowning face sinks into its own jowls. "Which I goddamn well didn't."

When Barnes opens the door to leave, a stray chick dashes from beneath the sofa, passing between his legs and tumbling over the threshold to the grass below. Barnes stoops to pick it up, but the chick flows between his fingers, a boneless bit of fuzz.

Clevis curses. "What are you waiting for? Shoot it."

"*Shoot* it?"

"Fine, then. Fine. Let the foxes eat it."

The chick scurries across the yard and vanishes, swallowed by burdock and spurge. Where does it think it's going? A few leaves quiver, then don't.

Sugar Hill at one in the morning is a clutch of clapboard houses, a gas station, a church. Doc follows the road into the hills. His headlights snake over a doe knee-deep in the waterlogged ditch. In his mirror, she scrambles up the clay bank and springs into the woods. Other than that, he's alone on the road.

The Carroll farm is just a notch cleared from the forest, a small house downslope, a brushy pasture climbing out behind. Kim, Del's wife, meets Doc at the gate. She wears muddy galoshes and a housecoat and looks cold. Doc rolls the window down.

"It's Hunter," she says, pinching the housecoat closed at the throat. "Del and the boys are with him."

"How's he look?"

"You know, I think he'll be okay." She holds up her pinkie. "The hole's just so small."

Doc drives them both out to where Del stands with his sons—redheaded, jug-eared boys who beam Doc with their flashlights as he pulls up. They're chasing one another around, sleepy and excited not to be sleeping, whatever the reason. Kim goes to corral them while Del clasps Doc's hand and says, "Goddamn it, Doc."

Along with their chickens and goats, the Carrolls keep a handful of shaggy mutt horses, runty and tough as mules from grazing on tree bark and dogwood buds. Doc knows them all. Hunter, a dark little gelding, winter coat still scabbing his flanks, lies with his legs folded beneath him. From a distance, his silhouette is a Viking ship, beached and abandoned.

"Where?" Doc asks.

Del touches his own chest.

Hunter aims his long head at Doc, who crouches, watching the horse's ears and lips, the ropy muscles in the neck, waiting for the animal to calm. In the dark, wringing Betadine over his hands, it's easy to let his thoughts wander to a certain stretch of Crab Creek Road between home and the hospital where Susan once worked as an emergency-room nurse. Off a ways, Kim has given up on catching the boys. They're playing flashlight tag, spotlighting one another. The younger one, pinned by a beam, throws up his arms to shield his eyes. The light leaches color from his clothes and skin. He looks like a tiny sopping creature shucked from its shell.

Doc steps into the murky cloud of Hunter's breath. The horse lays his chin on Doc's shoulder like a dancer. It takes a moment to find the wound. Kim was right—just a hole smaller than a dime, a knuckle of flesh bulging like a bitten tongue. The blood, though, is pink, foamy as spit. The tumbling bullet must have opened a lung. Doc runs a hand down the long neck and Hunter chuffs softly in his ear. It doesn't matter whether he digs for the bullet or not.

"Gunshot," he says, postponing worse news for a moment. "Best call the sheriff."

"You sure?"

So Doc shows Del the hole Del's already seen for himself, says, "Right here, entry," and watches Del's face fall as he's trapped into admitting what he's known from the start. Doc thinks of Crab Creek Road again and the tall patrolman who walked him through the scene of the accident a few days after. Here, the patrolman said, speaking from behind the mirrored lenses of his aviators, was the furrow Susan's Camry had plowed through the clay when it had gone off the road. Here was the stand of shorn-off saplings that had overturned the car. Here was the oak that had driven the steering column into her lap.

Del coughs into his hand and stares at his palm as if expecting to find a piece of something there. "Maybe you can tell me, Doc, just why anybody would do this."

Across the pasture, his boys have snapped off their flashlights. They pick random directions and go sprinting through the dark, screaming like bats, pretending to be lost.

Doc's loading a syringe with a solution of sodium pentobarbital when the cruiser starts up the Carrolls' drive, turns at the gate, and creeps across the pasture to park beside his truck. Kim has rounded up the boys by now; they lean against her, sullen with exhaustion.

The deputy's little more than a boy himself, skinny wrists wreathed in hair, Adam's apple balanced above the top button of his shirt like a golf ball on a tee. Could they step to the house a minute, he asks Del and Kim, so he can take a report? He looks everywhere except at the dying horse.

Doc catches Del by the elbow, shows him the needle. It's the law: before he can do what needs to be done, he needs Del's permission.

Del's expression tightens. "Just a minute, Doc, honest to God. Then we can decide." He turns to the deputy. "You said just a minute, right?"

Won't be any easier in a minute, Doc doesn't say. The young deputy glances off into the dark, combing his teeth over his lower lip. Doc's seen this act before—the impatient, studied professional sympathy of officialdom. Doc put a palm to the spot where bark had been peeled from the oak by the nose of Susan's car while the patrolman polished the lenses of his aviators on a chamois square, blinking his pale, red-rimmed eyes against the sun.

In the Carrolls' bright kitchen, Barnes sits at the table and the woman sets a mug in front of him. Instant coffee: chalky, strong. He works up some spit and swallows.

"Kids," the man says. "Right? It's got to be kids."

Barnes hasn't told them about the stolen truck or the rifle he didn't see wrapped in blankets. They'll find out soon enough, he knows, as the investigation continues. For now, other deputies are worrying about those things. There was no reprimand when he radioed in Clevis's information, no time for one, but one will come soon enough. He'll welcome it, in fact. Down the hall, through an open bedroom door, the two boys are whimpering. "Just overtired," the Carroll woman apologized, hustling them off to bed as her husband led Barnes to the kitchen. Still, Barnes can't help but listen now for the soft snuffles, as if each were directed at him.

And then there's the look the veterinarian gave him in the pasture, that brief glare from beneath his shaggy brow—as if the man had known just how easily Barnes could have prevented all of this. A flush had run up the side of Barnes's neck like a wetted finger, and he'd been glad for the dark.

"Probably," he allows.

Every time he tries to imagine it, though, he fails. He pictures the boy bracing the rifle against the frame of the open window, drawing a bead. But what about the girl? He remembers how she hid in the folds of that sweatshirt, unable to meet his gaze. Guilt—that's what that was. Did she ask him to stop, and find herself ignored? Or did she, for some reason, hold her tongue? In any event, there's a gap in his account—between the aiming of the rifle and the squeezing of the trigger—that he can't seem to close. He listens to the dry scratching of his pen as it draws a trail to the end of another sentence. The man and woman are both watching him across the table. "Just a few more questions," he says. But he can't remember what he's supposed to ask next.

"I'm sorry," Doc tells Hunter, whose ears twitch at the sound. Doc rolls the syringe between his palms. The liquid inside is clear. It looks just like water. Mostly, it is. A few silvery bubbles cling to the plastic. He ticks a fingernail against the syringe to burst them, then wonders why he bothers. A shape swims across the Carrolls' kitchen window—Kim fixing coffee or Del flicking a match stub into the trash after lighting a cigarette. Both of them concentrating on the deputy's questions, as though the right answers might seal a punctured lung.

Blood dribbles into the grass. Doc's seen wounds worse to look at, abscesses in flanks he could fit a fist into and from which he's siphoned blood, pus, bits of necrotic flesh. But though they leave puckered scars, those wounds heal. He thinks of Kim holding up her pinkie. Seeing that, Susan would have smiled one of the thin smiles Dani likes to imitate. She told Doc once about a deer hunter who'd been rushed into the emergency room, shot through the kidney by a drunken friend. The bullet hole looked like a hungry mouth, so Susan fed it her thumb.

"I thought it might plug the bleeding," she told Doc that night. "Inside, though, all I could feel were tatters. And I *knew*." When she'd blinked at the man, the man had blinked back at her, as though they were communicating in code.

"You poor boy," Doc says. Then he says, "All right."

He rubs Hunter's ear, soft and firm as felt. The horse is steady. When Doc is, too, he sinks the needle. Thirty seconds later, Hunter lays his head in the grass, and Doc thumbs away the pinhead of blood so no one will see.

Nothing to be done, he tells Del and Kim and the deputy who follows them up from the house. Blood in the lung, suffocation. They make the expected noises. Del should probably know better, Doc thinks. Given time, he may grow suspicious. Then again, he may be grateful.

While Del trudges off for his tractor with the front-loading shovel and Kim crouches by the body, stroking the still-warm shoulders and neck, the deputy follows Doc back to where their vehicles are parked. Doc scrubs his hands with no-rinse soap. The deputy opens the door of his cruiser, folds one leg inside, and stops. Uphill, Del's tractor stammers to life. The deputy rubs the back of his neck. In a tentative voice that curls toward a question in a way Doc doesn't expect, he says, "Guess you see these things all the time?"

Doc looks at him, struck anew by how young he seems, the heavy badge dragging his shirt collar down his neck. Yet there's something careworn there, too—a sickly glow to the cheeks and forehead that reminds Doc of Dani as a little girl with the flu, her face sunk among the pillows. He sat at her bedside, his palm on her pale brow as the shocking, clammy heat of her fever soaked the bones of his hand. He had to play down the panic bubbling up in his throat, covering it with a joke: "Milk fever, no doubt about it."

Her face contorted with fury; she was in no mood for games. "That's what *cows* get."

He managed to laugh, wondering even as he did if he was convincing her.

In bed that night, he couldn't sleep, listening to his daughter's dry, spiky coughs through the wall. His wife squeezed his hand just hard enough to hurt. "It's the *flu*, Doc. You've probably heard of it?" That was Susan: like any good nurse, she knew when to flash her steel. But she was awake, too. She was listening, just like him.

The deputy knuckles the corner of his eye. "Sorry," he says.

Doc, embarrassed by what his own face might have revealed, looks away. "I can take it from here, fax the paperwork tomorrow morning. I know the number."

"Old hat," the deputy says.

"Sure."

In a red burn of taillights, the cruiser creeps across the pasture, wet grass whispering against the undercarriage, leaf springs creaking over uneven ground. Doc takes the empty syringe from his pocket and drops it into a biohazard bucket. Then he returns to where the Carrolls are burying their horse. The sound of the front-loader's hydraulics isn't human, he thinks, but it is alive, a hurt dog's whine. The shovel bites earth.

The realization creeps up on Jimmy Barnes while he's parked along the shoulder of Highway 70, running radar on the semis barreling out of the mountains or gearing down for the long climb toward Asheville. He listens to the sleepy radio chatter, tongues instant coffee from between his teeth, and stews over the night's mistakes, of which there are many. Still, the veterinarian's dismissal stings. *I know the number.*

Barnes had turned to him desiring—he searches a moment—reassurance, perhaps, that what had happened, however awful, wasn't unique. The impulse seems childish to him now as he watches the radar gun's digital readout. Shameful, even. And the veterinarian's reaction, both his words and the distressed look that had passed over his face before he spoke, seems to confirm that judgment.

Daily, after waking and after gulping his coffee, after stepping into the grass-scented afternoon to collect the newspaper that's been sitting on his front stoop for hours—which, more often than not, he tosses without reading—Barnes buckles and buttons himself into his uniform while people everywhere are returning from work, their children returning from school. A gap has opened up between him and the rest of the world, an infuriating inability to understand anything quite as well as he should.

It's while thinking about the veterinarian, though, that he begins to understand what he saw in his rearview mirror, an image captured in the glare of taillights as he guided the Crown Vic out of the pasture. That surreptitious hand in the pocket, withdrawing something: an empty syringe. But full, Barnes recalls, when he first arrived.

The name is there in his report: Dr. Arthur Jeffries. It takes only a minute to call up the truck's registration, which includes an address. The Crown Vic lurches into gear.

The downstairs windows are bright as bullseyes. Dani meets Doc in the kitchen, carrying one of her mother's stoneware mugs. "You took your time."

"Is that coffee?"

Smiling, she tips the mug so he can see the brown mouthful sloshing at the bottom.

"I wish you wouldn't," he says, unable to muster more of a reprimand.

"You made too much," she says. "You always make too much."

He's surprised she's noticed. Her eyes are glassy and dry, fixed upon him.

In the den, the muted television flickers. A bearded man with inky, angular eyebrows brandishes a knife and shouts into the camera—saying what, Doc can't imagine. The man's gestures are sweeping, hysterical. The camera pulls back, and he plunges the knife into a watermelon. A 1-800 number appears over a montage of the knife sawing through tomatoes, loaves of bread, copper pipes. Doc flops into the recliner, feeling foolish for allowing himself to be spooked, yet spooked just the same. He turns the television off.

"I wasn't watching that," Dani says. "I just wanted some company."

She sits on the sofa. Through the window over her shoulder, Doc can see the end of their driveway, the two red reflectors on their metal stakes burning dimly.

"What happened to the horse?"

"It was shot, Dani. It died."

She folds her arms across her chest. "Did you have to kill it?"

It never occurs to him to lie until after he's already nodded.

His daughter hugs her knees to her chest, her shoulders pinching toward her chin, her body tightening around some central knot. He watches her finish off her mother's share of the coffee. It reminds him of married life—how Susan would wait up for him when he returned from nighttime emergencies, drinking the coffee he'd brewed for them both before leaving. "How was it?" she'd ask, never flinching when he told her the truth. He talked about cutting rotten piglets from a sow, piling the pieces in the straw like jigsaw puzzles of animals while the farmer, who would pay with a couple of crumpled bills and a scribbled IOU, jerked his thumb at the dead little things and asked, "Those are still good to eat, right?" And Susan, after her night shifts, could answer with stories from the ER: the mother who'd put her cigarette out in her baby boy's eye, the teen who'd flooded himself with meth and poured himself through a fourth-floor window, the husband who'd notched his wife's nose with a broken beer bottle and then driven her slowly, both of them weeping through an opioid haze, to the hospital. Afterward, Doc and Susan would slip down the darkened hall to peek into their daughter's room. "Sleeping," one or the other of them would say, whispering the word like *Amen*. In their own bedroom, they would lie awake, caffeine twitching in their joints.

In their first days alone together, Dani resisted Doc's efforts at comfort, standing rigid in his arms. With her chin on his shoulder, he could hear the snick of wet eyelashes beside his ear, a sound like a jackknife closing. Her grief was the folded blade, its edge positioned where it could cut only her. But now he sees the phone still tucked into her waistband, and he recognizes—belatedly, and with a wordless sense of having been an absolute fool for not understanding right away—just what it meant: her need to know where he was going, her need for him. It's every bit as simple as that. A wave of gratitude blows warmth into his fingers.

"Darling," he says, rising.

The word surprises them both. He's never called her that before. Dani stares, her expression as blank and frightened as a spotlit deer's.

Just then, a car turns at their driveway. Its high beams cut across the yard and the windows ring with light. Pinned in place, Doc throws up his hands. Dani gasps and springs to her feet. Retreating, she steps around the coffee table, toward him.

Long before he reaches the end of the dead-end road where Arthur Jeffries lives, Barnes can feel himself wavering. He's far from his assigned patrol area, and one incident, one call he can't answer, could mean his job. Does it matter to him, this job? It must. It must still, despite everything: a surprise. The farther he drives, the more acutely he feels the risk, and the harder it becomes to ignore the fact that he doesn't know what he's supposed to do when he arrives. His anger begins to feel untenable, stale, a role he's playing.

But it's not until he turns at the driveway, his headlights raking the front of the house, that the last of his resolve fails him. Through the front window, he sees a man and a woman. Arthur Jeffries and his wife. The wife steps toward Jeffries. Their shapes merge.

Later, lying in bed with his blinds drawn against the light, Barnes will wonder why, after driving all that way, he immediately backed to the road and wheeled about in the direction from which he came. Something about that glimpse, the tidy domesticity of the image. The private moment of affection he wasn't meant to witness. His sudden amused embarrassment.

But why was *that*, in the end—and not wisdom, not knowing better—the thing that turned him around?

In the half-dark, Barnes will roll over, pulling the sheet over his head. Pointless question, he'll decide. Who knows why people do the things they do? Maybe you have to learn to forgive, he'll think—yourself most of all, though you deserve it least—or else you'll never sleep.

In the white Sierra, the girl rests her cheek against the window. Durham blurs by in the dark, sodium lamps suspended like fuzzy tangerines over empty parking lots and gas stations. The boy says something to her. She closes her eyes, pretending to sleep.

The rifle went off in her hands, she half-remembers, half-dreams. Though of course that's not exactly true. The boy was showing her how to hold the gun, how to squint down the sights. He was proud to know these things, she could tell. And because she liked him then—*then*, she thinks, because things are different now—she was eager to prove she was a quick study. There was nothing else to aim at, so she aimed at the horse. "Like this?"

A ten-minute joyride, the boy promised. But then came the gun and the horse, and then the cop at the gas station who scared the boy so badly he drove them straight onto the interstate. "On the lam," he kept saying, until she began to suspect he simply liked the sound of it. He says he's driving them to the ocean, a place to clear their heads and decide what to do next—though surely they'll be caught long before then. Doesn't she want to be caught? Again and again, the horse sinks to its knees. Or would she rather just disappear?

When she opens her eyes, Durham is gone. They're in a land of open fields. Beyond the reach of their headlights, the road just keeps unscrolling.

She wouldn't have thought she was the kind of person who could have squeezed the trigger like she had. Strange, she thinks, how one little thing—an accident, really—can split you from your life so completely. Can throw you in with company you'd never expect. The boy's still talking, trying to describe what the ocean will look like at dawn. Soon the girl falls asleep in earnest. She walks straight into the sea and slips into the depths, where unthinking fish flit past one another in the dark.

Of course it's only someone who's taken a wrong turn. But that step, Doc keeps thinking, that step toward him is what matters. As the car reverses back to the road, its high beams drag a flock of shadows across the walls, and in the middle of all that movement it feels as if he and Dani are the ones moving. They tumble forward through the night.

THE LITTLE FLASHES

I didn't think of myself as lonely before I met Thom, which may be the same as saying I wasn't, not quite, until he came along—that he made me unhappy. Papers had been placed before me; I'd been told to sign and sign. Keys had been deposited into my hand while my fingers still echoed my name. A white clapboard bungalow on Hemphill Street in Ypsilanti, Michigan, three bedrooms, one bath, detached garage, aluminum awnings lidding every window. Starter home, investment: my realtor said it could be worth half again as much in five years. In the meantime, she said, I should make some updates. I wanted white oak cabinets for the kitchen. Thom was the carpenter I happened to call.

"I was a lonely child," I told him, and as soon as I said it, the word drew a line, an arrow through the years, between the child I was describing and the woman I was—ear to his sternum, listening to his heart the way a child, as I recalled, could listen at a locked door for the sounds of the ones who were leaving, the ones who had left her alone.

Thom once saw a man's finger partially degloved when his wedding band caught the spinning chuck of a sander. Like many carpenters, then, he never wore his ring while he worked: "You only need to see a thing like that once." He told me this before anything actually happened between us: it's not as though I was tricked. Large, callused hands, salt in his close-cropped curls. Handsome not in spite of the crooked nose, the knurled ear, but because of them, the strong particularity they imparted.

In law school I'd been married, too, something my husband and I had soon agreed was a mistake. Instead of seeking the clerkship that might otherwise have been mine after graduating, I'd returned home, to Ypsilanti, where'd I'd grown up—though my mother was long dead and my father was living in Surprise, Arizona—to pass the Michigan bar and join the practice of an old friend of my mock trial advisor at a small firm specializing in estate law, a position promised around the time of my divorce, a net in case I needed one. I would not have said I needed one. Yet here I was.

Sometimes I saw people I recognized. In the Kroger parking lot, I helped my eighth-grade English teacher heft a forty-pound bag of Ol' Roy into the back of her Subaru. I shepherded an estate through probate, and the grandson of the deceased turned out to have been on my high school debate team. Sometimes I was recognized. "Didn't know you were still around," the grandson said. He told me about his family, his job down in Dayton with a company that manufactured plastic blanks for credit cards. My old teacher adjusted her glasses when, approaching, I greeted her by name—as though waiting for me to come into focus, as though I were only a blur, perhaps not so different from how I'd appeared in the eighth grade: an unfocused, unfriendly, unloved blur of a girl. She said, "Have we met?"

Drinks sometime, I suggested, around the time Thom finished hanging the cabinets. This was before I learned about the ring— very shortly before. And then came one of those pauses, the hush of impending mortification. He wasn't sure, he finally said, what his wife would make of that. "Well, of course," I replied, "but why would you tell her?" At the time, I didn't think I meant it. It's just that I had to say something, and I come from the school of comedy that believes the best way out is through.

The cauliflower ear was from wrestling, he told me. Third-team all-Michigan in high school, a scholarship to Grand Valley State, but it hadn't worked out: "Partied." He was happier, anyhow, working with his hands. By now things had happened we couldn't take back, and in the same easy tone he told me how he and his wife had separated for six months when their daughter was small, how she'd actually been speaking to a lawyer—he grinned: "Maybe someone like you"— both of them reasoning that if it were going to end between them, it should end before their girl was old enough to remember, and when I asked what the trouble had been, he told me, neither apologetic nor proud but faithful to all the mistakes that had led him this far, that he'd cheated.

Eventually the phone rang: Thom's number. "I was just thinking of you," I said, but it was a woman's voice, asking who I was.

What did I think, she wanted to know next—did I think I was somebody special? I admired her resolve in that moment, her steadiness of voice as she maneuvered into striking distance, waiting to land like a blow news of that past affair, the one she'd outlasted, the one that meant nothing to anyone anymore. Anne was her name. Annie, Thom sometimes referred to her as, though I'd come to believe—already, even then—that his sudden fondness in such moments had to do with the guilt that followed his pleasure at how I made him feel, which meant it was fondness for me, too, that I was hearing, or fondness for me, *actually*. With a feeling familiar to me from mock trial— something like a wrestler's proprioceptive sureness, I imagine, of balance shifting in a grapple—I asked her what she meant. "To the universe," I asked, "or to Thom?"

Dot was his daughter's name—a little girl, seven years old. Now that he was staying over, I heard more about her than before. *Staying over*: I couldn't say *moved in* when he pulled clothes from a duffel each morning. His shaving kit sagged over the ledge above the bathroom sink, as it would have at any motel. His girl was gifted, he told me. "Should see the fat books she reads."

She had sneakers with lights in the heels that flashed with each step; she wore them everywhere. She woke in the night for the bathroom and put on these sneakers just to go down the hall. I knew when Thom woke: his breathing changed. I opened my eyes and his were open, too—looking out the bedroom door, as if waiting for the little flashes.

In the beginning the sex had been good because we were compatible, our pheromones were attuned, we liked the same things and were glad to be able to surprise one another with what we knew or were willing to try, and for all the other reasons one might expect—the danger, I mean, the wrongness, the sin, if you'd like, as well as the freedom that comes from having nothing expected of you beyond this moment, and this one, and this—but now it was even better because when he took me he seemed to want to destroy me, to wear me down to nothing, to make me go away so his normal life could resume, and my job was to withstand all this, enduring and absorbing everything, harder than he was in the end and more permanent than the life from which he'd been thrown. I was still here, holding him after we came. And now, certainly, I was lonely.

Beside him in bed, I watched him watch the hall. "Thom," I said, and he twitched the way a sleeping dog twitches when you touch it. "In the morning," I said, "you should probably leave," and hated myself for that *probably*, for the door some part of me seemed determined to prop open. But I needed to say this, needed to be the one who said it first, who made it my choice. I said, more firmly, "You should leave," and even though he didn't say anything, and it was too dark to see whether he even nodded, the tense few inches between us relaxed, I want to say, warmed by relief and, yes, at last, a kind of love.

One lunch break I walked to the Frog Island bridge and, leaning at the railing, called my father. His new girlfriend answered:

"He's taking his morning swim." He lived in a white stucco complex surrounding a turquoise pool. I'd seen pictures on Facebook. The river swifted brown beneath me, the sun flicking riffles downstream of a snag, as I tried to remember the girlfriend's name. "Is it important?" she asked. Not terribly, I admitted, and afterward I did something I hadn't done in a while: I dialed my husband. I still thought of him as my husband, as though it weren't a generic title from a legal arrangement we'd chosen to dissolve but rather his most intimate name, the name no one could call him but me. Frightening to think I could think this way still. After two rings, a woman's robotic voice began reading off his number, pronouncing each digit separately, as if it had nothing to do with the ones before and after. I hung up before the beep.

Frightening because—well, obviously. Men. Dependence. Shoved to the verges of my own life. Always waiting for something: his attention, his approval, whoever *he* might be at the moment. What I needed was a friend, someone to talk to, but I'd been, I told myself, so busy since moving home: what friends? Sixty-hour weeks, seventy, new at the firm and earning my keep. Somehow I hadn't expected the sadness of the work, the way families could claw themselves apart for what the old friend of my mock trial advisor, long in this business, called their forty pieces of silver. "It'll be better for everyone," he liked to say, when these sorts of conflicts arose, "on the other side." Our job was to get them there. I wondered what this meant in my case. Where was my other side? How could I get there, and what would I find when I did?

My mother, dying slowly and then very quickly, had been too frightened and in too much pain to impart anything I could turn to now as wisdom, and I'd been too young and too certain that what was happening was really happening to me to have attended closely to anything she might have told me in any case.

My parents, too, had been divorced, acrimoniously, a cloud over almost every early memory, and my father—after recovering from the curiosity that had briefly followed his initial alarm at my suddenly increased presence in his life, in his home—had not been cruel or cold but simply elsewhere: neither misbehavior nor overachievement could hold his glance long. There'd been girlfriends, some of whom had taken an interest in me, none of whom had lasted, none of whom I'd wanted much to do with, my sense of loyalty to my mother having arrived too late to do either of us any good.

I would have to start over somehow, here in the small city where I'd begun. When I'd told my eighth-grade teacher I was a lawyer—trying to force myself into focus for her—she'd glanced nervously around, as if some sort of trick were being played. "Here?" she'd said.

Still, it was possible. I had certain advantages: a job that, despite everything, I didn't hate, with income enough to honor my sizable debts plus a little left over besides, as well my privilege in all its various forms, a bungalow on Hemphill Street that promised to deliver that slippery, polysemous word, equity, and kitchen cabinets redone in white oak with soft closes, an entire system of doors and drawers easing themselves soundlessly shut.

Except for this: a knock. The door opened, and there on the front porch, shifting from foot to foot on boards that sagged and creaked because I hadn't yet found a new carpenter, beneath a porch lamp mobbed by moths, stood—well, of course—with his cauliflower ear and graying curls, saying everything you'd expect about loving, about being unable to live without, consequences be damned, et cetera, and if I'm glossing over this part, it's because I had a choice, and despite all my recent intellectualizing, all my high-minded self-analysis and firm resolutions to no longer be that lonely little girl, I chose, in the end, grubby conventionality and my own bawling needs. What I mean is, I stepped aside. I loved him back. I told him so, and let him in.

I had one condition: this time, we'd do nothing halfway. The best way out, after all, was through.

He didn't have to say, "There she is," but he said so anyway—offering one last chance for me to back out of this, probably. He could still drive around the block, drop me off out of sight; I could Uber back to Hemphill Street. But I only nodded. From the passenger seat of his idling truck, I'd recognized her already, and without his help: a little girl in pink corduroy overalls, standing with her friends on the sidewalk outside Eastbrook Elementary, which had been my elementary, after the final bell, and turning now to the familiar truck, here to pick her up as usual, she must have thought, and running over to us—not noticing me yet, and so from moment to moment preserving the contours of an unfractured life—running astride flashes of light.

"No," he'd said at first, of course. "Absolutely not." For the first time, I'd felt sorry for him, though he was perhaps the one person in this whole situation who deserved nobody's pity. He wanted everything, relinquishing nothing. He wanted me on one side of the door, the rest of his life on the other. That little girl listening for voices from locked rooms felt less like my distant past than like someone who was with me now, someone I was going to have to care for if I could. This wasn't a negotiation, I told Thom, squaring myself, lawyerly. These were the only terms there were ever going to be. I was going to meet Dot. She was going to know me, to know my face and name. Because only then would I would be *in*—through the door and on the other side.

She stopped short when she saw me. I opened the passenger door. "Hey, baby," Thom called—sheepish, weak. "It's all right."

But she just stood at the curb, face still. She knew he was a liar. I wasn't sure whether to get out so she could climb in and sit between us or slide over on the bench seat so she could sit by the window, so I did neither at first. I was waiting for her to recognize me, it seemed, as though once having been a little girl lonelier than she was, less loved, perhaps even someone she'd have wanted to help, was more important than now being someone who was here to ruin everything—as though the child I'd been, the one I'd brought with me, could somehow atone for this person I'd become.

YOU ARE THE GREATEST LAKE

We're at the tip of the thumb of Michigan. The sky threatens
sun, so Thom's run to Caseville for groceries. His kayak lies
belly-up in the yard. His waders, latex and neoprene, hang in the
mudroom, smelling sourly of rubber and sweat and preserving
the shape of his legs. In the quiet rental cottage, I put a pitcher
of lemonade in the refrigerator to chill. From the back porch, I
can see Dot in the bay, practicing the dead-man's float. Dot is
Thom's daughter, nine years old.

"I love you," I say.

Distantly, she stirs in the water, as if she's heard me.

The yard rolls down to the lake, grass giving way to pebbles
and shells, pebbles and shells pouring smoothly into the water to
form the firm gravel bottom that Thom says draws bass into the
bay on cloudy mornings and afternoons. I know nothing about
smallmouth bass except what he's told me: a striped bronze fish,
football-shaped, with the slung jaw of a linebacker, that he paddles and wades for, casting. I know that in broken light they rise
from the depths to prowl the bay for crayfish and leeches, mayfly
larvae and minnows. I know the bay is broad and flat as a pan.
A mile out or more, there are shoals where Thom can anchor,
slip into the water, and walk. A hundred yards out, where Dot
is floating, it's only three feet deep. Still, I worry. Thom makes
allowances for her I could never imagine for a daughter of my
own. She's so small.

"Dot!" I call from the edge of the water. "Hello, Dot?"

Dot lifts her head.

I cup my hands around my mouth. "I made lemonade!"

After a moment, her voice comes back to me: "What?"

"Lemonade! Want some?"

No answer. She may not understand; she may not care. Out

in the bay, her body looks exactly like a tiny floating body. I wrap my arms around myself, though it's late spring—the second plague spring, the world fitfully itself in places, though only in places—and warm. I climb the yard and pour a glass of lemonade. It hasn't chilled yet.

"Too soon," I say, just to break the silence. On the porch, I lean against the railing, sipping lukewarm lemonade and watching Dot and waiting for Thom.

Thom would like to marry me, he thinks. I'd like him to keep thinking this, and eventually to believe it. Of course it's not so simple. He and his wife are separated, not yet divorced, though proceedings have begun. It's a process, as I would know. "How do you get over a person hating you?" he asked me once. "Real hate. Like you didn't know you could make a person feel."

I told him I didn't know, and I don't. I don't hate my ex-husband, and I hope he doesn't hate me. We were married for fifteen months, back in law school together—a floating dream, at the end of which we unclasped hands and simply drifted apart. He met the woman he's living with now, and I met—eventually— Thom. I took Thom from his wife.

Tonight I lie atop the stiff mattress in the cottage's only bedroom. Dot's in her sleeping bag on the floor, sweetly snoring. Thom curls like a comma, his hairy back to me. It's not easy— he's a tall man—but I do my best to hold him. The back of his neck smells bluely of minerals, like the lake. When he stirs, I run my fingers through his hair.

"You're a good man," I whisper, not because I believe it, necessarily—we're past the point, he and I, of staking such claims—but because I know it's what he needs to hear.

He's going to lose custody, an adulterer, left to accept whatever arrangements are offered. This is what he fears. Even now, he sees Dot mostly on weekends. He hasn't moved in with me, into my bungalow on Hemphill Street in Ypsilanti, where we first fell in love, or into something else first and then into love, but keeps a separate apartment for himself, for Dot, for the impression it offers to the world—and perhaps also to himself—that he has not chosen for me but simply against the marriage, that throughout the pandemic he has remained committed to his wife and daughter, in a way, podded with them, as people are calling it, shielding them from disease vectors such as strange women. Thom and I are both vaccinated at last. Still, this trip of ours, together with Dot, as the first vacation rentals begin to reopen, feels somehow as secretive, as full of the potential for scandal and hurt, as anything we've ever done.

Thom leans his dreaming body into mine. I am his one regret.

I practice the ugly side of estate law, the parts that get gnashed out in court. It's not so different from divorce, in a way. A central loss—of love, of a loved one—unglues a family, leaving each member to claw for advantage. They take sides, cementing fierce new loyalties. I mouth Dot's name into the back of Thom's neck. It forms an ellipsis: *Dot, Dot, Dot.* Below the bed, she growls sleep at the ceiling. I close my eyes and follow her down, arms open, sinking.

Near shore, the bay is the color of the pines it reflects. The open water is the depthless gray of the overcast sky. Thom rises before dawn. By the time I pour my half of the coffee, he's already stepped into his waders, into the kayak, into the water. I can spot him only by the distant hint of patterned motion against the irregular surface of the bay as he casts. There's no opposite shore here and, for a little while this morning, not even a horizon. Sky and water merge. When I stare too long at the place they should meet, I begin to feel ill. We are at the edge of something vast.

Dot pads into the kitchen, knuckling an eye.

"Good morning," I say.

She doesn't look at me. "Morning."

"Like some breakfast?"

"Huh." She pulls a chair out from the table.

"Would you like cereal? Maybe an Eggo?"

Dot folds her arms atop the table and lays her head down, concealing her face. Her downy hair will soon darken; Thom and his wife are both brunettes. But her scalp is softly, pinkly visible through her hair, and I can't help but hope this never changes. My ex-husband and I didn't have any children. I never thought I wanted any.

"Eggo," she mutters at last.

So I place a frozen waffle in the toaster, heat the bottle of syrup in the microwave, spread a pat of margarine once the toaster spits the waffle, douse everything in the warmed syrup, and set the plate in front of her, along with a glass of milk.

"Fork," Dot says.

I bring her a fork.

"You know," I say, "that looks so good, I think maybe I'd like an Eggo, too. Could I eat my Eggo with you?"

"Huh."

It's an all-purpose sound, the thing she says when she has nothing else to say. Dot often finds she has nothing to say to me. She's only recently stopped wearing a mask in my presence, even in Thom's apartment, treating me, perhaps not inaccurately, as a threat. Does she understand what I've done, what her father has done for my sake? Does she hate me for it? I'm waiting to find out. And while I wait, I make myself an Eggo. We sit across the table from one another, eating our Eggos together.

Around ten, Thom paddles back, boat and body growing as they slowly cross the bay. I watch from the kitchen; Dot watches from shore. She's been lying in the grass, reading *The Black Stallion*—a book I remember from my own childhood, about a boy and a wild horse marooned on a desert island together. I wonder if she's reached the part where the boy gathers moss to feed the horse, or where the horse first pushes its soft nose into the boy's waiting hand. But of course I can't ask her; I wouldn't know how to begin. I keep hearing the ringing falseness of my voice this morning, inviting myself to an Eggo. Meanwhile, Dot's concentration—flat on her stomach, bare feet swaying like seaweed—is complete. She only tears her gaze from the book to look out across the water at the blur of distant motion that is her father, the man I love.

For lunch, I'll make sandwiches.

Ashore, Thom opens his arms. Dot leaps into them, book forgotten in the grass. He carries her up to the cottage.

The fishing's been good: for the first time all weekend Thom's smiling, at ease, pleased with himself. "They move so silently," he says of the bass he has caught and released. "The big ones have this effortless gliding motion, like whales." He slides his broad hand across the table. It becomes a gliding bronze bass, swimming over to the plate of sandwiches, pausing to nip at a pickle spear. Dot giggles. The bass takes notice: Thom's hand tenses, fingers arching. Dot snorts, stifling laughter. Thom's hand darts out at her and she grabs it, squealing, and bites down on one of his fingers.

"Yowch," Thom says mildly. "Let me go, little fish."

Dot releases his hand and beams up at him.

I am amazed at the red toothmarks just behind Thom's cuticle, the saliva shining his nail.

"Do you like your book?" I ask.

Dot's face drains.

"*The Black Stallion*," I say, "was one of my favorite books when I was a little girl."

She studies the bubbles in her apple juice.

Thom takes my hand. His finger is wet. It burrows into my palm and I hold it there, squeezing tightly.

After lunch, Dot becomes a superhero. She drags the garden hose into the backyard, using the trigger to launch jets of water in all directions. "I am the Greatest Lake!" she announces. "I'm made entirely of water!"

Thom sits with me on the porch, placid and happy, his long pale legs splayed in front of him. "Give her time," he says.

"You could help me out a little."

"This *is* helping," he says, watching Dot. "Time is helping. Hanging out. Not pushing things. Just *being*. Just time."

Thom's better at patience than I am. A carpenter, he's spent his life measuring twice to cut once. These days his daughter disappears every Sunday night and he doesn't see her again until Friday afternoon. Deep down, he feels he deserves this. I want us to pool our lives together. One day, he promises. I'm waiting, I say. But I can feel him measuring, measuring, preparing for the cut, and I can't help but wonder which side of the blade I'll be on.

"I can communicate with fish!" Dot shouts, hosing the forsythias.

In her bright swimsuit bottom and drenched, billowing shirt, she appears costumed, streamlined, aquatic. I imagine her slicing through the water of the bay, easy and graceful, a little whale. The image brings an ache to my chest, as if she were swimming away from me. Dot fires water straight into the air and does a stomping, stiff-limbed rain dance as it showers down.

"She hates me," I say.

"Hey." I smell fish on Thom's hands. His lower lip leaves a rim of moisture beneath my own. "She's a little girl," he says. "She hates peas and carrots and fruits with pits in them. She still hates bathtime and the boy at school who put an earthworm in her hair. It's not that way with you. With you, she just doesn't know."

For Thom, this counts as a speech, a performance. I'd like to believe him. A précis of my childhood would include my own parents' unhappy marriage, infidelities, and contested divorce, shortly followed by my mother's early death—ovarian cancer, though by the time it was caught it hardly mattered where it had begun—and after that my father's cool, watery bemusement at my surprise return to his life, an attitude vacillating between half-fond distance and half-distant fondness. But recounting these things to myself has started to feel like being forced to listen to someone else's dull, garish, idiotically eventful dreams. Turn the page, I think.

Dot, at these moments, is who I'm thinking of. Mooning over. This little girl, someone else's child.

Thom slides back into the waterproof skin of his waders, but instead of marching to the lake, he joins Dot in the yard, clomping around in his felt-soled boots. "Fear not!" he cries. "It is I, the Master Angler!"

I stay where I am, happy to go unnoticed. I'm not ready for Dot to make a supervillain of me—the Vector—or else grow suddenly silent in my presence, her face as still as the surface of the bay. Once their game has carried them around the side of the cottage, I step quietly into the yard and pick *The Black Stallion* from the grass—miraculously, it is dry—and carry it inside. Dot has folded down the corner of the page she is on. I'm impressed by the attentiveness of the gesture. In the living room, I turn the armchair toward the window that overlooks the lake and arrange an end table and a floor lamp on either side. I set the book on the end table. This would be a comfortable place for Dot to read. She could look out the window and watch her father fish, if she wanted.

I understand that I am trying to trick her into staying inside, close to me.

At the heavy oak table in the mudroom, I open my laptop and log onto the firm's intranet, where there are always PDFs awaiting me. I remind myself I'll always have my work. Outside, heroes are springing into action. "Dot," I say. Her name in my mouth is round at one end and pointed at the other, a raindrop. My fingers, tapping keys, are a clock.

The next day is Sunday, the end of our long weekend on the shore, and Dot wants to fish. After breakfast, Thom unpacks her small rod and ties a golden hook to the line. The knot he uses is a complicated, twisting thing, his fingers moving faster than my eyes can follow. Along the edges of the yard, he and Dot pry up rocks and rotten logs to gather angleworms and grubs. I watch from the kitchen. Dot is fearless, plunging wrist-deep into dirt.

Today, Thom paddles out into the bay until he's disappeared from sight. I scan the horizon for him, but there's only the endless rolling of the waves. Dot is unconcerned. Rod in hand, she walks the shore, catching tiny fish. I steel myself and approach cautiously, as I might a wild animal.

Dot, however, is aglow with success. She shows me a fish as round and flat as a little tea saucer. "This one's called a bluegill." This may be the first time she has ever spoken to me unbidden, words offered like a gift.

"Bluegill," I say.

I learn that another fish, with the same round shape but prettier, speckled colors, is called a pumpkinseed. Dot pops the golden hook free from the fish's mouth and lowers the fish gently into the water. It darts away, pauses for a moment as if to catch its breath, and then flits farther into the green reflections of the trees where it cannot be seen.

"Pumpkinseed," I say. Dot nods, very serious.

I follow her down the shore, my head empty as a sleepwalker's. I move like Dot, with fluid gliding steps so as not to frighten the fish, and keep my careful distance so as not to frighten her. The clouds feather open; a white sun appears. Dot's hair lights like a lamp. Frowning, she turns to the sky. Looking at her, I see Thom, hip-deep atop a distant shoal, squinting as the light burns his shadow onto the water. UV rays, he's told me, are the problem. They drive the bass deep. Dot rubs the back of her neck. In her mind, I imagine, she follows the fish, sinking down and down. She is the Greatest Lake. Sweat glistens on her upper lip.

"I'm thirsty. Are you thirsty?" I'm thinking of the lemonade in the refrigerator.

Dot blinks up at me, reminded of my presence. I might as well be the sun, spilling my dangerous heat.

"No," she says.

I smile and don't press my luck. This has been a good morning, something to build upon. By the time I've reached the top of the yard, the clouds have knit together again.

For an hour, I try to work in the mudroom, but how can I concentrate on the boilerplate language of quitclaim deeds? The words drift away from me. "Pumpkinseed," I say, picturing Dot's face. I close my laptop and sit in the armchair by the window. Down below, Dot's toes are in the lake.

I'm sitting there, drowsy and warm and contemplating lunch, when Dot screams.

Something has happened. Her small rod bows sharply to the water. Out beyond the reflected pines, a small bright patch of bay turns to froth. A heavy brown fish flings itself clear of the water, crashes down, and flings itself tumbling into the air again: one of Thom's bass. The fish thrashes across the surface. Dot, at the other end of an invisible line, is hooked to it.

I've never heard Dot scream before. There's no ragged tremble of adult emotion, only a high, pure tone that reaches through windows and walls to pluck me from my chair and carry me out the door and down the lawn without my feet ever touching the ground. Still, it seems to take a very long time to arrive. "I'm here," I keep shouting, lying, "I'm here," but by the time I finally reach her, it's over: the bass has torn the rod from Dot's hands. She stands open-palmed and shaking.

"I was pulling in a little fish," she gasps. "And then this bass came up and—it *took* it."

Thom, I'm sure, patient as he is, a carpenter who builds things piece by piece until at last they stand complete, would know the right thing to say now. But I'm not Thom. I'm nobody's parent, and lately it seems to me I've hardly ever known how to understand myself as anybody's daughter. The bay is empty, and I'm dry-mouthed with love. So I leave my sandals on the shore. The water is cold; my skin prickles. My hands trail in the water. The pebbles are smooth beneath my feet, the broken shells sharp as teeth. I find Dot's rod and draw it, dripping, from the bay. The bass is gone. At the end of the line is only a tiny fish, fins stripped and body crushed, a golden hook fixed to its cheek like a pin. A pumpkinseed.

The red gills flex. I feel little muscles pulling against my palm. The mouth opens and closes as if trying to speak.

"Let it go." Dot's voice is small. "Let it swim away."

"Dot," I say, "I can't."

I mean that it's too late now; the damage is done. I can't stitch torn fins, affix lost scales. When I pop the golden hook free, it leaves a hole I can't close.

"No," Dot says, as if I've misunderstood. "It needs to swim away now."

"I'm sorry," I say.

Her eyes wash over me, the dying fish in my hand. She pins elbows to ribs, fists to thighs, as if she were the one being squeezed.

"I'm sorry." Spoken at last, the words keep bubbling up unbidden. I'm a primed pump, spilling stale, wet, mineral-scented regrets. "I'm sorry, Dot, I'm sorry, I'm so sorry."

Her reflection wavers in the water a moment.

"Huh," she says.

She boils up to the house.

The yard is empty; Dot is gone. The windows of the cottage are filled with the bay. I clutch the tiny body because I cannot bear to watch it float away. Against my palm the little muscles pull, and pull, and pull, and stop.

A scream must carry a long way over water: already there's a flicker of purpose out there, slowly assembling itself into Thom. I wait for him on the shore. Dot waits in the house.

"What is it?" The lake streams from his waders. "What happened?"

"Oh, boy. Thom, I don't even know." My breath keeps galloping. "If I could've saved it, if I could've made it better somehow—" A rising wind blows waves up the beach, plastering my hair across my face no matter how I try to shake it away. "'I'm so sorry,' I kept telling her. That was all I kept saying."

Thom takes my hands and tells me—reasonably enough, accurately enough—there was nothing else I could have done. "You have nothing to be sorry for," he says.

"But I *am* sorry," I say.

I look at him until he understands.

"We," I say, "are the worst thing I've ever done."

The wind plucks the bay into curls. Thom raises my hands to his mouth. We must smell the same now: algae and mucus and minerals, the wet scent of fish.

Yeah," he says. "Yeah, I know."

After a quiet lunch, we pack our bags and clean the cottage. It starts to rain. The wet lawn shivers. The lake steams into the air.

Thom checks the forecast again. "Better leave now. It's only going to get worse."

Dot turtles her heavy backpack out to the car. We've said exactly nothing to one another since our exchange on the shore. I straighten the living room, returning the armchair, end table, and lamp to their original positions. *The Black Stallion* is still where I left it yesterday, the same page folded down, untouched.

Thom leans inside. His pickup is idling in the driveway, kayak complexly lashed into the bed. "Ready?"

"Almost."

I pour the lemonade down the sink.

In the narrow backseat, Dot sleeps. Her mouth moves stickily, making big and little Os. Driving rain skins the windshield; Thom leans low over the wheel. "Pull over," I say. "We can wait it out." But he shakes his head. We both have work tomorrow, and he has to return Dot tonight. He'll drop me off at my bungalow on Hemphill Street, and then he'll take Dot home. It occurs to me we haven't said whether he'll come back to stay with me after that, or whether he'll go to his apartment instead. I don't want to bring it up. I'll have to wait and see.

The storm brings early night. The tires hiss. I begin to feel ill. It's the loss of horizon again: sky bleeding into water bleeding into sky, nowhere to fix my gaze.

"I need to get in back," I say.

After Thom pulls to the shoulder, I get out. The rain soaks me in an instant, cold through my clothes, as if I've waded in again, or plunged overboard. In the back of the pickup's cab I am sodden, dripping, leaning away from the little girl snoring beside me. Just now, I'd do anything not to disturb her. "Try and get some sleep," Thom says. And even though this doesn't seem possible, it happens. A long day, a long weekend, a long few years. As the heater breathes over me, my skin begins to steam. I close my eyes and sublimate, drifting to the ceiling. From some-where far above, steaming, I touch Dot's hair. The fine strands mat beneath my fingers, revealing delicate pink scalp. My hand slides behind her head. My heart pops like a cork. Thom pilots a submarine through the rain. We are sinking deep. I cradle Dot's head as if she were my own. Little fish, I say. And she turns to me now, she recognizes my soaked and shining body costumed with water, and she calls me by the name of her hero.

Thom touches my knee, waking me. We've stopped. He says, "It's time."

A HIGH SCHOOL PRODUCTION OF
TITUS ANDRONICUS

She was Alarbus, dragged offstage to be dismembered. She had no lines, but at least got to thrash in the arms of her captors and offer, from the wings, a piercing scream. "Bloody murder," the new drama teacher said, the first of his two notes for her.

At the Peace and Purpose House they couldn't go inside but instead sat out on the patio, at a cement table where potted geraniums sprouted through twisted butts. Her mother joined them there, all luminous eyes and wispy silences, glancing to the windows as though they were being watched. Her hands swam to her lips as she smoked or to conceal a smile. She never smiled when she should've. "She could get a pass and come see us if she wanted," her father remarked once, bitterly, on their way home. "But she don't want it."

Human sacrifice, cannibalism, mutilation, rape: "Sounds nasty," her brother said when she told him about the play. He'd called long-distance from Camp Lejeune—calling just for her, as he'd never done before. "Hey, how you holding up?" She might've asked the same thing. The fall of '97, another buildup in the Gulf: she kept waiting to hear he'd been deployed.

Sad-dam, her father pronounced it, with a hard *a* and an emphasis on the first syllable. "Means dog in their language." But recently his face had begun reminding her of the one on the evening news, mustachioed and heavy-lidded, the rundown handsomeness of strength gone to seed. He managed the deli and seafood counters at the Food Lion—tipped back in his recliner now, pushing stoppered snores at the ceiling while she did homework in the kitchen. The refrigerator was packed with leftovers from supermarket cold cases. Grease had congealed in the hood of the range; shrimp tails and chicken bones gleamed in the trash. The snores hitched, buckled, dropped into silence. She paused her pencil, waiting to hear him breathe.

After school, cast and crew mixed gallons of blood from Kool-Aid and corn syrup, hammered together a tilted platform to be placed atop the stage. This was where the killings would occur. Gore was to stream toward the audience. The new drama teacher wore a porkpie hat, brown felt with a brown silk band. Sometimes he took it off as he lectured, turning the brim in his hands, tonsured gleam at his crown. Other times he sprang about, liquidly athletic, reciting Shakespeare's stage directions: *Enter Titus like a cook.* "So he's literally dressed as a chef when he feeds her sons to her." No catharsis here, no suffering trans-figured into art, only bloody farce. "Seventies grindhouse meets Buster Keaton," he said, "just as the Bard intended." And though she understood neither reference, she felt some mysterious permission being granted. Her lungs loosened in her chest.

"I'm going to be in a play," she said. Her mother nodded, smoked, didn't smile. For a time that fall she'd stopped smiling com-pletely, stopped speaking, stopped eating, stopped getting out of bed. Then came the Peace and Purpose House. Now when she smiled, she wouldn't say why. The cement table was warmer than her mother's hands. She went to see *Titanic* but missed everything after Rose let go and Jack slipped beneath the waves. In the bathroom she spluttered over a running sink, Celine Dion swelling through the wall. She couldn't explain afterward to her dazed and jubilant friends just how much she'd hated the movie, how pretty it tried to make everything, how it wasn't that kind of story.

Backstage at rehearsals, her castmates bit down on spare squibs, chewing bloody-mouthed through all of the best lines:

> Oft have I digg'd up dead men from their graves,
> And set them upright at their dear friend's door,
> Even when their sorrows almost was forgot . . .

Years later, she saw the man who'd been the new drama teacher on a slushy February sidewalk outside a West Asheville bar. Alongside another man, he came toward her in the dark, wearing a long wool coat, a houndstooth scarf, and the hat by which she knew him. Shuffling on salt, she veered his way. She wanted to say it had helped her to scream. She wasn't sure this was true, only that those sounds had been all she'd had. But she must have appeared merely drunk—which she was—and oblivious: the men parted around her. Their intimacy crackled over her own skin as they passed.

Her brother reenlisted after 9/11 and was eventually caught in a roadside blast on the highway between Ramadi and Habbaniyah, in the aftermath of what was being called the Surge—a victory—in a sector that had been declared pacified, safe for travel. They'd hung Hussein by then; her father had sent a link to a video of the body swaying. Repulsive, she'd said. Butchers deserve what they get, he'd replied. Later he went into the hospital, his heart leaking, furiously panting as though a rope were tightening around his neck, too. "In Jesus' name," her mother prayed, her hand to his chest, shortly before the end. She'd returned long ago, but Christ and the hollow between her palm and his heart were the most she had to offer anymore. Choking beneath the respirator, her father chewed for air. Her brother had his leg sawn off above the knee.

For three straight Fridays, twice on Saturdays, and again on Sundays, she'd twisted and spat at the centurions who dragged her away, and in the darkness off stage-right, where no one could see, she'd uncorked howl after howl. Act 1, scene 1: her job was to let everyone know what was coming. Minutes before curtain on opening night, the new drama teacher called her over, offering his second note. "Remember," he said. "No one is coming to save you."

TEN THOUSAND YEARS

Carter lived with another woman before Claudia, but that was another life, decades ago. She's barely a memory anymore, that spooky girl with her delirious grin. Andrea: pronounced, she insisted, with a swooping emphasis on the second syllable. And-*ray*-uh. They lived in a mobile-home development over in Wausau.

A mobile-home development over in Wausau. This is the language Carter uses at meetings in the basement of First Presbyterian. They were bad for each other, he says, pausing to sip decaf from a Styrofoam cup. It was worse than being young and stupid, he says. They fed off one another.

One night, they were plinking an old Buick in the woods behind the development with a .22 rifle. Carter was strenuously drunk. Andrea, six months pregnant, was simply herself. When he handed her the rifle, she turned it on him. "Stick 'em up!"

It seemed like a joke until she fired. The bullet burrowed into the sky behind his head.

Below her shirt hung a sliver of belly, a pink grin.

"What did you say?" he asked.

Laughter sat them both in the grass.

When Andrea's father came to the trailer, she barricaded herself in the bedroom. There had been some falling out between them; she'd never explained. In any case, the father pounded on the front door, demanding to see his daughter. Eventually, he began to weep.

"My baby," he called. "My darling little girl."

Carter opened the door holding an empty fifth. "What would you like?" he remembers saying. "Like me to bust this across your face?"

"You'll never live down what you're doing," her father called out, on his way back to his car. "Not in ten thousand years."

Later, Andrea emerged, slick eyes downcast. It was impossible to guess how she felt.

At the meetings, Carter can smile at the bullet that nearly killed him. He can laugh, describing how they laughed. He's allowed this ridiculous tenderness; the years have come down like a gate. As long as that tenderness turns, by the story's end, to remorse.

Their son was born, Brady, miraculously whole. Carter loved him. A sloppy, overfull emotion, always threatening to spill. When Brady wailed, Carter wailed, too. When Brady raged—rigid, snorting tirades against hunger, filth, neglect—Carter made fists. Clutching Brady to his chest, he stumbled around the trailer.

"Carter! Carter, you're crushing him!" Andrea cried, wresting the child away.

Her love was different. It transformed her. Even now, this hardly seems possible. She became a mother all at once, without deliberation or transit. Her final trick, the one she'd been planning all along. Even her name changed. She began calling herself, as her parents did, *And*-rea. She began calling her parents.

Andrea and her parents on one side, Carter alone on the other. In Carter's arms, Brady stiffened, his red face clenched. It wasn't as if he were afraid; it was as if he were indignant. As if Carter had no right. "Why?" Carter asked the child, squeezing.

Finally, when their son was a year old, Andrea and Brady left.

There was no marriage to dismantle, no lengthy courtroom process or lingering contractual stain. Her parents came to get her. Carter hasn't seen any of them in years. Still, Andrea's name comes up sometimes, particularly when he's over in Wausau. She married a man from her parents' church, he's heard. She, her husband, and her parents have all moved down to Florida. She and her husband have a family, three children of their own in addition to Brady, all raised together under one roof.

Carter wishes them well. He's happy for them.

He's found a happy ending himself. He got help, got sober, got into heating and plumbing. He's a homeowner now, a citizen, sole proprietor of a successful small business. In the basement of First Presbyterian, he tells his story to applause.

He lives in a rancher at the edge of town. Beyond the backyard is a cornfield. The fields stretch empty all the way to Green Bay. Silage corn sprouts in stiff green rows, thickening and twisting, turning brown. On autumn evenings, Carter rests on his back stoop with a can of cream soda, listening to country-western radio and watching combines drag the fields, corn crackling in their combs. The world dwarfs him, providing perspective.

He senses the workings of a higher power, out there in the fields.

It's not a bad life. Certainly not lonely, the way some people— the ones who feel compelled to mention Andrea, for example— seem to think.

Claudia has crooked pinkies that pain her in the cold and a long, classical face he's heard people describe as handsome. Several months in, her presence in the rancher continues to surprise. He wakes in the night: there's Claudia. She puffs heavily through sleep, a marathoner. The mattress sinks beneath her body. Like a moon, he wants to roll toward her.

She's a social worker, state-mandated counselor to victims and perpetrators of domestic abuse. Last summer, she attended a meeting at which Carter spoke. She does Al-Anon herself—her father was a drunk—refers clients to the program sometimes, and sits in on the occasional AA meeting. Carter had seen her at meetings a few times before, hadn't realized she wasn't a drunk herself. In the parking lot, she caught up with him.

"Thank you." For telling his story, she meant. "It gave me hope."

Hope for what? She didn't say. It surprised him. He told his story mostly because he felt he ought to, periodically. It was expected of him. He expected it of himself. Everything, that blue evening, seemed to be covered with a fine layer of dust, as if drawn long disused from a drawer. She gave him a card: her name, LMSW. Her phone number. He waited a few days before calling.

"I'll cook you dinner," she said.

She coaxed a daube from his cramped galley kitchen, filling the rancher with the earthy scent of beef, mushrooms, onions. The windows silvered. Heat pasted little bouquets of ringlets to her temples. The daube arrived bubbling inside a glazed iron casserole.

Later, during sex, he felt her attention lift away—floating above the bed, observing them both from a distance.

"There," she kept saying, "there," as if comforting him.

Claudia could be perturbed but never angered, unsettled but never surprised. Week after week, she made plans for them. He found himself comfortably rolled up in another's cause. At the same time, he was reminded of his weaknesses, defects of character he could bury but not redeem. Days without her turned impenetrable, ominous, vaguely evil. Maudlin sentimentality eroded the edges of his thoughts. Nights alone in the rancher, he snapped on the police-band radio scanner he'd ordered from a catalog years ago. A soothing habit: conversations parsed into numbers and code, invested with purpose and power. The bed smelled like Claudia. He listened until he slept.

Her lease over in Wausau was expiring. "Live with me," he said.

Claudia pressed her lips together. "Let me think about it." The next morning, she agreed. It was not as if he'd come up with the idea himself. He'd merely anticipated her.

Here they are, then. The wind burns into the shingles. *Love* isn't a word he cares to use. Still, it's a kind of life together, more than he'd come to expect. Outside is a world sketched in charcoal. Trees drag low clouds to tatters. Snow dribbles down. Deer wander in from the fields at night, slipping along icy streets to strip birdfeeders from branches. Every morning, Carter pilots his van past the tiny, colorful wrecks.

Toward the end of January, he receives a confused call.
"The metal things are cold," a young voice says.
"The metal things."
"The ones in the corners. They're supposed to get hot."
"The radiators."
"Yeah. They're cold. We got ice inside our windows; it's bad."
The address leads him into the fields. One of those failed farmettes, Carter thinks, the cropland long ago repossessed and auctioned, split into tracts for housing developments that were never begun. A black-roofed cottage, a huddle of ruined outbuildings, a windbreak of rattling poplars. Ice veins the drive, unsplintered by tires. An ancient Vanagon tilts in the yard, heaped with snow.
Carter knocks.
"Who's it?" the young voice asks.
"Greeley's Heating and Plumbing."
"Oh. The furnace guy."
The deadbolt shucks loose. The door peels open. A boy stands there, black curls parting around the white stone of his face.
"The metal things are cold," he says.

This is Preston Tanner. He tells Carter's he's nineteen, but he looks younger, sitting on the basement steps with his socked feet one atop the other while Carter inspects the furnace. There's a girl, too. Carter's afraid to ask her age. He saw her on his way to the basement: doughy doll's face, elbows lost in rosebuds of loose skin, enormously pregnant. The subterranean air clings like cellophane. Condensation has clogged the furnace's fuel nozzle. Carter waves the boy over. "Watch." He cleans the nozzle, reinstalls it, restarts the burner. The boy's blank face might suggest concentration, boredom—anything at all, really.

After a minute, warming water clicks through the pipes overhead.

"You saved us, man," the boy—Preston—says. "All three of us, you know?"

Carter frowns, fitting his screwdriver to the starred eye of a screw, reattaching the access panel. "Just remember what I showed you, this happens again."

"Sure, man. Cake."

Upstairs, beneath the rotten plaster arch connecting kitchen and den, he shakes the boy's soft hand and folds into his wallet a check he's sure will bounce. The girl hasn't moved. She lies atop the sofa, swollen feet slung over an armrest. Figures on the television wander a blaze of static, calling out in garbled barks.

"When are you due?" Carter asks.

She heaves onto her side. Her voice is as high and petulant as any little girl's. "Far as I know, never."

"Lily's just ready for it to be over," Preston explains.

At dinner, Claudia makes a face. "That's sad."

"Sad." It's not the word he wants.

"Well, what would you have me do?"

"I didn't say anything."

"You don't have to. You look like Droopy Dog."

"Sorry," he says.

That's all they say at first. Claudia has made Swiss steak with pearl onions, carrots, and winter squash. The onions lie translucent in the juice, feathered open. The meat flays itself across the tines of his fork in delicate brown strings.

Years ago, nailed to his bed by sobriety, Carter memorized psalm after miserable psalm. *Great are thy tender mercies, O Lord: quicken me according to thy judgments.* These days, the words bring a metallic taste to his tongue. Still, he can't keep them from bubbling up: *He leadeth me, He leadeth me,* timed to the beat of his pulse. He survived those first weeks by doing nothing, being led, waiting each moment for the moment to pass.

In the weeks following his visit to the farmette, he finds himself whispering verses again. Sometimes he listens to the police-band scanner as he drives.

Once, as part of the program, he wrote a letter to Andrea, asking forgiveness. *I do not know how I can but if you tell me how I will do my best to make amends.* She was gone by then, down to Florida. He had no address, so he drove to Wausau to deliver the letter to the minister at the church she'd attended. In the minister's wood-paneled office, Carter sat with his hands in his lap while the man looked him over. Leaded glass carved the sun into blocks. The minister wore a suit of dark wool. When he inclined his head, heavy light poured over his shoulder, obscuring his face except for a fringe of beard and the band of deep shadow beneath his brow that marked the hollows of his eyes.

I know I have done wrong but he is my son too even if he is yours alone in the eyes of the law. I hope you will find it in your heart . . .

In that office, with his head lowered, powerless to meet the minister's gaze, Carter began to cry. It was not an act of release. It was a newer, deeper humiliation, a heat that came over him.

He never heard back from her. He doesn't even know if the minister mailed the letter.

But surely *God is good to Israel, even to such as are of a clean heart.*

Claudia can tell something's wrong. "Your face moves when you think."

Caught mouthing psalms, he turns away, spitting his toothpaste. In bed, he douses the lamp without a word, and Claudia sighs through her nose. Carter gives her his back. It's not that he takes pleasure in disappointing her, in opening this small hurt. It's just that he's confused. He needs time to appraise his feelings before he talks.

But in the middle of the night, he rises suddenly out of sleep. Claudia breathes deeply, blasting through a backstretch

of dreams like a thoroughbred, and in the brief twilit clarity
before all the lights in his head come on, Carter understands
how the urge to roll over and loop his leg through hers is a
hunger that leaves him beholden. For just a moment, it's an
impulse worth hating.

In the morning she's up before him, grinding coffee. Snow blots
the windows. He moves with a sluggishness similar to hangover,
a sense that he's only alive at his core. His body is a collection
of distant, icy extremities. He pours cornflakes, listens to the
cereal crackle in milk.

Claudia sets a warm mug in front of him. "It's not those
kids, is it?"

He looks up sharply. How does she remember? No, of course
she remembers. It's her job to make these connections, after
all, and she knows his story. For the first time, he feels himself
the target of her shrewd professional interest.

"Because there's really nothing you can do," she says.

At the end of the month, a surprise: the boy's check clears.
Through the jeweler's loupe he uses for fly tying, Carter scrutinizes the bank statement's miniature copy. The name in the corner isn't Preston but Duane Tanner. A Wausau address. Claudia's
watching a nature program in the other room. A lioness sprawls
on a rock, gazing with sun-drenched disinterest at a herd of
springboks while the rapt Scottish narrator pursues his busy
exegesis. Carter closes the door and dials.

A man answers. "Yeah."

"Mr. Tanner?"

"Who's this?"

"Carter Greeley, Greeley's Heating and Plumbing. I recently
did some work for—I suppose it was your son, Mr. Tanner?"

"Yeah, what? Little retard stiff you on the bill?"

"No, no, nothing like that. The check, though, was in your
name, so I guess I just wanted to confirm—"

"Gave him some blank checks. Yeah. There a problem with that?"

"No, Mr. Tanner, no. I'm just calling to confirm payment from your son and—his wife?"

A pause.

"Think you spotted something?" the voice says.

"Excuse me?"

"Think you spotted something unusual? Something unusual about my family?"

Carter grips the phone. "You tell me, Mr. Tanner."

"*Mr. Greeley.* You call me to talk about my family, Mr. Greeley, Mr. Carter Greeley? That's your name, right? Yeah, that's your name."

"Greeley's Heating and Plumbing," Carter says. "You can look it up."

"Yeah," the voice says. "Yeah, yeah, yeah."

Carter hangs up.

He sees the thick fingers working the phone, pulling up his website, yellow smear of overgrown cuticle, red crease of a hang-nail. He hears a beater pickup roaring to life.

Let this be true. Let the father be coming for him.

The fields cast blue light into the room. Eventually, Carter sets his phone on the desk. His fingers have left damp marks on the plastic case. Evaporating, the marks look like fingers, then feathers, then nothing at all.

Beneath the church, Carter rises and speaks, a ritual he hopes will steady him. Instead, it raises questions. Would it be unfair, for example, to ask what the point is? Would it be ungrateful to wonder what he gets from it anymore? Always the same fond, self-effacing laughter, the same mousy groans of commisera-tion and disgust, the final plaudits rising like a flock of startled pigeons. He nods to the familiar faces and tops off his decaf for the drive home. It's snowing again. A small ghost flickers over the

Styrofoam cup. He climbs into his van and starts the defroster, waiting for a fan to open in the fronded glass.

There's something postapocalyptic about the whole arrangement. A higher power intervenes; the past is buried in snow. You're left to beg forgiveness for all you can't repair. You offer to make amends, but if those offers go unanswered? You can never go back—it's over. You can never do the one thing that really matters. *Not in ten thousand years.*

But Carter has begun to imagine a different life. A door has opened, revealing a darkened room. He puzzles its dimensions dimly, wondering what he might find. It's clear, at least, that the space hums with powers long ago abdicated.

On his street, houses slouch like bunkers. Deer tracks trail across a yard. The impulse to return to the farmette is ridiculous, even dangerous—Carter understands this. Didn't he believe, every time he squeezed his son's wet face to his chest, that he was saving him? He pulls the key from the ignition. Soft plosives of snow overspread the windshield. The kitchen window pours light into the yard: Claudia. She spins him in an eddy of contradictions. She doesn't feel like a new presence in his life. She feels like something he lost, but found again.

Several times over the years he has approached a backslide like this, always managing to turn away in the end. He crosses the yard, buoyed by a giddy sense of threat. Claudia's voice greets him from the kitchen. He smells the white beans and duck confit in her cassoulet as he pries apart the frozen laces of his boots. He is not merely happy but shaken, not merely excited but desperate. A third helping only sands down the edges of his hunger. Across the table, Claudia assesses him with a flat, mathematical gaze. This look has grown familiar in recent weeks. He's a latched case; she's searching for the hinge.

He escapes to the den to build a fire. At the tip of a match, he scratches to life a wet orange drop and touches it to a twist of paper. The flame drips up the edge of the crumpled page and disappears into a crease, where for a time it remains hidden, smoking furiously. Just when it seems extinguished, it reappears all at once: a small fire teetering atop the kindling, lengthening as it spins, casting a glassy ball of heat. Carter feeds it logs.

"Carter." Claudia crouches beside him. "Talk to me. Please."

He smiles. It's as if he's peering through the wrong end of a telescope.

She brings his hand to her lips and sinks her teeth into his knuckle.

He grabs for her.

They spread pillows and blankets in front of the fireplace, a nest. Then she trips him, her eyes bright. She brings him to one knee and rolls him to the ground. She's much stronger than he expects. Their teeth click together. His arms are pinioned within his sweatshirt. Freeing them, he hears a seam pop. Claudia works the buttons of her blouse. Her face in the firelight is angular and drained. In the end, he presses a knee between Claudia's thighs and she guides him inside, where he comes so quickly he laughs, flushed with embarrassment and pleasure.

She touches his cheek, trying to turn him toward her, but there's no force in the gesture and he buries his face in her neck until sleep moves over him, the shadow of a wing. He wakes in a tangle of blankets, soft ropes. Claudia is gone. The fire has collapsed into a riffled pool from which rise the wrecks of charred logs. But heat still emanates from the ash.

The deer skitters into Carter's headlights and stops, pinned by the beams. The brakes lock. The van slithers forward on a carpet of slush. For a moment, Carter sees everything clearly. A yearling. The head swivels to face him. The white tail goes up.

At the last possible instant, the deer springs out of the way of his van and into the path of an oncoming car.

He meets the other driver in the middle of the street, in the shared strobing of their hazard lights. For some reason, they shake hands. It's the middle of town, a street of shops, a law office, a credit union. "Where'd the bastard come from?" the man wants to know. He has a loose red face. "I'm telling you, he came out of nowhere." The corner of his hood twists inward like a bitten lip. One headlight is blacked out. Carter follows a smeared brown trail through the slush, up the street, behind a parked car.

A small whitetail, haunches twisted and hind legs splayed bonelessly behind. Storefronts gaze blankly down. The stoplight at the end of the block turns yellow, then red, the crosswalk indicator chirping to no one. Above the body floats the faintest slick of steam. The other man calls his insurance agent and the police department, the gears that must mesh in a situation like this. Beneath verdigris-scented blood, Carter can just whiff the living deer—richly pungent, like black loam. He strokes the felted triangular head, fluted bones narrowing toward the nose. It doesn't react, doesn't even blink.

For years, he's carried a mental map to every liquor store in the county, the location of beer and wine in every gas station and grocery. Only occasionally does the knowledge rise to break the surface of his thoughts.

He is less than two blocks from the nearest liquor store.

Looking back, Carter can see the crumpled body. His boot prints up the snowy walk connect him to it. He opens the door. The overhead sensor emits its two-tone cry.

O spare me, that I may recover strength, before I go hence, and be no more.

The world elongates to the point of stasis, a series of moments he's dropped into from above. Crossing the kitchen takes an eternity; lifting the Dutch oven full of leftover cassoulet takes another. Carter remains patient. Golden light suffuses everything. He understands his sacrifice. The whiskey is something he'll pay for, perhaps for years. But it's worth it. "It's worth it," he says. Speaking takes an eternity.

Outside, the cold snaps him half a step back to himself. He shifts the heavy casserole, unlocks the van, and places the dish on the passenger seat. Claudia is working late. If he hurries, he can deliver this meal to the farmette, return, shower, and crawl into bed before she arrives. Tonight will remain a secret. At best, it will sit between them, invisible, possibly poisonous. This, too, is part of the sacrifice.

A warm meal in the farmette kitchen, the three of them sitting down together. No, four: the baby bounces on Carter's lap. He dips a finger in the rich, dark sauce, and the baby's mouth opens. He touches food to the little tongue. He will say something next. He will tell them all they need to know. The van roars, heater blasting. In the farmette kitchen, Carter reaches for words, but the hot marbles keep skittering through his fingers.

As he backs from the driveway, he turns on the police-band scanner. It's unbearably lovely: everything codified and condensed, every request simply made and immediately answered, each call and response crystalline and perfect.

"Please copy."

"Copy."

Tears spring to his eyes.

A mile outside of town, he hits a patch of black ice and the van rises as if drawing breath. Flung from the seat, the casserole unlids itself, spilling helplessly. His headlights swing wide, sweeping a lighthouse's arc over the fields. The ground falls away. Over he goes, into the ditch.

In the broken light of the following weeks, full of unglued hours and sudden clouds across his thoughts, Carter hews close to Claudia. She sets the rhythms of his days. "Time for bed," she says each night. And in the morning, after the alarm has been silenced: "Time to get up." Each second is precarious, an opportunity to continue losing the ground he's gained over the years.

His head ticks like a cooling engine. His fingers curl and twitch, wanting to grab something.

One evening after work, he visits Claudia in the brick building in downtown Wausau where she works. He doesn't know why, except that he can't stand to be home alone. A secretary directs him down a narrow hall. The narrow window in Claudia's office is veined with wire and dimmer than the overhead fluorescents. Claudia sets down her pen. "Carter? Are you all right?" There are papers and manila folders on her desk, forms in triplicate: goldenrod, lavender, mint. She offers her hand. He watches himself take it.

"Goddamn it," he says.

"What?"

He can see them driving home together, his dented van following her car like a giant, ungainly duckling.

"Why put up with me? Goddamn."

She seems distant, as though her arm must span a chasm to reach him. But she manages it. She presses her arthritic pinkie into his palm.

"Carter. Feel that?"

He nods.

"My father broke my fingers with a hammer," she says.

Somehow, it doesn't shock him. He recognizes the worn cadence of the words. Half his life he's listened to similar sentences, the practiced unscrolling of hurts, while First Presbyterian squats overhead like a lid. Claudia is stony, handsome: the chisel blows around her eyes and at the corners of her mouth give her this quality, the absence of finer, more subtle etching. She's a sculpture half-completed, her face a series of hard, primary planes.

A finishing hammer, she says. The kind used to tack up small pictures or replace delicate pieces of trim. In his fist, it looked like a toy. "Spread," he'd say, and she'd have to spread her fingers—left or right, he let her choose—atop a table or the bathroom linoleum, a carpet if he was feeling kind. One swift strike followed, always to the smallest finger. If she flinched, he struck her again. She learned how not to flinch.

Claudia's mother had died. Her father, drunk, had walked away from the wreck. This was when Claudia was five years old.

He offered no explanations. For a time, in fact, the punishment was meted out so regularly and arbitrarily she ceased thinking of it as a punishment at all. Her aching hands, which she carried in front of her like teacups, were a natural human frailty, a consequence of living, like sickness or sleep. Surely children everywhere were spreading their fingers atop kitchen tables while fathers gripped their wrists and reminded them of the consequences of flinching.

That fall, when she began kindergarten, her teacher took her into the hall.

"Honey," she said at last, "where are your fingernails?"

"They fell off," Claudia said.

She was sent, finally, to live with her mother's parents, whom she was told she had met long before. They had never bargained for another child. Mostly, they left her alone.

Her father died years ago, in Milwaukee, of renal failure.

The furnace comes on, a *whump* of breath in the ducts. The building adjusts its massive, institutional weight around them. The fluorescents buzz like something passing overhead at a great height. Claudia wears a tailored black blazer with a brilliant white scarf at her neck.

"So," she says. "That's why."

March ends in blasts of sun and rain. The fields flood, freeze, flood, freeze, flood, and finally thaw. Yards turn shiny and soft. Crocuses mob through the mud. Tractors grunt in sheds. A sour wind rolls in from the fields and geese vee north, yawping.

Spring.

He still listens to the scanner as he drives, though not as often as before.

Sump pumps preoccupy Carter's days. The ground gives up what it's held all winter; basement walls weep water black with sediment. Claudia packs his lunches, heavy sandwiches on dark bread that he eats with greased hands. It's possible to believe that this is what life will be like from now on. Their hurts could be complementary, their scars marking them for one another. They can live carefully, divided from separate but shared pasts, paired survivors.

It gave me hope.

Carter goes fishing on the Big Eau Pleine, and Claudia makes a bouillabaisse with the fillets.

A wet April morning, patchwork sun. Clouds align, scrolling by as if on strings. Rain freckles the windshield. He's driving to his first job of the day, another pump, when the scanner crackles. It's a paramedic, gasping as though she's sprinted to the radio, though of course the handset would be right there, clipped to her shirt.

"I need everyone," she says, not bothering with code. "Now. *Now.* I need all the people you can get."

She gives an address Carter knows.

Cruisers from various agencies herringbone the farmette yard, lights spinning. First responders are arriving, and Samaritans like Carter. Voices echo through empty outbuildings. A German shepherd whines and rears at the end of a leash. Burly troopers tear logs from the woodpile, aiming flashlights down crevices, shouting, "Hello? Hello?"

As if an infant would know to answer.

A search party fans through the fields, eyes on the mud that sucks at their shoes. Carter is among them, though he's not the one who finds the shovel lying in the milkweed beside a little hummock of turned dirt.

The year rolls over. On a Friday in November, he wakes to a yard crisp and white, the air turned to glass. Behind the rancher, late corn rattles. Before the rime burns away, the combines will be out. By Monday, the field will be stubble.

He's in Wausau all day, laying the baseboard heating for a house. A landscape contractor he knows is there, too—not a friend, exactly, but close enough to serve. Leaving the site that evening, they share a few words, planning. It's the weekend of the statewide antlerless hunt.

Beneath First Presbyterian, everything smells of Folgers and Pine-Sol. He steps to the front of the room for his nine-month token. Last winter's relapse has imbued him with a new identity, an air of wisdom bound to brokenness, like a blind prophet. "I choose to live alone," he can say. "I choose not to look back." In the crowd, people nod. He can say, "Hold up my goings in thy paths," and at least a few voices will mutter, *that my footsteps slip not.*

Evening arrives, fiercely starred. Reaching the stadium behind the high school midway through the second quarter, he settles at the fence in front of the home bleachers. Grass glows beneath banked lights. Boys sprint upfield, pounding each other into the turf. A whistle blows. Unharmed, they rise, loping into formation to do it all again. Others slump beautifully on metal benches, cheeks flushed, hair in their eyes, gnawing orange wedges.

At halftime, he joins the line at the concession stand for a cream soda.

"Carter?"

Claudia.

"I thought it was you." She touches his arm. "How have you been?"

"Fine," he tells her. He can still feel the momentary touch through his sleeve.

She's begun attending these football games, Friday nights, Claudia explains. In fact, though she's never really watched the sport on television, she enjoys herself here. "The things people find to do when they won't go to bars." She shrugs. "I'm babbling."

"It's okay."

"I'm just surprised to see you."

"Me, too."

"Actually, Carter, I've been meaning to get in touch."

The kid working the register looks at Carter expectantly.

"Meet me here after the game?" Claudia asks.

"Sure."

"There's something I want to talk to you about."

The soda sits fuzzily on his tongue, too sweet. Before the third quarter begins, he drops it into the trash and drives home.

She doesn't call. Before bed, he disassembles and cleans his rifle. The alarm goes off at three-thirty. He wakes gasping, his chest clenching at the bottom of every breath.

Where is his son?

He supposes he could find out if he tried. He imagines contacting Andrea—it's easy enough, these days, to get back in touch—and simply asking. Years have passed; she might even tell him. But that's not the point. The point is that, in all this time, Brady, a man by now, has never once tried to contact Carter.

The question is always more urgent in the dark.

Where is his son?

He keeps his rifle unloaded. It's enough to be outside, climbing through cloud after cloud of his own breath up a slope of dead leaves, bare hickories, and blackberry canes for a view of the Flambeau—from this distance, just a series of riffled black thumbs folding through the low hills. It's a good hike. It empties him.

He hears the report of a rifle.

The landscape contractor is smoking a Swisher at the truck by the time Carter arrives. A doe sprawls across the tailgate. "Scraggly little bitch," the man says, grinning. "Shouldn't of wasted the bullet." He offers Carter a few cuts from the haunches. Meat enough for two.

Carter spends a day mulling things over.

On Monday, he dials Claudia's office. Fresh venison: is she interested?

"Carter. I'm glad you called."

At her apartment in Wausau, near the university's satellite campus, she fries venison steaks in a skillet with pepper and sage, serving them with creamed parsnips and a beet salad. They eat in a nook off the kitchenette. Someone else's music thumps through the walls. Her neighbors are students. She's saving up, she explains. "I was half a homeowner for a winter. I suppose it rubbed off on me."

That's how it goes at first: small talk, nothing asked or offered. He compliments the food; she refills his water. Finally, she sets down her knife and fork.

"I'm working with the girl."

"Who?"

"Lily Adrienne Jamrozik."

He hardly recognizes the name, freighted with additions that suggest a history, a family, a life beyond the farmette where he saw her exactly once. He pictures a child's face, pouting. Claudia describes how tiny she is. It's difficult, she says, to imagine the girl pregnant. "She must have looked awful, truly awful."

He cuts a wedge from his steak and plows it through the parsnips.

She summarizes the state's involvement. Probation, counseling, supervision from all sides. Lily's still a minor, adrift between the age of consent and legal adulthood. Preston, who wasn't lying about his age, is serving manslaughter time downstate.

"Serving," Carter repeats. The word is exact. *The sacrifices of God are a broken spirit: a broken and a contrite heart.* The walls throb with bass, trailing wisps of human voices.

"I shouldn't be telling you this," she says. A HIPAA violation, her license on the line. "But I thought you needed to hear. They meant something to you—a lot more than I guessed at the time. So I thought you needed to know"—she's reaching for his hand now—"how someone *you* know is looking out for her, or trying."

A single combine still works the stubbled field, its headlights grinding across the horizon. Carter watches from his stoop until he grows cold, and then he goes inside.

"I don't want to think about it," he told her, pulling his hand away.

Not at all, not anymore.

After Andrea left with her parents and Brady, while the screen door still shivered in their wake, Carter grabbed the .22 rifle from the bedroom closet and thumbed a cartridge into the chamber. Her parents had parked up the road, as if to arrive in stealth. Carter shouldered open the screen door. They were walking away, three backs turned. The little boy's face regarded him soberly over Andrea's shoulder. He raised the rifle and aimed—first at the father, then at the mother, and then at her. Nobody saw.

Desperately, he aimed at the child.

Just before getting into the car, Andrea looked back at the trailer.

Was she reconsidering? Did she love him even then? Did they still—up until she saw him with the rifle—have a chance?

In any case, she didn't say a word. Her parents never knew. She got into the car with Brady, and the doors chunked shut. They all went away.

The body was carried across the field, a little girl. Carter glimpsed her only briefly. Like an onion, her skin was translucent, flecked with dirt. She was taken from the arms of whomever had found her, taken away. At some point an officer grasped Carter's elbow and led him back to his van. This was a crime scene now. The volunteers, the good Samaritans, could leave. The authorities would take it from here.

Were they lying from the start, or just too frightened to tell the story straight? Both, perhaps. Even the initial 911 call was a muddle. Someone was hurt. Who? No, someone was already dead. The paramedics, the deputies, a lieutenant of the state police—all asked the same questions, all received the same answers. What happened? The child had been crying. The child wouldn't stop crying. The child had died. How? They had killed the child. No, the child had stopped breathing. She'd died in her crib in the night. No. She'd gone into the grave alive.

The grave. Where was it?

No matter how many times the two were asked, their answer remained the same.

The child. Where did you put her? Where is the child?

The child.

Brady.

"Out there in the fields."

A STRING OF LAPIS BEADS

He lives with his daughter at the end of a dead-end road, in a house he and his wife chose for its seclusion. They were newly-weds then; what they'd wanted was to be alone together, wild with love. He thinks of those idiot bursting annuals, begonias and impatiens, he convinces himself to plant in the shade near the mailbox for no better reason than that she used to. Dry stalks by the end of the season. But they were better than that, finally. They settled into themselves, settled into one another, and began a slow greening: marriage. Susan was her name. She died twenty-seven months ago, in a single-car accident.

Dani, his daughter, will turn eighteen this summer. She plays volleyball in the fall, runs cross-country in the spring. One Saturday, tentatively warm, at the end of March, she sets out from the house with the bundled, smoothly shuffling stride of a distance runner, everything held in reserve. There's a trailhead a few hundred yards up the road, a public right-of-way over the nearest ridge to the Pisgah National Forest. On fair weekends in the spring, Dani runs the trail.

He worries about strangers. Anything is possible; again and again, the world has taught him so. The worst things are pos-sible. As she departs he raises a hand on the front porch, and she raises her fist in return: the gleam of metal there, key ring wrapped around one finger like a promise, and hard against her palm the canister of mace.

An hour goes by. The wind works cirrus clouds into horse-tail sprays. From the next parcel of land, the Kuykendall place, their nearest neighbors, comes the ragged nasal roar of a chain-saw. And when Dani raggedly lopes up the drive, he's out on the porch again, waiting. She could almost be Susan's double: long-limbed, small-breasted, narrow-shouldered. Reaching his truck, she bends, hand to fender, to spit a white bullet into the dirt.

"Nice run?"

"Ugh," she says. "Rat king."

Head thrown back, she gulps down water from the Nalgene she left on the porch rail. Her abandonment at such moments amazes him. He remembers how she used to sleep, face smashed into the pillow, neck sweating, sprawled across the backseat on long car rides. *Down and out,* Susan used to say, and when Dani woke there'd often be several dazed, blinking minutes before she'd speak or even acknowledge their presence. As if she couldn't quite place them, or had come to question their connection to her, given the cosmic distances she'd traveled.

She sweeps past him now, into the house.

He's a veterinarian, a solo practitioner. *Doc,* clients call him, which is what he's come to call himself. Most days he spends driving to and from farms, south as far as Cedar Mountain, west sometimes nearly to Tennessee. Dani begins college in the fall: Tulane, in New Orleans, shockingly distant, supported by loans he's cosigned and is determined to pay. So these rare afternoons when he isn't working and she isn't off somewhere— when they're alone together—are precious to him. He rests socked feet on the porch rail, front door open behind him, faint music rolling down the stairs, the bubblegum pop she likes to listen to in the shower.

Later, in the kitchen, she smears Nutella on toast, wet hair darkening the shoulders of the green and blue hoodie she ordered as soon as her acceptance letter arrived. He finds her there and asks, "Rat king?"

"Mmm-hmm." She chews and swallows. "In the woods by the trail. All tangled up dead."

Not tangled but heaped. He learns this later. Dani's gone into town to meet some friends. After a brief, stony climb from the road, the trail flattens out for a hundred yards or so through spindly pines.

It's his land on the left, the Kuykendalls' on the right. Every third tree sports a pink ribbon, Todd Kuykendall marking his territory. Venus is out, plush sky deepening into blue.

By the shed, she told him, so when the trail bends close to the pole barn at the corner of the Kuykendalls' yard—just before it begins switchbacking up the ridge—he flicks on his flashlight, combing fallen needles with the dusty beam.

Here are the bodies, heaped.

Rats. Twenty or thirty. Poisoned, by the look of them: their tiny, swollen hands.

Doc's brought gloves and garbage bags. He fills the first bag and doubles it within the second, hefting the bodies back down the trail, down the road, to his truck.

His headlights darken the night around him. Driving is like sliding down a wet, bright tunnel. The rural waste center is ten minutes away, a gravel apron off the side of the road, some dumpsters for trash and recycling, a Salvation Army bin. Someone's leaving as Doc arrives, a dazzle of high-beams sweeping his truck, but by the time he swings the bag into the dumpster the evening is still. Just the wind simmering in the trees and the distant hum of the interstate reflecting down from above, a trick of the mountains, as though a road's been cut across the highest portion of the sky. He stands there for a moment, one hand pressed to the cool slab of the dumpster.

This still happens sometimes—dragging himself along like a swimmer in waves, up and then down again, careful of his breath.

The Kuykendalls are having a bonfire, Todd Kuykendall burning the brush he cut back earlier today. "Arthur," he calls, his shadow detaching itself from the blaze as Doc swings his legs down from the truck. "Hey, there."

"You put out rat poison in your barn? Coumadin?"

"What's this, now?"

He spent the drive over measuring out words. You can't just shovel the bodies into the woods, he means to say. They're still toxic. Anything could get into them, poison itself. A bad death:

slow bursting of capillaries over days or even weeks, joints and extremities growing hot and baggy with loose blood, aching with it. There are probably still bodies in the walls Todd hasn't found, bodies in the woods Doc hasn't, exhausted bodies still scrabbling for darkness, concealing themselves, because the last need that still holds for an animal in pain—he's seen it often enough—is the need to be alone.

You could set out traps instead, instantaneous. You could just get a fucking cat.

But he says almost none of this. He bites the words back. Faces flicker in the firelight, pieces of Todd Kuykendall's wife and children, his grandchildren, his friends. Fifteen or twenty people in all, lawn chairs and blankets in the grass, a stereo playing the Ronettes. Todd's face swings toward Doc's, fleshy and whole, as if assembled from the pieces phasing in and out of sight in the yard. "Hey," he's saying. "You all right, Arthur?" *Be my, be my baby* . . . Above the bonfire, a continuous whorl of sparks disappears straight up into the sky. And how can Doc even begin to answer this other man's question? They hardly know one another at all.

Weekly at first, and then every other week, and finally once a month, his daughter's been seeing a therapist in Asheville. Corinne is her name, a tiny woman, bird-boned, half-buried beneath ropes of beads and the heavy scarves and shawls she apparently crochets herself from skeins of sparrow-colored yarn. Dani found Corinne herself in the *Psychology Today* listings, having rejected, sight unseen, the names offered by the school counselor. "This is who I want," she said. Doc was surprised— he'd have expected someone younger—but of course he made the call. Corinne has a smoker's voice, a rare thing nowadays; over the phone, he found this oddly reassuring. She sounded a little like Joan Rivers. He explained the situation, why he was calling, and she said, "I'm truly sorry," in a tone both brisk and sincere. A relief: they could go ahead with business.

Still, there's something in Corinne's stern, professional gaze Doc's found himself flinching from, the few times it's been turned upon him.

Sometimes he drives Dani to her appointments. More often, now that these sessions are less frequent and, apparently, less intense, they make an evening of it: dinner afterward, maybe a movie if there's anything they can agree on, though she'd usually prefer to pop into the stores on Biltmore Avenue or stroll through the open studio spaces and artists' collectives that have pushed out into the factory buildings and warehouses along the river. Usually he thumbs through magazines in the tidy reception area until Dani reappears, but once over the winter she slipped away after her session—just to the restroom, she said—leaving him alone with Corinne.

"And how are we, Mr. Jeffries?"

The same brusque warmth as before, only now he couldn't trust it. He sensed her probing intent. "Well," he managed, "you know."

"Actually, I don't." She smiled. "Hence the question."

Later, he followed his daughter into a small shop strung with prayer flags, shelves stacked with odd implements, folded fabrics, and packets of powdered incense, display cases crowded with jewelry and statuettes in brass and jade, the air thickened by patchouli puffs from an oil diffuser beside the cash register. Dani ran a dowel around the rim of a singing bowl, coaxing a high, clear tone. "Dad, listen." But Doc was distracted by the music—if that's what you were supposed to call it—playing from hidden speakers. Over distant, gently resounding bells, a woman spoke as smoothly and somnolently as a hypnotist. *Now you are wandering in the bardo of becoming. If you look into water, you will not see your reflection, and your body has no shadow . . .*

"College can be a difficult transition in the best of circumstances," Corinne had said, back in her waiting room. "Which, can we agree, these are not."

Difficult for *him*. It had taken Doc a moment to understand what she meant, that this was something his daughter must have asked Corinne to bring up with him. He was fine, though, he said. Yes, it was a big transition. No, it wasn't easy. But he'd be fine.

Corinne had prepared a business card. Inked on the back, in spiky, intricate handwriting like the prints of tiny birds, were names, phone numbers, e-mails. "These are good people," she said, as though he'd suggested otherwise. "People who might be a fit. In case you ever wanted."

What had his daughter been telling her?

"Do you like that?" he said in the shop. "Should we get it?"

Dani dropped the dowel; it clunked against the rim of the bowl. "*Dad,*" she hissed, glancing at the clerk, who'd paused in the act of dripping pale green fluid into the disperser, "it's like 130 bucks. Jeez."

Although she did end up buying something with her own money, a string of chunky beads, lapis lazuli, not so different from something Corinne would wear.

The possum pouchlings appear one morning, three of them curled together in the coil of hose beneath the spigot at the back of the house. Little Star, their tricolor terrier mutt, an old rescue dog, mustachioed and sweetly stubborn about nearly everything, keeps snuffling around, ignoring Doc when he calls from the porch. Investigating, then, he finds them. Tiny things, each barely bigger than his thumb, atop a pile of something soft like rags.

Dead, he thinks at first, nudging Little Star back with his boot, but as his shadow stoops over them they move. The largest even raises its head to bare its teeth, a mouthful of icy pins. Not rags they're lying upon, either, he discovers, but the body of the mother and four more pouchlings. The mother's been poisoned—whether from the bait itself or one of the rats, who can say? The other pouchlings are dead of neglect.

"What do we do?" Dani asks. She's brought her breakfast outside, nibbling one corner of the Pop-Tart, chewing thoughtfully. "We can't just leave them, can we?"

No. That would be cruel. But now Doc must consider what he *does* intend. He can picture quite clearly the bottle of pentobarbital in the locked cabinet in the garage. One box with needles, another with syringes. A call to the shelter to see about burning the bodies, as he should have done with the rats before. He'll have to do that anyway for the bodies already here.

But this must not be what he intends for the survivors. If it were, he wouldn't have called his daughter out to see. He'd have done it in secret, stowing the memories away somewhere—another locked cabinet, an inward place he imagines many veterinarians and others in certain professions must have, where things can be crumpled up and left to degrade in darkness.

Bending down, Dani offers a fragment of Pop-Tart to the largest pouchling, which hisses through its grin. Little Star, jealous of the offering, moans.

"We can't just leave them," his daughter says again, firmly.

For a year or so back in junior high, Dani kept a pair of rabbits as pets. Now the hutch Doc built for them is hefted up from the basement to the laundry room, lined with torn newspaper and old towels, an electric heating pad tucked within the towels. The heating pad is Little Star's, another sacrifice the old terrier will have to make. She watches it go into the hutch with a shaggy look, Doc thinks, of martyred endurance.

"We're lucky it's her who found them," Dani says. "Deacon would've eaten them."

Deacon was their last dog, a dysplastic old blockheaded Lab. He died of renal failure about six months before Susan. "Probably," Doc admits.

The pouchlings lie together in a fold of fabric. They look stunned, helpless, simply breathing. Occasionally the largest one stretches, tail whipping, as though preparing to waddle off somewhere, but it never does. All three are dehydrated, exhausted, perhaps slightly anemic. One by one Doc has cradled them, each little body as soft as a palmful of jelly atop the chalky second skin of his nitrile gloves. With a pair of tweezers he has plucked off the deer ticks that must have crawled from the mother's cooling body, dropping them one by one into a glass of rubbing alcohol. Dani has watched him do this, brow tight, gaze fierce. "Gross," she said once, but didn't look away.

Later, he drives over to the shelter with the bodies of the mother and the other pouchlings. Win, the manager, meets him around back. "Poison," she says, letting him in through the fire door. "The bastard." Todd Kuykendall, she means. Doc's called ahead to explain. "People don't think, is the problem. Or else they think and don't care."

"Just get a cat," Doc agrees, the line he'd rehearsed returning to him now.

But Win shakes her head. "No. The songbirds."

She's a small, sturdy woman, her hair buzzed short, her nails bitten down, with a taut, flexing intensity about her, an air of perpetual judgment. It's easy to wind up on Win's bad side. Opening the bag, she reaches in ungloved and frowns.

"Only four little ones?"

She knows four's too few. Doc didn't tell her about the survivors when he called, but now he has to. Otherwise she'll have him searching his yard for the rest. She'll be there herself at the end of her shift, on her hands and knees in the high grass, asking questions.

He and Dani are going to try their hands at fostering the other three, Doc explains, glancing away from the look she gives him, washing her hands at the sink. Of course he knows it's illegal: he doesn't have a rehabilitator's license. Still, they'd like to try.

"Dani's idea," he hears himself add, lamely.

"Dani's idea," Win repeats, in a tone of caustic amusement. "Tell her Flopsy and Mopsy say hello."

This is a poke, a reminder. Dani named her rabbits not Flopsy and Mopsy, of course, but Haystack and Clover, after the hutch does in *Watership Down*, a book she'd loved since childhood. The rabbits were a Christmas present, something she'd long claimed to want. All the typical pledges had been made: care and cleaning, lifelong devotion. Finally, he and Susan had relented.

For a time, Dani adored her charges. A framed photo in his office at the back of the house shows her on her stomach in front of the television, one rabbit perched atop the small of her back and the other at her elbow, seeming to watch along with her. Deacon would have been huffing and slobbering in the kitchen, barred by a baby gate and his own bad hips from unleashing whatever bloody mayhem he had in mind. Later, he'd forage the carpet for turds.

Things changed. The rabbits rarely left their hutch, which Dani rarely cleaned. "I'm *busy*," she protested. He had to order to do it, threaten punishments. He tried to explain. "It's cruel," he told her. "You're being cruel." Of course this didn't work. Nor was it quite what he meant. But he'd noticed the rabbits growing strange. Not that they cowered from him like wild creatures, but that they couldn't decide. When he was the one to clean the hutch, they snapped at his fingers and one another. They jostled for his attention, then sat miserable and shivering while he stroked their soft fur. The soured need of discards: he'd encountered this before, but never under his own roof.

Doc has never known what to do with anger. It leaves him choked, blushing, shaky. "We knew this might happen, didn't we?" Susan said when he complained to her about it. He stood there, shaking. So Susan called Win, and Win came to the rescue.

Flopsy and Mopsy. As if Dani might've already forgotten their names.

Watch out, Win's saying. And Doc understands. Forgetful: that's what he'd meant when he'd said *cruel*. He'd meant it amounted to the same thing. He sees it often enough. After a week of wet weather, for instance, an old bay warmblood penned in its own manure finally steps from a rotted hoof as if from a bloodied slipper, tripping about in the sucking filth with the meat of its foot exposed. No remedy but death, and Doc's the one who'll be called. Of course there will be someone leaning at the gate to the pen while he does what needs to be done: the owner. "I didn't know," they'll swear, as if that weren't precisely the point. No evil intent is required. The act of leaving, of leaving alone, will do. That's how fragile things are.

The pouchlings are stupid, feeble, helpless in ways he never would have guessed. He mixes dishes of water and calcium glubionate syrup for them; they use these as a toilet. The biggest one bloodies its nose against the chicken wire of the hutch, scraping it back and forth like a prisoner with a tin cup, so the wire must be replaced with fabric mesh from the hardware store. He works in solid foods—wet kibble, mashed potatoes, jars of strained carrots and peas—but these need to be supplemented with puppy formula. He stretches surgical tubing over the nib of his smallest syringe, which they suck at until they choke, tiny nostrils fizzing. Their shit smears like toothpaste.

Where is Dani, during all this?

On her way out the door in the morning, wrinkling her nose: "Stinks in here." Or with a friend, taking a break from what is supposed to be an AP Lit study session, though the music and laughter from behind her closed door has suggested otherwise, the two girls cooing now at the little creatures and scritching fingernails against the mesh. The pouchlings ignore them. Or at the kitchen table with a pouchling curled in the crook of her arm, doing the real work of care. These moments are fitful, unpredictable, yet she performs them with absolute devotion. "There you go," she says, offering the syringe. Not too fast, he warns, not for the first time, and she replies, not for the first time, "I *know*." Ignoring him, continuing: "There you go. There you go."

Two weeks is all Win has allowed. On the last night, they watch a nature documentary on Netflix, a new series, startlingly beautiful, produced at enormous expense. Little Star sleeps at the foot of Doc's recliner; the pouchlings, increasingly nocturnal, clamber about in their hutch. "What I heard," Dani says, falling across the sofa with a Sprite, setting her calculus homework aflutter on the coffee table, "is they had trouble finding footage without trash in it. They had to have this whole team out there picking up litter before they could film anything."

Where could she have heard this? Almost anywhere, possibly—she flashes through page after page on her phone far faster than he can follow—or nowhere at all. It may simply sound true to her, a matter of belief. The music swells. They're treated to shot after gorgeous aerial shot of sprawling savanna, with not a single speck of trash, not a glimpse of human encroachment to be seen. He wants her to be wrong, but fears she's probably not. He wants to know how such stories make her feel. Not exhausted, it seems. Not afraid. Her griefs weigh differently from his—maybe simply less. Drone footage is nothing like the swift sweep of a helicopter, the aircraft's shadow racing along the ground, parting the herds below. Instead, the camera floats along in silence, invisible, like the disembodied, soaring eye he becomes sometimes in dreams.

Carol Ann Chesnutt is the name of the woman Win put him in touch with. She's been advising him over the phone, scolding him sometimes: "Chicken wire? For Pete's sake."

The number must be a landline. Once a man answered, grunting a single inscrutable word. "Salvage." When Doc tried to apologize, thinking he'd misdialed, the man laughed. "Got it. You're the guy with the possums." And in a moment Carol Ann was on the line—her firm, patient, convicted voice with its undertones of amusement: tut-tutting, almost motherly.

"So. What is it now?"

The address she's provided leads them down an access road along the interstate. A Burger King sign hovers over a glassed and netted play area; strung pennants snap above a used-car lot. "I like ours better," Dani says, sitting shotgun, and he knows without having to ask that she means the children in the play area and the pouchlings in the towel-lined box she holds in her lap. She's in a sunny mood, skipping school to join him.

They turn at the promised sign: Cedar Creek Salvage. A steel gate stands open. "All the way back," Carol Ann said, which means they don't park in the lot out in front of the steel barn with its attached office. A Doberman lies heavily on its side in the thin shade of a sycamore, not lifting its head as they pass. A man in canvas overalls leans out the office door to give a curt nod and squirt tobacco juice into a Styrofoam cup. The gravel lane circles around back, through the ruins. Cars and trucks, tractors and vans, heaped appliances spilling their mechanical innards, the rusted gantry of a crane like a dinosaur's spine. Everything glitters: old chrome catching sun, the powdery glint of crushed glass. Flowers blinking in the weeds seem dull by comparison.

All the way back turns out to be a single-wide trailer sidled up beneath a stand of skinny pines. They park in the worn grass, beside a vintage two-tone Ram Charger sitting high on a lift kit—"Somebody's toy," remarks Dani, who's inherited her mother's wry appreciation for the hypertrophies inflicted upon trucks in this part of the world—and before he can step around the front of his pickup to help his daughter with the box, a woman calls out from the shade of the pines, raising an arm darkly sleeved in ink.

This is Carol Ann Chesnutt. She's not what Doc expected. It's a girl who grasps his hand—*girl* is the word that comes to mind. She might be twenty-five, broad-hipped in jeans and a racerback tank patched with sweat beneath each breast and across a thick, almost babyish roll of belly fat. She has a pair of work gloves shoved down one pocket and a grip that says she's testing him, or is used to being tested herself.

"And these must be the munchkins," she says. "Well, come along. I was just putting on the finishing touches around back."

Munchkins. Come along. Such quaint constructions. But then there's her left arm, a crawling portrait in green and red and blue, no distinct forms Doc can pick out, just scales and fire and the muscular, rushing water of Japanese woodblock prints. At the back of her shoulder, distinct from the rest, a snake clutches its tail in its jaws, forming a circle the size of a curled hand. "Nice ouroboros," Dani says—adding, more shyly, "Did it hurt?"

"My first. Nothing hurts like your first."

"But after that it's easier?"

It might alarm Doc, the interest she's showing. But he's more startled by the sound of that word in his daughter's voice: *ouroboros*.

Carol Ann grins. "Would you want it not to hurt?"

The enclosure is shaded by pines, steel-roofed, screened on three sides. Old stumps have been dragged in, bundled branches, plywood platforms constructed as perches. Pine straw has been scattered and stacked in bales. Gaps in the stack form caves, and an old section of culvert runs through the stack at the bottom.

A midday transfer is best, according to Carol Ann. The pouch-lings will sleep through everything, waking to a new world. Not that they're pouchlings anymore, technically. Young possums. She'll offer water in a dish but not food. She'll hide kibble and diced yams and thawed mail-order mice to teach them to forage, release crickets into the enclosure to teach them to hunt. She tips the box gently onto its side, facing away from them, leaving a small gap between it and the stacked bales. Latching the door to the enclosure, she offers Doc a level glance. "You don't need the towel back, do you?" And he realizes—another shock, though it shouldn't be—that the thing they've come to do has already happened.

An airhorn sounds and the runners set out, jogging across the open field. An eager few sprint off into the lead. Stupid rabbits, his daughter calls them. She'll run them all down in the end. But for now, Dani's lost to him, somewhere in the pack. He searches the flashing faces for hers, for her neon green compression socks

in the churn of legs. A momentary glimpse, a bouncing ponytail, and she's gone, the pack jostling down to triple-file as they
approach the wooded trail, disappearing finally into the trees.

He knows this is her favorite part: elbows clashing, clipped
heels, gasps and curses, the struggle to wrest herself free.

Together with the other parents and family members, he
follows coaches from various high schools across a cleat-torn
soccer field to where the runners will eventually emerge. It's
the final meet of regionals, a week before Dani's graduation, and
he's surrounded by people he knows, people with whom he'd say
he's friendly, people who've greeted him by name—*Hey there,
Arthur*—which is to say they're not quite his friends. Even Susan,
who knew him better than anyone, mostly just called him Doc.

"Listen," she used to say, those first ecstatic weeks alone in
their new house together, lying in bed. *Listen.* So they closed
their eyes, stilled their breath, and listened to the house as it
settled, the slow, spare music of nails squeezed by lumber and
water shifting in pipes. And the longer they listened, the more
there'd been to hear. The silence revealed its hidden textures,
as perceptible in the dark bedroom as an electrical charge—as
though their presence together, their daily movements, had
gently rubbed each floorboard and wall, generating these vibra-
tions, this not-quite-imaginary hum. She rested her hand on his
heart. He rested his on her stomach, where their little girl was.

First come the new frontrunners, a cluster of tall, skinny
girls pressing hard, shockingly leggy in bibs and bright shorts,
every mud-spattered sinew revealed. Dani's not among them; he
knows not to expect her here. "They're built for it," she's said
of these girls, with their track scholarships to Duke and Chapel
Hill. "They don't suffer like the rest of us."

She's thirty seconds back, part of a long umbilical connecting
the leaders to the pack. Two of her friends are running with her,
all three in stride, close enough to hold hands. Coaches trot
along, shouting things like "Focus! Focus!" But Dani doesn't
look at them, doesn't look for Doc. Her cheeks are flushed, her

ears aglow as if in mortification. Together with her friends, she follows the flagged path around the perimeter of the field and returns to the trees.

One more lap. The crowd shifts to the finish line.

At some point in the woods, Dani will kick free of her friends. Running hard, chasing the leaders—on a good day even cutting into the gap between them—and emerging, at last, alone. Most parents cheer their daughters across the finish line, but Doc never does. Something in her face warns against it. Any sound he might make would be superfluous, and his chest is too tight to cry out besides. He just tries to breathe with her.

Afterward, Dani and her friends pose together, phones held out in their usual post-race ritual, a triple-selfie. She smiles for the flash, her whole face crimson and white in patches, the same colors as her lips and teeth.

He confronted her exactly once about her college plans: didn't she want to at least apply somewhere in-state? What about her friends? His daughter just glared at the question, glared down at her dinner, glared at the four walls of the kitchen, measuring the space for her escape. But Doc understands—of course he does. He doesn't need Corinne or anyone else to explain. To go where she isn't already known, where she won't be The Girl Whose Mother Has Died: for Dani, escape must be precisely the point. He's seen her studying these selfies on her phone, flicking and tapping, changing things. A touch of her finger and a reticle appears, framing her face, bringing it forward and smudging the rest. Her friends blur into the background. Another touch: they reappear. Touch again, and they're gone.

"Darling," he says. "Wake up."

A starry evening near the end of August. They're approaching the end of a ten-hour drive. South of Slidell, Louisiana, the interstate leaps out over the water, everything dark above and below, headlights and taillights floating in their windows and mirrors, all neatly aligned and so apparently still he could convince himself, if not for the hum of the road and the rhythmic thud of the bridge spacers, that they aren't even moving at all. But from over the horizon a distant glow has begun spreading upward into the sky. In the humid air it looks more solid than light: a vapor, a fog.

Their first glimpse of New Orleans. She wouldn't want to miss it.

"Darling," he says again, but glancing over he can see she's already awake, her eyes open, dully gleaming. She doesn't acknowledge that he's spoken, doesn't acknowledge him at all. She may have been awake for a long time already, watching the light ahead in silence.

Three more things happen. Three things of note.

He catches himself organizing his thoughts like this in the following weeks and months—almost as if he really had called one of the numbers Corinne had offered, as if he were talking to someone, a sympathetic stranger, for whom his experiences must be unpacked and arranged, presented as if they had meaning.

In truth, he doesn't know where he put Corinne's card. He's allowed himself to forget; he may even have thrown it away. It's not that he has no faith in therapy. He's watched his daughter, after all. The very first spring she planted impatiens with him out near the mailbox, and he caught himself staring at her long-fingered hands working gloveless in the dirt. She stopped what she was doing and placed a lovely hand on his arm. "Corinne says it's okay to cry."

He nodded and kept nodding as waves crashed over him.

But perhaps it's as simple as this: he just wants to be alone. Home in the evenings, he paces from room to empty room, Little Star's nails ticking along behind him in the dark. And in the dark, pacing, sometimes he puts his thoughts in order.

The first thing that happens is an e-mail from Win, forwarding a video from Carol Ann. *You didn't leave her your contact info,* she writes. And then, at the end, *Hope you're doing good.* The closest she'll ever get to asking after him.

The video is in three parts, three quick clips shot by a smartphone in low-light mode, everything blazing green. Three times Carol Ann's voice sings out: "Shoo-shoo, little munchkin, shoo-shoo-shoo!" And three times, a low-slung form trundles away, disappearing without haste or hesitation into an undifferentiated thicket Carol Ann has chosen, presumably, for its distance from roads, homes, dogs, poisons, guns. Three times the camera zooms silently in on some spot in the undergrowth rendered conspicuous by the fact that a possum is no longer there, a last known location, before cutting away. The last time, it cuts to black.

He forwards the video to Dani, who texts back only *Goodbye!!!* followed by a row of little hearts. "The Possum Lady," he remembers her saying on the way back from the salvage yard—as though it were the title of something, Carol Ann's title. "You think she really lives there in that trailer, with that guy and the Doberman, surrounded by all that junk?" Doc just shrugged. It was more than he could explain: the things people chose for themselves, the lives they wanted, and with whom, and where. He offers no reply now but a little heart of his own.

Later, on one of his wanderings, he finds her lapis beads. This is the second thing. They curl at the bottom of a cup on her nightstand, as though she took them off one evening, dropped them into a glass of water, and forgot them entirely. The water is long evaporated. He lifts the beads out. They rest rugged, cool, and dense against his palm. He rolls first one and then another carefully between his thumb and forefinger, moving forward bead by bead, as Dani used to do, until something stops him. The shape of certain beads, a hidden regularity.

Every few beads, the shape he keeps coming back to, is a skull.

And on an October afternoon, brisk and bright, when he fires up the Toro for one last mow, the third thing happens. For a few moments he isn't paying attention, lost in the rhythms of the ride. And then the grass ahead glints and twitches, a muscled ribbon racing along. He has just time to think *snake* before running it over.

A black racer, enormous, four feet from the tip of the oil-dark tail to the brightly bleeding stump where a head once was. The body whips and thrashes, and when he picks it up—not knowing why, but maybe just to hold it still, just to stop that awful writhing—it lashes around his forearm and constricts. Doc hears himself gasp: impossible something dead could be so strong. Try as he might, he can't tear it away. His fingertips fizz, darkening like matchheads. All he can do is wait.

Down on his knees, skin printed with scales.

SOMEBODY'S BLOOD

She Never Came Back

The phone rang. Her father's voice through the wall: slow words, long pauses. The creak and thump of bedsprings, floorboards, feet as he got out of bed and dressed. But midnight calls were not unusual. A down cow somewhere, difficult foaling, palsied retriever. Something he'd have to see to. She was asleep again before he'd left. That her mother might not be home as well, not back by now from the county hospital, swing shifts in the ER that rotation—that her mother might not be just on the other side of the wall never occurred to her.

Now a woman staggers up as though Dani were a gale, a blinding light. This big dumpy woman in cowboy boots and jeans, bright blue eyes in crinkled nests. "Driving," she says in a flattened tone of wonder, because Dani's leaning at the fender of the driver's ed car outside the creamery—the sort of place they drive to during class, a gesture toward something like fun. The other student, her partner today, is still in line, still waiting for his ice cream. The instructor's around the corner of the building with a vape pen.

This is somebody Dani's supposed to recognize: a family friend, another nurse. "If only she'd come back to us," the woman says, meaning Dani's mother, meaning from the crumpled Corolla on Crab Creek Road, halfway between the hospital and home, "we could've done something. But she never came back. Not to the ER." There's a paper napkin, spattered with strawberry, tucked into the collar of this woman's western shirt. Her small eyes glitter, pinched in skin. "She was one of us. Family."

Dani turns away, rum butter dripping down her fist. She's like a stubborn child but also like a bride in her new life, forsaking the past. She woke dazedly, that first night, hours after the call, and heard everything stirring, moving about, being moved. On socked feet her father shuffled and slid, nudging her dirty clothes along the floor, rustling the homework on her desk. His face was wax, his eyes wicks, and when she sat up, asking what was wrong, he wheeled around, dropping to one knee and seizing her hand as if he intended to marry her.

Big Hungry

The girl in the papers, the one with the dogs: Dani knows her. The girl who walked miles through the rain with her baby in one arm, her other hand wrapped in rags and crammed down her pocket, picking her way down the mountain, down from the deer camp off Big Hungry Road where she'd been living, down to one of the glass-and-cedar mansions set back in the woods above Pulliam Creek, striking the door with her elbow, asking to use a phone.

Kristy's her name. A senior last year, when Dani was a sopho-more. They ran in different circles. Or, rather, Dani ran—cross-country—and played volleyball, and was taking her first AP classes, while Kristy wore a man's camouflaged coat in every weather, her ragged nails poking out the sleeves, white rings worn into the back pockets of her jeans by the canisters of Skoal she carried when she wasn't in school. She was small, stick-thin, nearly lost in that coat, though at last even the coat couldn't conceal what was happening.

Who was the father? Kristy wasn't talking. A man, people said. A stranger. For a few weeks she walked the halls with the coat unzipped to reveal her firm, mounded belly, bright eyes darting from face to face as if challenging someone, anyone, to meet her gaze. And then one day she wasn't in school. No one knew where—she was just gone.

Dani knows *gone*. For a time her mother worked at an outpatient surgery center up in Asheville, but then she returned to the county hospital for less money and longer hours. She needed to be where she'd be needed, she said, and in a year she was gone, running her car off the road, plowing into a tree. No explanation, only guesses. A grueling shift. A stretch of dark, winding, rainswept pavement. A deer in the headlights, a moment's distraction, an overcorrection. Whatever. Needed and gone.

That was the year before Kristy disappeared, when Dani was in the ninth grade.

The stranger: he came for Kristy, or she went to him—into the woods. A poor place, Dani's father, who was there at the end, tells her. He's a veterinarian; he came for the dogs. Twenty-three in all, chained in the yard or locked in what the man, cuffed by the time her father arrived, called kennels, but which were really just board boxes lined with soiled straw, or else loose in the Quonset hut, bleeding corrosion at the riveted seams, where the man and Kristy and, eventually, the baby, too, had lived among them.

What was it like inside? Her father, a tall, bony man with a sun-creased face, thin sandy hair whipped upward to curl like a quail's feather, simply shakes his head. "Bad," he says. "Yeah. Pretty bad, I guess."

Not all the dogs could be saved. *Destroyed* is the word the papers have used.

"Bad how?" she asks, though she knows better.

The glance he gives her: neck bent, eyes briefly searing. She owes him more than her questions, it seems; she owes him silence. She's all he has left in this world.

Two fingers gone, people at school are saying. No, say others, it was the whole hand. Someone says they cut Kristy's fingers from the belly of the dog that took them, but Dani knows better than to believe it. And then the volleyball team makes the regional semis and no one's talking about Kristy anymore. On the bus home after the match, a girl lays her head across Dani's bruised knees and sobs. What can be done? She strokes and strokes the sweaty, matted hair. Later, she finds the damp tangle still printed whitely, faintly, into her thighs.

Dani wakes, wondering what woke her. There's only the furnace sighing, the mountains out the window wedged black against the sky. No sound from the hall, no quiet tread retreating, though she knows he looks in on her, nights he can't sleep.

The man didn't wake when Kristy left in the night. What was left of her hand must have told her it was time. If the baby fussed as she lifted it from the nest she'd managed to make for it, the sound was lost beneath the moaning of dogs, the drumming of rain.

In the school auditorium on the day of the PSAT, ten rows back from the darkened stage, Dani bubbles in answers atop a wooden tray that folds down, locking her in place, solving and solving for x. Later, bells ring; afternoon light floods open the steel doors. She lingers a moment before raising the tray. Her hand aches from offering solutions. Volleyball season is over. Cross-country season is over. She's needed nowhere now more than where she's going, the only place left for her to go: home.

She lives with her father outside of town, at the end of a dead-end road. "*There* you are," he says sometimes, if he's home already when she returns from school, from practice, as though her whereabouts are ever a mystery, as though something's achingly open inside him, a gate left creaking on its hinge, and only she can clang it shut again.

They love each other; she collects college brochures. Both things are true.

In Dani's bedroom, on the bookshelf beside the desk, is a book from her childhood, one her mother used to read her, a heavy clothbound anthology of fairy tales illustrated by Doré

and others in a similar style. She thinks of the ogre in "Hop o'
My Thumb," his hands all wormy vein and horny nail, his knife
poised over his sleeping daughter's throat. She's developed a
nervous habit, one hand working the other, with three fingers
pinching at her pinkie or ring finger, squeezing at one knuckle
and then the next. In the end something must be sacrificed,
something offered. Somebody's blood.

Knock, Knock, Rabbit, Rabbit

"But first," she says, trying out the joke, "first, my *dog* died."
Nobody laughs. At the lunch table her friends look away, look
at each other, look off into the middle distances of the cafeteria like she's invisible, like *she's* the ghost. And nobody wants
the ghost, knocking on walls in the middle of the night, to be
angling for a laugh.

Knock, knock . . .

Deacon was his name. A Labrador, black with silver whiskers,
silvering eyes, fatty tumors plumping like grapes beneath loose
rolls of skin. When the time came, her father did it himself.
He asked if she wanted to be there, and she said no. Dani was
fourteen. She lay on the living-room sofa with her head across
her mother's knees, rewatching *Azkaban*. But then came the
parts with the dog, the big black dog Sirius turned into when he
needed to protect Harry, and she felt like such a baby, looking
away, but she couldn't help it, couldn't help herself—rolled onto
her belly, pressing her face to her mother's thighs, her nose and
chin seeking the space between them, burrowing. Her mother's
fingers in her hair.

Something awful they used to say to one another at school:
Go jump back up your mother. A line from some sitcom, a show
they'd chosen as their own because it was so clearly not intended
for them and no one else their age watched it. All through junior
high, Dani and her friends were telling one another to jump
back up their mothers. Shut up, it meant. You're too much. I

love you. But no one is saying this anymore, in high school. In high school, they're small again. Much of their time is spent like rabbits in the grass: sitting up suddenly, ears perked, waiting to sense what's coming.

One day a slice of pizza falls from the sky—whirling down wonderfully, landing in the middle of their lunch table with a greasy splat. Someone shrieks. Their chairs skitter back. They are standing, all of them—Dani, too—looking for faces looking at them.

From a few tables over, laughter. Boys.

Dani kept a pair of rabbits for a time, but she didn't love them. Couldn't, though she tried: their dense and miraculous fur, their tarred eyes intensely private, their noses twitching at the tips of their delicate faces like the time-lapsed movements of flowers. But their privacy never included her. She took them out to the yard but they just huddled, shivering, in the grass, leaning into the warmth of one another's bodies. Deacon sat in front of their cage in the laundry room, watching them through the wire with the steady, remorseless gaze of a hitman. The rabbits footed back and forth between water and food, pressing themselves into hollows in the cedar shavings as though to disappear.

Her father brings home a new dog, a mustachioed terrier mutt the color of leaf litter, squat and sturdy as a raccoon, front paws outturned as though ready to head in two different directions. When Dani reaches down, the dog flops heavily over, revealing warty teats from a recent litter on either side of a fresh spaying scar, her warm belly oddly hairless and spattered with moles. "Somebody loved her once," Dani's father says, admiring, it seems, this fearless expectation of a gentle touch while also noting—*once*—the damage. She'd been a stray before arriving with her pups at the shelter, thin and wounded, a wet fistula below her ribs that has since healed, grown over with a patch of snowy fur. At the shelter they named her Little Star.

A new dog. They're trying to piece things together, edging

forward into the awful expanse of the future. *Rabbit, rabbit,* Dani used to say, whispering the words first thing in the morning on the first of each month. An incantation, for luck. Though it began to seem strange to her, after she gave away her own rabbits, after she couldn't love them, to keep saying this. She's never loved anything the way it needed to be loved.

Burying her face in her mother's lap, she turned away from the worst of the movie, turned away from her father when he came back inside. One night, a few weeks after Little Star's arrival, Dani dreams her way back to that moment. A blind dream, no images, only sensation: hot denim, hot tears, warm fingers through her hair, an experience that clings like cellophane as she wakes, so that for a few moments she knows she's awake, knows herself to be lying in bed, but still feels those fingers, stroking. It's all so real, so absolutely *happening*, that it must be a haunting, this must be a ghost.

Mom?

She almost says it aloud, and in the effort of nearly speaking the last of the dream boils away. Like in a bad joke, everything reverses: not her hair being stroked but her fingers doing the stroking. Little Star has wandered into her bedroom, nudging open the door to position herself, firm as a hassock, beneath Dani's dangling hand.

A shaggy terrier face moons up at her now, asking why she's stopped. No spectral shadow, no beloved presence, just her awful, unfunny life. Still, she thinks: okay. In this world, pizza falls from the sky. She was the one who grabbed the greasy slice while everyone watched, cramming it into her mouth for an enormous bite. Turning to the boys, shouting with her mouth full: "Like what you see, shitheads?"

So they've seen her now; now what? Whatever comes next, she'll need all the luck she can get. It's not the first of the month, not the first of anything, but she runs her fingers through the fur and says the words she has to say.

Discover

For a while her mother still received mail: glossy advertising circulars, cardstock flyers for the continuing education seminars she attended as a nurse, once even a credit card offer. Dani filled it out; she sent it in. The card arrived, plastic made to look like brushed steel. Beneath her mother's name, an expiration date years in the future. DISCOVER.

Dani pressed the card to the back of her phone and slipped the phone into its case. She kept things hidden from her father. They'd had a fight; he'd gone through her backpack, looking for Kools. "You're fifteen," he'd said, pleading, as if her age meant anything at all, as if anything in her life could be age-appropriate anymore. At the funeral she'd stood beside him in the receiving line, accepting people's hands.

She'd wanted to explain this, but could not. Instead she'd threatened suicide. She'd kill herself if he went through her things again, she'd heard herself say. His face: like she'd slapped him, slack with shock. She couldn't stop. "Then you'll be alone," she'd said.

But it was true, she'd taken up smoking in the mornings before class, and not just cigarettes. Past the soccer fields, a hundred yards down the cross-country trail, six or seven of them stood in a circle, sharing. Steve Crawley was usually the one to slit a cigarette with a razor, tapping out tobacco and repacking with whatever he was holding. He resealed the paper with a flick of his tongue. The skunky stuff mostly just made Dani's ears ring all through first period, made her want to squeeze her molars together until her fillings squeaked. Her English teacher, Miss DeWitt, took her aside. "Now, I'm not going to ask if everything's all right."

Still, Dani enjoyed the intimacy of the act: her fingers brushing other fingers, her lips pressed to a filter wet from other people's lips.

Steve Crawley's mouth was girlish and full, his long dark hair unwashed, his typical expression bruised and sleepily pleased, as though daydreaming about the night before. He'd graduated last year but was still hanging around, taking classes at the community college and dealing, Dani supposes now, though it didn't occur to her at the time, from his old black Rabbit with the squealing fan belt.

"You," he said one morning. "Yeah, you. Come here. Show you a trick."

Dani is tall; she didn't have to tip her head back to receive the finely threaded stream of smoke he blew over her teeth and tongue.

Sixteen by then, she had her own car. Secrets came easier. She was going to a friend's house after school, she told her father, and when he asked what friend she dared him to challenge her—just made up a name: "Lyndsay." He didn't even ask *Lyndsay who?* Maybe he thought he was supposed to know. Maybe he was scared of her now. She thought *she'd* be scared, alone with Steve Crawley in his Rabbit, cornering on mountain roads, his hand on hers as he showed her when and how to work the stick. But she wasn't. Even when they parked, when he leaned into her, and then when he leaned back, arching his hips to fumble with his belt, she was never afraid. She thought of the card. Tucked against her phone, inside her backpack, between her feet, was an artifact from another world, a universe where her mother was alive. Dani had grazed that universe somehow, hadn't she? She'd brought something back.

The first penis she'd ever actually seen: half-hard, slung over the waistband of his boxers like the arm of a little climber trying to lift himself over a ledge to safety. She wasn't afraid, but she must have hesitated. She must have, because he spoke.

"Come on—please."

She'd never heard him like this before. A high note, strained, like the Rabbit's fan belt. He tugged at her fingers, a child.

"Don't leave me like this."

A year later, and already that feels like another life. Sometimes he turns up online, in her feed. PEOPLE YOU MAY KNOW. A grid of faces, some familiar, one his. The same dark eyes, hair pulled back in a ponytail the way it never used to be. Unlike hers, his profile is public; anyone can see. Fair Play, South Carolina. Another state, though not far. A cable installer. His unimaginable, unremarkable life.

Whatever. Tap the screen and he's gone.

As for Dani, she survived; she survives. Obituary language: *survived by* . . . Fifteen, sixteen, seventeen. Sophomore, junior, senior. PSAT, SAT, ACT. Her college applications go out. She awaits the e-mails announcing her future. And sometimes, alone in her room, she locks the door, removes the card from its hiding place, and holds it, mostly steady, within the opened angle of a pair of scissors. *One day*, the card used to promise. *One day you'll need me.* But that hasn't been the case. No dramatic developments, no emergencies or inspirations, no escapes lifting her into another life. It should be easy, she reasons, to make the first cut.

But it isn't; she doesn't; she never does. At the last moment a voice always rises in her, pleading. It pleads the way Steve Crawley did, full of whining want. Once she thought it was her he wanted. Now she thinks he just wanted to grow up.

No Fear Eyes

Saturday morning, seventeen, home alone and half in bed, one leg dangling to the floor like an empty promise: she'll go for a run today. Instead, Dani finds herself down in the kitchen, poking around. An ancient box of brownie mix, unopened. Ghirardelli, the good stuff, the kind her mother loved. This, she decides. This is what she needs.

She's aware she's being impulsive. Awareness like this, stepping back from herself, is a big point of emphasis with Corinne. In Corinne's office this week the blinds were lowered and the drapes tugged closed, turpentine light bleeding around their edges while Dani's hands braided nervous rope from a tissue. Just a time of year, Dani insisted, not even the first anniversary but the second. How could her body know? How could a body know when to grieve?

Off in her corner, Corinne sank back in her armchair, spidery, suspended in a brown webwork of hand-knitted scarves and shawls and leaving, as always, the space of one long breath, in and out, for Dani to keep speaking before speaking herself: "It knows."

Dani would have to watch herself, was the point—watch her body as it remembered everything, roiling and contracting in bizarre ways. Stiff shoulders, sore neck, sudden appetites, sudden headaches, a psoriatic rash flaking behind one ear: all her secret storehouses of hurt. She must remain mindful. Be patient. Be kind. Practice self-care. Resist impulse. Go for a run. Be wise. Be brave.

"Nevertheless," Dani sings, gathering ingredients from the fridge, belting words tunelessly out: "Nevertheless, she per-*sis*-ted . . ." Her father is off somewhere, driving between farms or wringing his hands with iodine, preparing for a surgery or a birth. He's taken the terrier with him, as he sometimes does. There's no one to whom she must answer. It's like being an adult, which makes her feel like a child, giddy and loose, left alone.

In the pantry, she discovers a stack of unopened mail addressed to her mother.

Her father has tucked these things away, she imagines, an impulse probably too thoughtless, too reflexive, to be quite shameful to him, stashing them nearly out of sight between the food processor and the mixing bowls, other items long disused yet not discarded—still potentially useful, if only in a future no one can imagine.

Atop the stack, most recent, is a mailing from the local offices of the Democratic Party. SURVEY ENCLOSED, the envelope says, OPEN IMMEDIATELY, so Dani does.

Susan, she reads, *which of the following actions by the Trump administration makes you angriest? (check all that apply),* and she's halfway down the column below, pressing invisible marks into empty boxes with her thumbnail, when her breath stops and her body decides: nothing to do but fold forward around the pain, lay her head to the torn envelope, and howl.

Near the house, a public trail switchbacks up a red clay ridge to national forest land. Today there's a truck at the trailhead, not one Dani recognizes, not likely to belong to any of the local hikers, birdwatchers, and retirees she typically encounters on her runs. A rustbucket pickup, lifted and straight-piped and slapped with decals. Smirking Calvin pisses on the number of a NASCAR driver. A pair of angry cartoon eyes squint above the caption NO FEAR. A rattlesnake coils on a bright yellow field, above a caption so at odds with the snake's wincing, submissive expression, like a patient saying *ahh* for the dentist.

Sometimes in her office Corinne says, "Let's just breathe for a bit, shall we?" and the trick then, the one Dani's been taught, is to breathe with her belly but not her chest. She's trying to root herself to the immediate present, where nothing is actually wrong—just a girl out for a run—and everything else, her past and her future, is just a wind through her leaves, moving her hardly at all. But she can't manage the trick this time. It's not like being punched but like having been punched, rage rising like an old bruise. She staggers to the truck, presses her housekey to the fender, and drags it forward. Paint curls up, a fine fringe like frost. Underneath is steel.

Taut bunch and swift spring of muscles, hard rhythms of heart and breath: up the mountain she goes. But even though Dani runs the web of trails until stitches sink into her kidneys, she's only ever alone. She can't seem to find him—the asshole, the one responsible, whoever he is—and by the time she returns to the trailhead, bent and gasping, the truck is gone. More invisible marks: has her rage signified anything at all, among all the other dents and scratches? The hard little cylinder in her fist, her canister of mace, is a joke. "You don't know how the world can be," her father said, presenting it to her for the first time. But how could he say this to her—to her, of all people?

Be wise, Corinne has said, so Dani will try: she'll crack eggs. Succumbing to the least of her temptations may be the most she can manage today.

But not right away. First, she lies on the sofa as sweat dries to powder on her skin, doomscrolling the headlines and picking at the itch behind her ear. She allows her resolve to harden, until at last she gets up, grabs the survey from the counter and the stack of mail from the pantry, and dumps everything into the brown grocery bag beneath the sink where they keep the recycling.

A glimpse before the cupboard closes: her mother's name, waiting to be pulped and reprocessed. Dani feels herself making No Fear eyes. Breathe, now. Breathe. The oven warms, ticking like an engine. Her father will be home soon, tugging his boots off at the door, his little terrier skittering around him, his loose old socks blackened at the toes. And then he'll smell the smell. On this anniversary morning, two years to the day, Dani cracks the eggs and whisks, knifes open the ancient powder, and fills the kitchen with the scent of bitter chocolate.

Screaming in the Trees

"How'd you do?" Lara asks, splayed in the grass at cross-country practice the afternoon following a practice exam in AP Lit. Lara's still not shaving: a fine golden pelt overspreads her inner thighs, honeyed into whorls where the grass has wetted it and more beautiful, somehow, than skin. Dani, who initially made the no-shave pact with her, lost heart as soon as the wiry black stubble appeared. Her body's not like Lara's—just as compact, rounded, blushing, and desirable as a peach. Tipping on one leg, drawing her other foot back to feel the stretch in her quads, Dani's a stork by comparison. Lara folds forward between forked legs, reaching far past her toes. The small of her back appears, gently fuzzed like her thighs. Of course boys notice, jogging by. At the apex of her stretch she emits a little mew of distress and, relaxing, says, "There was that essay-thing we had to read, the one with the peacocks. 'The peacocks screaming in the trees.' That one weirded me out."

"Joan Didion," says Dani, who has read *The Year of Magical Thinking.*

"Creepy Joan," says Lara.

Which will have to be the last word, because here comes Coach Joy, barking and slapping her paws together, clapping girls to their feet, Dani's chest suddenly flooding, her heart thudding away in response: time to run.

She found the book in Ms. DeWitt's classroom last semester, pulling it from a shelf in the silence after seventh hour. "A masterpiece," Ms. DeWitt called it, which did not incline Dani to crack the spine, before adding the comment that did: "But I don't know—it may be too much. Put it down if it feels like too much."

They're friends, or something like it, Dani and Ms. DeWitt. Between classes or before or after school, she can wander into Ms. DeWitt's classroom, with its view of the tarred roof of the vocational wing, its posters and portraits of authors from beyond the domesticated paddock of the curriculum. Margaret Atwood, Jeanette Winterson, bell hooks, and of course Joan Didion, young and sylphic and devastating with a smoldering cigarette between two slim fingers. Dani can browse the tall shelves for striking titles—along with the Didion, she's read *Lives of Girls and Women, The Temple of My Familiar,* and *Oranges Are Not the Only Fruit*—or just sit quietly in the armchair by the window, in the peaceable, purposeful calm Ms. DeWitt at her desk seems to exude, in the gaps and margins of the day. "Dani," Ms. DeWitt might say, looking up from the papers she's grading, when Dani enters the room. Just that, just her name, in a tone, firm but warm, that reminds Dani so much of her mother. The way her mother was.

A surprise, then, not entirely pleasant, to encounter Joan Didion on a multiple-choice exam, with easy meanings to be extracted and bubbled in.

Pacing Lara around the perimeter of the soccer field, Dani silently chants. The jouncing couplets match her strides.

> To get an A in AP Lit
> if you're a girl, take Ms. DeWitt . . .

The song runs on, growing filthier as it goes. Easy rhymes: tits, clit, Alice DeWitt.

Who knows who made these lines up, or how long they've been bouncing around the halls of the high school? All lies, in any case: despite their friendship, or whatever you want to call it, Dani's found Ms. DeWitt's classes to be among her toughest. A note at the end of an essay, underlined: *You can do better!* Still, it's true Ms. DeWitt is a lesbian. It must be dangerous, or at least frightening, Dani sometimes thinks, here in this place of rolling green mountains, spit-bottles of tobacco juice in the roadside weeds, pickups streaming American flags and worse. It's hard to imagine where the peace that surrounds Ms. DeWitt, there in each day's interstices, could come from.

Dani's father knows Ms. DeWitt's wife, who operates a local animal shelter. "Just two people, the way I see it," he has said, as if Dani were the one who needed to hear this—speaking with uncharacteristic ferocity, the way he must speak to the farmers he works with if the subject arises. Typically a quiet man, inward, he shakes his head like a horse flicking flies, ready to defend what little he has left: "It shouldn't matter."

But it *does* matter. It matters to Dani.

To know that there are others out there—everywhere, presumably—who've borne everything she has and more, much more, and more bravely, and more creatively, and who've said in the end *let them go, keep them dead*, as Creepy Joan has, smearing her heart all over the page, page after page, and then just letting go, and never mind which ghosts may be listening. Fuck what anyone thinks—the living or the dead.

The cross-country trail leads down through the woods, down past the bend overlooking the stream where a picnic table has been set, and where, in that first miserable year—it seems like another life—Dani went to get high with a few other students, people she hardly knows anymore. "I'm not going to ask you what's wrong," Ms. DeWitt said after class. Dani stood before her, swaying: the beginning of things between them.

And it is typically here, past the picnic table and the bridge over the stream, as the trail curls back uphill, that Dani leaves Lara behind. Her stork legs have a kick Lara's lack. She's on her own now, somewhere between the frontrunners and the main pack, alone.

Fuck what anyone thinks, she and Lara told one another when they made their pact. They'd want what they weren't supposed to want for themselves and be seen wanting it. But Dani's not as brave as she needs to be, or else the problem's her sad conventionality: she only wants what she's supposed to want, only wishes she wanted more. What does this mean for her? A wife one day, a mother? Just trying to become the thing she lacks? *You can do better!* There are moments like this, under the trees, running alone, when the bitter sweat beading her upper lip tastes like her future, like her own future amazement at the strength she once had in her legs.

The Girl with Nine Fingers

Say they meet again. It seems impossible, but say it anyway. They meet again at last: the girl with nine fingers and the girl whose mother has died.

Eleven at night. A Marathon station at the edge of town. At the back entrance to the hospital, a lighted sign shines an arrow up a darkened drive, EMERGENCY, pointing where Dani's mother would be tonight, otherwise. And *otherwise* may be the conjuring thought, because when Dani comes out of the store with her Monster drink—she leaves for college in two weeks and tonight, she's decided, she will stay up; she will stay out; she's told her father she's staying at Lara's but told Lara her plans have changed, and now the night is hers—an old Dakota has swung in next to her at the pumps, and the driver's door is open, and a woman's sitting sideways with her boots on the running board, and it's her.

Kristy.

With one hand she's lifted her tank top to her collarbones, while with the other she steadies the baby in her lap, whose mouth is latched to her breast, who's hardly a baby anymore but a miniature man wearing miniature sneakers, and if the hand that lifts the tank top for him seems twisted somehow, somehow ruined, Dani still can't look too closely because of the small heavy breast below those knuckles, and because of the rhythmic swish and click the little man makes as he sucks, and because of the curded pouch of loose skin above the unbuttoned button of Kristy's jeans, as intimate a glimpse of another body as Dani's ever seen.

But she must look too closely just the same, because Kristy's eyes find hers.

A squint at first, a challenge. But then something else.

Say she's recognized.

Yes: in the other girl's eyes, Dani sees herself seen. The girl whose mother has died. Later, driving around, parking here and there as the night slips by in green numbers on the dash—roiling mist off the river, electric clouds of insects mobbing the sodium lights over the truck stop, sour afterglow of Monster chased by truck-stop coffee and sugar donuts from a plastic pack, dark houses scrolling by in blocks, roads curling off into the woods, the humped and blackened mountains, the ramp to the highway, and twice again that glaring arrow, EMERGENCY—the encounter begins to feel like a dream, a story she's telling as she wanders, dry-mouthed and overcaffeinated, to still her twitching fingers and soothe her twitching blood.

Say it happened. It happened like this.

"Hey."

"Hey yourself."

Never mind who said what or what else was said—some explanation about driving the baby around so it would sleep. That's not important. Say, instead, that before anything was said, an understanding passed between them: two girls mutilated, missing parts so vital and so permanently gone that the absence had cleaved their lives forever into before and after. For each, seeing the other must have been like snapping on a light in an unfamiliar room and coming face to face with a full-length mirror.

In the last hour before first light, Dani finally follows the arrow. She passes through a blast of air conditioning to the waiting room and takes her place among the injured and ill and the muted television news. There she sits, anonymous, beneath endless images of disaster, until a nurse comes over, some friend of her mother's, to wrap a heated blanket around her shoulders and call her by her name.

"Dani. Sweetie. Honey. What are you doing here?"

Like looking into a mirror: surprised, you might see yourself differently, noticing what you'd never noticed before. Dani draws the blanket over her head. She must look like a child's drawing of a ghost. But inside the dark huddle she's made for herself, she's not actually sad. She's not grieving or deranged or dissociating, as the nurse at first seems to think. Instead, tingling from sleeplessness and caffeine, she's begun to register a feeling like—like gratitude, or joy, or just plain luck. Because she's not Kristy, after all, because they're different, too, because she is herself, she's *Dani*, and she wouldn't trade places for anything in the world.

She drives home to find her father awake, waiting on the porch as if summoned by the sound of her tires, his terrier at his ankles like a small shadow he's casting. "*There* you are," he says, and his tone lets her know the nurse called ahead. She clambers from the car, stands facing him. He's her blood, as they say in this part of the world, and she's his. But her blood is also, Dani knows, still her own. That's the difference between Kristy and Dani, the thing she discovered when she looked into the mirror. Whatever binds her to the past, she carries no link to the future but her own heart hammering away, her own blood rushing in her ears. So say a mist boils up from the river bottoms now; say it boils over the yard. Say for a moment it covers her completely, and when it lifts again she's gone.

Anything's possible.

She has her whole life ahead of her, into which it's her privilege to disappear.

SOUTH OF HAVELOCK

Once he walked into the public library instead of a bar after his shift and asked the woman at the reference desk what happened to people who died. "When nobody wants them," he said, making fists within the long unsnapped cuffs of a cowhide welding jacket. To the rain-strewn windows above and behind her, he said, "The bodies, I mean."

This is what she was able to tell him, after a few minutes' research: in North Carolina, unclaimed bodies were burned and buried at sea. Twice a year a boat sailed out from Morehead City to scatter ashes in the Atlantic, the ashes of dozens, one bag at a time.

No, he told her, that was all. That was all he'd wanted to know.

Years later, in Havelock, he ducked out from the angle of an overhead weld, out from within his helmet, gulped down water, thumbed sweat from his eyes, and ducked in again, nodding down the shield, to watch the bright keyhole bleed through blurred, molten metal. As a young man he'd been less careful than he was now, so the keyhole was always with him, whether there in fact or not. Darkness recalled it: a turquoise comma shivering in the dim stall where he showered in the travel trailer in the row of trailers trucked in for temporary workers. A candle guttering behind closed eyes in his bunk, fading teal to violet to gray.

Havelock dangled, a droop of roads, from the base at Cherry Point. They were twenty miles inland from where the Neuse spilled into the sea, bused in each morning through the main gates, bused out again each night. Salt haze smeared the summer sun. Brackish water rose into ditches when it rained. Week after week he lived like this, warehouse construction at the

Fleet Readiness Center, making arc connections in the super-
structure, pipe welds for the plumbing and sprinkler systems,
handrails along the access stairs, reinforced frames for each
emergency exit.

Cargo planes lumbered down runways. Jump jets snowed
from the haze, flashing overhead with a roar like circular saws.
At the strip clubs across the highway from the barbed wire and
hurricane fencing that marked the perimeter of the base, Marines
were everywhere, and what surprised him most was how young
they all looked, their smooth faces tipped back in the throbbing
dark. He was thirty-eight, not old, but he felt the difference. His
scarred corneas danced fire down the catwalk.

He'd made a mistake once, on a job, in the rain. Condensation
must've dripped from the sheeting erected to keep him dry.
Electrocuted: in an instant he'd been thrown down and emptied.
Direct current had saved him, the shock blowing him free instead
of sealing him to the power supply, as alternating current could
do. Still, he'd been gone a minute, stretched out in the dirt with
a head full of smoke, a child again, and the rain spattering the
sheeting had become the play of an overnight shower down
the length of the car where he'd slept and woken to his mother
stoned and asleep beside him in that humid, intimate, hutch-
scented dark where, for a time, they had lived. Afterward, awake
again, shaking it off—a vision—he figured she must have been
dead to have come to him like that. Okay, he said to himself. For
years he'd thought of her mostly as a thing that had happened
to him. She'd left him long ago; now she was gone. Okay. His
teeth were chattering. Take the rest of the day off, the foreman
told him, but he shook his head: no, no. What he wanted to do
was work.

South of Havelock the highway cut through the Croatan. No
exits here, no driveways, just sandy banks spiked with weeds,

dark pines piled against the silver sky. The oil light was on in his old pickup. He wasn't sure exactly where he was going and had to hope the highway would take him there. He'd seen the ocean once before, on his last government job, a six-week stint in Newport News, but that had been different. That hadn't been here. The first small clutches of houses began. In a truck burning oil he entered Morehead City.

Nothing at first. Strip malls, gas stations, used-car lots, fast food, power lines strung over the highway like netting. A dollar store, an urgent care, a gated subdivision, motels. Miles of this—and then the water. The highway lifted, and he was carried across the sound to an island thin as an eyebrow. He parked on an apron of sand where the pavement scalloped away. A foot-pocked path climbed the last wall of dunes.

The roar of the surf. The thick, dank, faintly electrical smell of a receding tide.

Children rolled in the cement-colored shallows. Gulls circled down for small creatures that blew holes with their breath through the wet sand that concealed them. Small voices cried out to be looked for, to be watched. He took it all in, as he'd come here to do, though he didn't know what this could change. It was a long drive home, inland all the way, to the foothills where he lived. He followed the glowing keyhole into his rented room, the dark air stale, the water shut off at the valve beneath the sink. Turning the valve, he heard water refilling his walls. Like wave after wave, like overhead rain—his eyes prickled. The keyhole flared. And for the first time, he took comfort in the scars: a light endlessly fading, endlessly renewed. A faith to sustain him on this side of the horizon, where sea and sky merged in an unbreakable weld.

THE SWEET NOTHINGS

Valerie and Mack met years ago, at North Carolina State, where she was studying elementary education and he played right tackle—second string—for the Wolfpack football team. They were partners in a chemistry lab, a required science credit Valerie had overlooked until this, her senior year. Mack, meanwhile, was a freshman, a hulking, overgrown boy from the western part of the state. He had a stiff brown brush of hair and a face like a thumb. Pencils snapped in his fist. Safety goggles bit rings into his forehead and cheeks.

Still, he was an athlete, and on Tuesday and Thursday mornings she watched him navigate the narrow classroom aisles with the heedless, galumphing grace of a big dog. When the first-string tackle graduated, Mack would be promoted to starter—if he maintained his grades. Valerie suspected that she, trained to cajole children into learning through charm, trickery, and force, had been made his partner in order to protect him.

Perhaps Mack sensed this as well. During lab exercises, his attention to her bordered on reverence. He wrote down measurements as she called them out, his flushed face squeezed tight. At the end of the term, having earned a B-minus, he asked her to a movie.

Boys did not ask Valerie to movies. Valerie's mother, kind and clueless, had once described her as *an ample girl*, words that still stung. Mack didn't seem to mind. A week before Christmas, the campus theater was screening *Miracle on 34th Street*. Near the end—"Faith is believing when common sense tells you not to," Maureen O'Hara was saying—Mack covered her hand on the armrest with his. His palm was warm, heavy, and damp.

So he courted her in his earnest, stumbling manner. For

Valerie, the experience was new and disorienting. What did Mack see that other boys had missed?

"Tell me what you love about me."

(A bad habit—addressing him like a difficult student who needed to be coaxed into speaking through clear commands. Still, the request was sincere.)

"Hey, now." He plucked at his lower lip as if trying to draw out the answer. "I'm not too good with words, I guess."

True.

But he was good at other things. His hand at the small of her back guided her through doors. At meals, his big foot rested between hers like a puppy. He put his tongue on her body. He slipped his fingers between her thighs with a gentleness so unlike yet so necessary to the happy, grunting work that followed. She hadn't been a virgin when they'd met—there'd been a boy her sophomore year, a series of brief and mostly unsatisfactory scuffles beneath dormitory blankets—but Mack was her first real lover.

Lover. That word, with its ponderous romanticism, had a way of shaming Valerie. It was difficult, some mornings, to look back kindly on her eagerness in the dark. All that flesh colliding, the sounds they made together, the smells. *Ample lover,* she thought.

Her parents, Diana and Ned, lived in nearby Cary. They approved of Mack in the same simple way they approved of nearly everything Valerie chose. Mack's parents remained distant. He came from a mountain town called Saluda. The son of a machinist and the grandson of a logger, he rarely mentioned his family.

"She wants to talk to you." He held the phone out to Valerie.

It was his mother.

"I don't suppose you've been baptized."

"Excuse me?"

"A girl what's done the deed with a boy she barely knows. I don't suppose you've been baptized."

Mack, hovering over her shoulder, stole the phone away.

In truth, Valerie found this exchange obscurely exciting. The threat of trouble bound them together somehow.

That summer, Mack tore ligaments in his knee during a blocking drill. After two surgeries, he began physical therapy to minimize the limp that would dog him for the rest of his life. Football was out of the question. Without his athletic scholarship, he'd have to return to Saluda. "I don't know," he said following one therapy session, still panting after the walk on crutches from Valerie's car to her tiny garden-level efficiency. "I could still run a metal press pretty good."

Valerie placed her hand on his thigh. Love was a new muscle sewn into her chest; it squeezed at the oddest moments. For days at a time, Mack was simply there, as steady and unremarkable as the summer heat. And then, without warning—*squeeze*.

"Stay with me," she said.

The disapproval from Saluda—and Mack's presence at her side through a flurry of phone calls and a brief, unannounced, and utterly poisonous visit from his parents—only hardened her resolve. Ned and Diana were less inclined to judge. They were easygoing, affable people, well matched. "He makes you happy," Diana said at Thanksgiving. She removed a rhubarb crisp from the oven. In the den, Ned and Mack were watching a football game. Something good had happened. They pounded each other on the back, whooping.

"He does." Valerie dug a corkscrew into a bottle of gooseberry wine.

In those first delicate days, it mattered more to her that she could say this with apparent conviction than that she actually felt convinced. Later, she'd recall her early years with Mack as the happiest of her life; at the time, however, they hardly seemed so. There was, for example—for the first year, at least—the apartment itself, small to begin with and made smaller still by their shared bulk, their inability to pass from the kitchenette to the closet-like bathroom to the futon sofa that doubled as their bed without brushing against one another. There was the terrible anxiety that overtook her each morning as she left for work, to stand alone before a room full of kindergartners, the rows of little upturned faces. Above all, there was the inescapable intimacy of a life shared. Nothing remained hidden for long. If she was cranky, sweaty, or had gas, he would know. And she would always know the same about him, whether she cared to or not.

Despite its proximity to Raleigh, Cary still had the feel of a small town in those days, and Ned, the assistant manager at the Chevrolet dealership, could claim a degree of local regard. Through what he liked to call his worldly connections, he'd helped Valerie secure her teaching position in Fuquay-Varina; now he turned his attention to Mack, finagling a job for him at the dealership's body shop. This kindness, as much as anything, cemented Valerie and Mack. It pulled Mack from the apartment, lending their days the rhythms of what finally felt like a real life together. It muffled the criticism from Saluda, since he was earning more than he would have in the machine shop. It meant Valerie and Mack could move out of the efficiency and into a starter home. It meant they could get married.

Marriage did not strike Valerie as momentous. It was simply a confirmation of fact. She'd already leaned into Mack while he groaned and flexed his knee against her weight. She'd wiped the sweat that stung his eyes and heard the chewy pop of scar tissue inside his knee. She knew his strength, and she knew where he was weakest.

Yet it was Ned, not Valerie, to whom Mack turned first when his own father died several years later, a stroke felling him as he crossed the blazing parking lot outside his machine shop.

That evening, Valerie carried their son, Kevin, to the bottom of the backyard, where a small stream gurgled. (This was their second home in Cary. They'd left the first when neighboring houses began dividing into apartments or else falling to make way for condos and duplexes. In a few years, the stream here

would be dry—diverted down an enormous grate and into the
sewer system for a new subdivision—and they would be packing
again.) She set Kevin to play at the water's edge. After receiving
the news from Saluda, she and Mack had called her parents.
Diana was in the kitchen now, preparing dinner. When Valerie
had tried to help, Diana shooed her away. "Take care of the
boy." Tears forked down her mother's cheeks, shed for a person
she'd barely met.

Before taking her son outside, Valerie had peered into the
bedroom where Mack had retreated with Ned. The blinds were
lowered, a baseball game on the television. A pair of beers
sweated onto the nightstand. On the bed, her husband pressed
his face into her father's chest and wept.

"Momma, look!"

Kevin had dug a crayfish out from under a rock, and now he
lifted the dripping brown thing for her to see.

Mack hadn't noticed her in the doorway, but her father had.
Over the top of Mack's head, Ned had given her a small, sweet
smile. She needn't worry, he seemed to say. He'd take care of
things. The sight of the two big men curled together, barefoot,
had wrenched a hiccup from Valerie's throat. She'd hurried out
the door with the boy.

Kevin yelped and began to cry. The crayfish had pinched him.

This would prove to be a pattern: Kevin pursued bad ideas
zealously, came to harm, and shrank back in remorse, only to
grow enraptured by his next mistake. Stiff in her arms now,
he glared down at the stream. "Where is that thing?" he said.
"I want to *stomp* it." And then he burst into fresh tears, wilder
than before.

When he was eighteen, Kevin showed up one day with a pair
of tattoos: FUCKING written in gothic script down one welted
red triceps, HOSTILE down the other. "What is that supposed
to mean?" Valerie asked. The boy only stared. He'd inherited
Mack's massive, slouching frame, and Valerie recognized his
expression—suspicious, gloomy, almost exhausted—as one of

her own. But *fucking hostile*? To whom did that sentiment belong? Surely least of all to Kevin himself. When her son had been fifteen, she'd watched from the bleachers as he'd torn off his football helmet and slumped to the sidelines, rubbing furiously at his eyes. He couldn't seem to grasp the calculated intensity of the sport. He took it personally: those other boys were trying to *hurt* him. And when Valerie had told Kevin he didn't have to continue playing a game he didn't enjoy, the relief that had washed over his face had been heartbreaking.

"But what will Dad say?"

"Oh, honey. Dad will understand."

A lie. Mack was, if anything, more easily troubled than Valerie by their big, bewildered, bewildering son. While she explained Kevin's decision to quit the team, Mack blinked at his shoes, as if she'd just posed a riddle.

"I wasn't like that," he said at last, looking up.

She imagined the world as Mack saw it, a foggy place he muddled through. If someone took his hand, he followed; if a door opened, he passed through. But where did the door lead? Who had opened it? The world receded into mystery the farther it extended from himself. She wondered whether Kevin found his surroundings so inscrutable. Perhaps, whereas Mack could resign himself, trusting the machinations he couldn't grasp, Kevin felt threatened.

More worrisome than their son's football troubles had been the incident with the Sharpie. This had been when Kevin was in the third grade, a chubby boy still growing into his bulk, a target for classmates' mockery. During recess, he'd retreated to the coatroom with a permanent marker. When the bell rang, he'd emerged, arms and legs and much of his face coated in ink.

Valerie was called into a meeting with the vice-principal and the school counselor. They were concerned, they said, about the possible racial overtones of Kevin's act. At her side, Kevin fidgeted in his chair. His skin, scrubbed raw, still held a blue shadow. (And who had scrubbed him? Years later, the question still rankled.) His eyes bored into his lap, his small body practically vibrating with misery and rage.

She rose, quite literally, to his defense: standing, pointing, assuming her ringing classroom voice. She didn't work with these particular men—she still taught in Fuquay-Varina—but she knew them by reputation. And she knew the administrative type, so eager to pigeonhole students according to patterns of behavior that meshed with prescribed institutional responses. But Kevin was not a bad child, she insisted; he was not looking to hurt anyone.

What, then, was he?

"Fucking hostile," Mack repeated, the night of the tattoos.

They were in bed. It was late. Over the years, this had become their place and time to talk, their problems temporarily softening like the lamplight through its shade.

"That's not him, though," Valerie said. Kevin had his own apartment. He had a job in the parts department at the dealership. He was only directionless, like so many eighteen-year-olds. Maybe he could enroll at the local community college. He was only anxious, only frightened.

"You could talk to him," she said.

"And say what?"

An honest question, she knew. Rising through the world of the dealership, Mack had remained himself, earning a reputation for honesty. "Pathologically scrupulous," Ned once had remarked, smiling. But what diminished profits in one way seemed to augment them in another: the body shop was one of the busiest in Cary. "Always good to have work, I suppose," Mack said, happily befuddled, as if he'd had nothing to do with it.

One upshot of this success was that, when Ned bought out his retiring business partner to become the dealership's sole proprietor, he promoted Mack to assistant manager, overseeing all non-sales operations. Later, he encouraged Mack to return to school for a BBA—which Mack managed, over several scrambling years of night and weekend classes, to do. And when Ned entered his own semi-retirement, he promoted Mack to full manager, a seemingly perilous height for someone without sales experience. (Watching Mack straighten his tie that first morning, the silk knot overlarge, his pink neck overflowing his collar and already beginning to glisten, Valerie again felt in her chest that terrible squeeze.) Yet this caused little stir at the dealership. Her husband, it seemed, was universally beloved.

"On the job," Mack said, lying beside her, "he likes to eat lunch alone."

As if this were the most difficult thing to understand about their son.

So Valerie tried to be enthusiastic about Miranda. She was the first girl to whom Kevin had ever introduced them; she might have been his first real girlfriend. He was twenty-three, still clerking in the parts department, still living in the same sweaty studio in a building full of college students. Somehow, he'd saved enough for a motorcycle. Meanwhile, he'd added two new tattoos: a rattlesnake coiling around his left forearm and an abstract tribal design that climbed the side of his neck, where it could not be politely concealed. Miranda was nineteen and worked at a bar in Durham. Valerie wondered what sort of bar Kevin might frequent. He'd said Miranda was a waitress, but she suspected the girl was a dancer. Still, she'd set her reservations aside, for Kevin's sake.

"Oh, my God, hello!" At a restaurant in Cary, Miranda slipped from beneath Kevin's arm to greet Valerie and Mack. Her spaghetti-strapped dress clung like a colorful mist to sun-crisped skin dusted with glitter. A sparkling glaze oozed down her cleavage. She spoke in bursts of emotion: "It is so good! To meet you!"

And if, ultimately, she was not the woman Valerie had feared she might be, she was also not whom Valerie would have chosen for her son. Kevin required a steady hand at the tiller, but

Miranda was as beautiful and empty as a doll. She could provide encouragement but not guidance—an enabler.

The motorcycle, the tattoos, Valerie and Mack's fear that Kevin was selling marijuana to his coworkers at the dealership and the students in his building—given this history of mistakes, these symptoms of damaged judgment, it should have come as no surprise that he ended up marrying her.

Mistakes. Kevin and Miranda moved to Asheville, where, together with a group of business partners whose names seemed to keep changing, they opened a head shop. (When Valerie explained what this was, Mack's face scrunched as it had back in the chemistry lab.) After a year, a police raid revealed several dozen marijuana plants beneath grow lamps in a windowless storeroom. Several of the business partners—if you could call them that—went to prison, while Kevin escaped with a suspended sentence and probation. Miranda, whose name had never been legally associated with the head shop, got off scot-free.

Valerie and Mack had loaned Kevin money to open the business. "How much did you spend on filth?"

"I had no idea, Momma, swear to God. I went to the cops the instant I found out."

Could it possibly have taken him an entire year to discover the secret of the locked storeroom? The authorities, incurious, seemed to have chosen to credit Kevin's account. Valerie wanted to believe it, too.

After that, Kevin and Miranda crossed the state to Elizabeth City, working for an elderly couple who rented kayaks, paddleboats, and bicycles to tourists. For a time, Kevin's voice on the phone sounded—Valerie thought, with guarded enthusiasm—truly happy. When the elderly couple offered to sell the business and Kevin again asked for money, it was difficult to say no.

But Kevin and Miranda quickly defaulted on their bank loan and burned through their scant savings in an attempt to expand the business into jet skis. This venture, too, failed.

So they returned to Cary. Kevin began clerking again at the dealership, while Miranda—they weren't trying to hide it anymore—went back to dancing. It was more difficult for her now, though, Kevin admitted. He and Valerie ate lunch together on Saturdays, when Mack worked half-days. Leaning back, Kevin ran a hand over his stomach. In a mortified flash, Valerie understood that he meant stretch marks.

They'd brought a son back with them from Elizabeth City—an infant named Doyle, in honor of Miranda's shiftless and underemployed father.

Was it still possible, Valerie wondered, that all could be forgiven? They were back where they'd begun, after all, her child and his childish wife. Worse for wear, perhaps, but surely wiser, less romantic, more defined.

But that winter, Miranda's dog, an ancient Boston terrier named Smurf, finally died. For Miranda, this prompted another reappraisal. "My one dream," she revealed during a dinner at Ned and Diana's, "is to breed dogs. Boston terriers, I mean. Like Smurf? Because he was a good, good dog, and what I want? Is for other people to know my joy." She spared Valerie a low, savvy glance over the gravy boat. "Three hundred, four hundred dollars a pup."

Unmoved, Valerie spent the next several nights bringing Mack around to back her refusal.

They would keep baby Doyle in diapers, formula, and clothing, she and Mack explained. If Kevin wanted to attend night school, as his father had, they'd pay for his classes—Miranda, too. One day, they'd help put Kevin and Miranda in their first home, and they were already setting money aside for Doyle's college. Valerie leaned forward, her hand on Mack's scarred knee. He needed support during the awful act of refusal. "But not this," she said. "We will not help you open a kennel."

"It's not a kennel!" Miranda cried. "It wouldn't *be* a kennel!"

There was more to Valerie's reasoning than she'd revealed. For the first time in years, money was tight. Dealerships everywhere were pinched. After their Saturday dinners, Mack and Ned sequestered themselves in Ned's office, talking in low voices. Would they be shuttered as GM contracted? The answer was out of their hands. Mack seemed confused and hurt. If people didn't want massive pickup trucks and SUVs, why did shipments of them keep arriving? Where was he supposed to put them all? Who was doing this to him?

Valerie had long declined opportunities to leave the classroom and join the administrative ranks; now she reconsidered. Charter schools were springing up all over Raleigh-Durham. Many were casting about for anyone with experience to take the reins. "It's a risk," she told Diana. They were at the kitchen table, sipping decaf. "A better salary right off the bat, and opportunities for advancement I don't have now. But these new schools go under all the time. And where does that leave us?"

"Worse off than before," Diana agreed.

Valerie had another, more personal reservation: the bland administrative masks of Kevin's vice-principal and school counselor as they'd refused to care for her troubled boy the way a good teacher, however strained by dwindling budgets and growing classes, still could.

She loved her work; she often said so. She said it to parents, nervous couples increasingly younger than she was, preparing to send a child alone from the home for the first time. "I truly love working with children," she said. It seemed to reassure them, as though they'd feared the opposite. Still, the words were thin: they captured so very little of the sweet, quenching, exhausting efforts of her days. She'd learned to distrust the comment, even as she made it habitually; she rarely spoke of her work outside of habitual remarks. The dealership was the public business of the house. Valerie's teaching was something else. She held it close.

Diana smiled. "Whatever you do, dear, I'm sure it will work out."

Her parents were well into their seventies, their bodies and voices slowly shrinking. Dimness gathered slyly in the corners of their home, as though the light bulbs were too weak. With her delicate neck, large gray eyes, and unnaturally orange poof of downy hair, Diana looked like the chick of some exotic bird.

"Please don't worry about it," Valerie said.

Soon thereafter, Ned caught a chest cold that developed into pneumonia. For several days he lay in the hospital, feverish, slipping in and out of an unconsciousness far more abandoned than sleep. At one point, Diana called: he was passing. Arriving at the hospital, though, Valerie and Mack found Ned sitting up, receiving fluids through an IV and blinking in apparent astonishment. "Hello?" he called to Valerie.

"Hello, Daddy." She took his hand. Across the bed, Diana held the other.

"Hello?"

"Such a scare," Diana said. "I'm afraid he's still a little out of it."

Valerie stroked the spotted knuckles, the putty-colored nails. "I'm right here."

"Hello?" he cried.

Afterward, Mack got into the car and lowered his head to the steering wheel. "I'm not okay to drive."

But Ned recovered, after a fashion. His strength returned, and Diana took him home.

"He's a little different," she said when Valerie asked how he was doing.

"Different how?"

"He's still getting better. Yes," she added, more firmly, "a little better every day."

At their next Saturday dinner, Ned ate poorly. For years, he and Diana had followed a low-sodium diet, but tonight he complained. "Bland," he muttered to his fish and vegetables. "You're bland." Looking up, he wore a strange, hooded expression. What was he thinking?

But the question couldn't claim more than a portion of

Valerie's attention. Another crisis had arisen. Perhaps the kennel had been the final straw: Miranda had gone to stay with her people in Five Forks, South Carolina. She was "thinking things through," Kevin had reported.

"What things?"

"I don't know. *Things.*"

She'd left Doyle, now almost a year old, with Kevin. In the past, he'd worked days while Miranda worked nights; they'd passed their parental duties back and forth like a baton. What was he supposed to do now? He couldn't afford daycare.

"We'll take the boy," Valerie had said. "Whenever you need."

She and Mack could've paid for daycare instead, or Kevin could've left the child with one of Mack's sisters for the time being. (A real possibility: without overture or apology, the years had effected a rapprochement. Mack and Valerie visited Saluda each Easter. The terms on which their marriage had begun, if not forgotten or even quite forgiven, had turned toothless—ancient embarrassments hardly worth mentioning at this late date.) Either option would have been wiser. They had their own obligations, after all. Yet to do otherwise was unthinkable. When she'd told Mack, he'd simply nodded: "Sure, sure." The arrangement needed no explanation.

The following Saturday, Ned seemed better. He was eating, at least, and when Mack mentioned a new hybrid car, he listened with apparent interest. Halfway through the meal, though, he turned to Diana, speaking around a mouthful of food.

"Pass the salt."

Diana lowered her fork. "We don't keep salt at our table, remember?"

Remember? The word flashed like a warning. Valerie tried to catch Mack's eye, but he looked away.

"I want salt. I want it." Ned still hadn't swallowed. "I have always taken salt with my dinners."

"No, dear," Diana said. "Not for years."

Ned reached into his mouth and hooked out a mass of

chicken and rice. It plopped to his plate. "Cow," he said to his wife, jabbing a dripping finger. "Fat, fat, fat, fat, fat."

Once, Cary had been a town Valerie could walk across from one side to the other. Now, though, the population was approaching 150,000, the city inextricably linked to the Raleigh-Durham metroplex by an umbilical of strip malls and subdivisions. She and Mack had given up outrunning the expansion. After sagging through a period of stately decline, their neighborhood now straggled toward second youth. Two houses on their block had recently been purchased by young families from up north; another had been stripped to its skeleton by flippers. In the backyard opposite theirs, neighbors were installing a pool. One Saturday, Valerie woke to a backhoe snorting and pawing at the other side of the fence.

"Awful racket," she said over breakfast.

Mack dumped coffee into a travel mug, his sports jacket already rumpled. "Don't think I'll make dinner tonight."

"Ned will miss you."

A cruel poke, but he'd avoided last Saturday's dinner, too, claiming to need the extra hours at the dealership. At first, the transparency of the ploy had stoked her tenderness for Mack, who loved Ned as much as anyone, but this morning, she simply found it irritating. Another month had passed. Ned was no worse, no better. This was simply who he was now: a bitter old child, quick to confusion and anger, occasionally crawling from beneath the rock of his own dismay to spit abuse at his wife. Different, Diana had said. No, Valerie thought, worse. Her mother's insistence that everything was fine was itself cause for concern.

"Sorry," Mack said. But he didn't offer to come.

Still, keeping with custom, she walked him to his car, where he kissed her cheek without meeting her eyes. After he'd gone, she stood listening to the blasts from the backyard. What did it cost to bring in work crews on a Saturday morning? Why dig a pool in such a rush?

Useless questions. The day's tasks presented themselves, a list.

Mack had assembled a crib in the spare bedroom upstairs. Kevin was heading to Five Forks to "clear the air," he said. The baby would stay here. (Valerie's idea. She feared that, were her son to travel south with Doyle, he might return alone.)

The morning passed in a fuss of cleaning, as if Doyle were a prickly guest, apt to find fault. It was possible, Valerie allowed, peeling foil from beneath a stove burner, that she was excited. But there wasn't time to explore the accusation. She soon discovered, in the little-used powder room beside the laundry, a brown blister swelling from the wall beneath the sink. Valerie crouched, groaning a little as her knees popped. The blister was warm and pliable, like skin. Through the wall, she heard the beat of leaking water: drop-drop, drop-drop.

Something to add to the list.

She met Kevin for a late lunch at a wrought-iron table beneath a striped parasol, a dining arrangement the restaurant advertised as *Parisian*. Lately, he'd taken to shaving his head and letting his beard grow. Valerie supposed the look might fool strangers, but she recognized the uncertain eyes peering out through the undergrowth, leaping from one thing to the next. He hefted Doyle in one arm, a diaper bag in the other. Following him to the table, she read, on his skin below the sleeves of his t-shirt, the words KING TILE, as though he were advertising a local business. Doyle was lowered into a booster seat; the belt mechanism seemed to fascinate him. A waitress placed three sets of wrapped silverware on the table.

"Excuse me!" Kevin called after her. "Did you just put sharp objects in front of my child?"

Blushing furiously—he was enough to scare *her*, at least—the girl stammered an apology, collected the extra silverware, and hustled away.

Kevin blushed, too. His beard seemed to brighten as his cheeks grew dark.

"You were protecting your son," Valerie assured him.

"I didn't have to do it like that."

"Well," she chirped, "I don't know if it's Paris, but it's lovely to be outside."

Too late: Kevin was already sodden with guilt. Before their drinks arrived, it had altered the course of their conversation.

"I'm sorry to put all this on you." The child, he meant? Yes, apparently, and more: "I know that you and Dad—you never wanted another kid. After me."

"Sweetie," she said, reaching for his hand. Where had this thought come from? Yet he was right. Kevin had been born late. Two weeks overdue, Valerie had sat by the rain-smeared window of her hospital room, waiting for the hour of her induced labor. Instead of fear, anticipation, or excitement, she'd felt merely a pressure between her hips: a constant, maddening, insatiable urge to pee. Curiously pained, resentful of it, guilty over her lack of more significant affect, she'd been nearly in tears by the time the procedure began. And then, of course, had come Kevin himself. Over the years, Valerie and Mack had occasionally broached the subject of another child, but such talk had never gone far.

Still, what was Kevin suggesting—that she loved him less because of his troubles? Oh, preposterous. More, she wanted to tell him, more. She'd known easy children, gliding through her classroom on soft wings of self-confidence. Their expectation that their every action would be met with approval, even applause, would be galling were it not so sincere. They were loved; they knew it and expected it; they returned it with ease. She'd watched such children become easy young adults, wearing their lives like exquisitely tailored fashions. But she'd never wished for anything other than what she'd received.

Still, saying *sweetie* did no good. Instead, she tried to steer his resentment away from himself. "Miranda and her kennel. What a fuss that's turned out to be."

"It wasn't about the kennel, Momma."

"Of course it was."

She recognized in her tone the same righteous certainty once aimed at her from Saluda, and from across the desk in the vice-principal's office.

"No," Kevin insisted, "it could have been anything. I mean, what are we, Miranda and me? What are we right now?"

"I don't understand."

"You and Pops, you're *something*. Grammie and Gramps, too. But how do you get to be something? You get these ideas, right, and you build them up." He was warming to the subject, brimming with the brittle enthusiasm she knew could quickly shatter into silence. "You get these ideas about what you could become. Otherwise, you only ever are what you are right now. And you don't have to tell me what that means for Miranda and me. I already know."

The waitress arrived with their food.

"Oh, thank you," Kevin said, absurdly grateful. The girl smiled stoically.

"Plash," the baby cried. "Plash!"

Kevin seemed to understand, leaning over so Doyle could pat his beard.

"The head shop, the rental stuff: those were my ideas. And she was so good about them. She believed what I said we could become even when I didn't anymore. You act like it's her fault," he said. "*I'm* the one who proved her wrong."

The baby grabbed a curly brown handful and yanked. Kevin's face went rigid. Doyle had Miranda's beautiful emerald eyes, and it seemed to Valerie that he'd never looked more like his mother than he did now, squealing as he tore at her son's beard. When Doyle released him, Kevin sank back, ebbing, and Valerie turned to her salad. She didn't have the heart to tell him he was wrong. There were no big ideas, no grand romantic sweeps of time. What were years but stacks of days, hours, minutes, seconds? Life was lived small.

Still, Kevin loved Miranda; that much was clear. He'd chosen her, as he'd chosen to mar his skin. That love, like ink, had insinuated itself. She could no longer have her son without it. When the waitress reappeared, Valerie seized the check over Kevin's halfhearted protests. As she lifted Doyle from his booster seat, though, she saw Doyle slip a twenty beneath his water glass. Did he think she wouldn't notice, wouldn't care? After Doyle and his safety seat were buckled into her car, she opened her pocketbook, removed the bills inside—not counting, lest she reconsider—and pressed them into her son's hands.

"In case."

His shoulders slumped. His face was an overcast sheet, as it had been years ago, before he'd pulled on his football helmet and slogged back onto the field. He stuffed the money into his pocket. On her toes, she kissed the corner of his jaw through his beard.

"Momma," he said.

They left the restaurant, turning in opposite directions. Kevin was off to Five Forks—to do what? Beg, cry, rage? Perhaps it would even work. They would return together. Their lives, for a time, would go on as before.

As for Valerie, there remained the day's tasks to complete.

First the supermarket, to pick up a few staples for her and Mack and the baby; next, a pedestrian mall where a boutique sold local vintages, including the gooseberry wine her parents enjoyed. For years, Valerie had disliked it—too cloying, too syrupy—but the winery had improved as Cary had grown. These days, their gooseberry wine finished with a tart, melancholy bite. The mall was crowded with people shopping, eating, or simply enjoying the day. Valerie wove her way, baby balanced on her hip. Amazing, how quickly the feel for this returned. At a playground, Doyle piled her toes with sand. Changing his diaper—the pink soles of his feet, his soft pink bottom, the tiny, silly pouch of his scrotum—was an act so familiar it seemed impossible that she hadn't done it daily for more than twenty-five years.

At six o'clock, she rang her parents' doorbell.

"Oh—Valerie!" her father said. He blinked down at the child. "Kevin."

No tantrums tonight, at least. Ned stabbed cauliflower florets one by one and pointed with his fork when he wanted something added to his plate. Only Doyle engaged his interest. As Valerie guided spoonfuls of strained carrots to the baby's mouth, which opened eagerly or bowed in a plump expression of refusal, but never did either more than twice in a row, Ned's own lips trembled.

"He's been so calm," Diana said after dinner. "His appetite's returning, too."

Ned was watching the baby in the den, an arrangement Valerie tolerated because it gave her these minutes alone with her mother. They'd cleared the table and loaded the dishwasher, wiped down the counters and scrubbed the pots and pans. Valerie opened the gooseberry wine and poured them each a glass.

"We should talk about what to do," she said.

"About what, dear?"

In the next room, Ned coughed and muttered something. It sounded like Latin.

"He takes care of himself just fine," Diana said. "Any help he needs, I can give."

How to say this? Ned was a big man still, his mind diminishing more rapidly than the rest of him. Valerie could envision—dimly yet firmly, as she might puzzle the outlines of an object beneath a shroud—an irrevocable act. Three decades with kindergartners had left her impatient with pretense, quick to anticipate trouble and engage it head-on. The reckless child who waved safety scissors at his classmates: you took his wrist and worked the scissors from his grasp. You gathered him up and sat him in a distant corner of the room. If he cried, you smoothed his hair. You dried his tears with your sleeve. But you did not return him to the class. Not if he couldn't settle.

"It's one thing if he just insults you, Mom. But it's another if—"

Diana's eyes narrowed. "If what?"

"I'm only saying, Mom."

"If *what*?"

"We need to consider the possibility."

"In fifty-three years, your father has never raised a hand against me. Not once."

"He's not himself anymore."

"He's my husband." She glared, suddenly fierce. "And you have never known him, Valerie, not like I have. He can still be sweet sometimes, as sweet as ever before. You have no idea the sweet nothings he whispers in my ear at night."

"It's not a matter of who loves who," Valerie said.

"Of course it is. Everything is."

Her mother drained her wine, settling the matter.

In the den, her father had sunk into his favorite armchair. Valerie kissed his cheek and gathered Doyle from the carpet. Ned's eyes tracked her to the door.

"You're a great-grandfather," she said.

He looked away, his attention sinking.

From the kitchen came the wet chuckle of a glass being refilled.

She drove home, softly singing snatches of songs for Doyle, whose head bobbed along in shallow sleep. Up the front walk, then, her arms strung with grocery bags, the baby hot against her shoulder. He patted her chin, searching for a beard.

"All gone," Valerie said.

"Puff," Doyle whispered.

It was nine o'clock, a clear blue evening. Exhausted, she tucked Doyle in before collapsing into bed herself. Mack was there when she woke, hanging his wrinkled jacket in the closet, disappearing into the bathroom to stuff his shirt into the hamper, reappearing in a yellowed undershirt and boxers, his white gut rolling over the waistband like a pooched lip. Before she'd awakened, he must have set a stack of promotional pamphlets on the nightstand; he selected one now before pulling back the covers.

"You're bringing those to bed?"

"Was going to." He showed her the pamphlet: a tiny car shaped like a teardrop, with a pleasantly meaningless name.

"These new models—the sub-compacts, the electrics—the next few years, they'll make or break us." Without football, his bulk had gone soft and loose. She, on the other hand, hadn't changed: ample girl, ample woman. He eased into bed, the springs creaking, and frowned. "I feel like I need to know everything now."

It was not a day Valerie would particularly come to remember, lost in all that lay ahead: the contraction of dealerships and the bailout, new jobs, new crises, her parents, her son. Mack's familiar end-of-day scent descended over her now, a cloud of burnt cinnamon, moldering cardboard, and lumber. He was enormous, an entire landscape of hills beneath the blankets, the only thing in all the world that could make her feel small.

She buried her face in his chest.

Setting the pamphlet aside, he gathered her up. "What's wrong?"

Valerie felt as though she'd been holding her breath.

"I'm going to try for one of those charter-school positions. I've decided."

"Okay." He stroked her hair. "That's good. I think that's a real good choice."

Always his faith that things would work out. He never flagged. She pressed ear to his ribs—that distant, watery beat.

At this hour, at least, the neighborhood was as quiet as the one that had surrounded their very first home. Then, too, they'd curled together at each day's end while a baby slept across the hall. She ached for that small, lovely, departed town.

Eventually, her hand trailed through the fur on Mack's chest, his belly.

"Hey, now," he said.

They'd never gotten more graceful. If anything, their means had grown simpler, more honest and direct, over the years. They stroked one another. When they were ready, he climbed atop her.

At the same time, however, she was remembering something; unaccountable yet insistent, it scurried across a corner of her thoughts. The leak in the downstairs bathroom. The plaster softening, drip by drip.

"Mack," she said.

He grunted. "Valerie."

But the old tidal pull of pleasure was already taking over, her head tipping back, her words unthreading. What was left? Only his name, a few simple profanities no naughtier than dandelions, and the weightless vocabulary of blessing and affirmation that rattled along in the wake of emotion, as clamorous and incoherent as cans fixed to the bumpers of newlyweds' cars. *Sweetie. Honey. Doll. My love.* These, at last, would have to do. Closing her eyes, Valerie surrendered the day.

TO WOUND, TO TEAR, TO PULL
TO PIECES

Years ago, recovering from a case of heartbreak, I met a friend for lunch in the small Wisconsin town where we both were living at the time. We talked for a while, and when we parted, I felt better. I can't explain why.

This is a ghost story.

A case of heartbreak. What I call it now. As if the only thing to do anymore is laugh—a little jaded, a little prideful. I abandoned graduate school to live for six months with an older man, a professor of linguistics named Jeremy Kite, and when, one might say, my shine wore off, he asked me to leave, and I left. I fled homeward, to my parents. In the town where I'd grown up, I submitted to their tender, suffocating attentions and readied my return to the life I'd been leading before.

Which I eventually did. That's all my great romance turned out to be: a bump in the road.

Some clichés save us more than time.

It's also too simple to say Joanna and I were friends. We'd known one another in high school—I played volleyball and field hockey; Joanna cheered; we knew many of the same lazy, athletic, breezily handsome, utterly thoughtless boys—but I don't believe we ever had a real conversation. I remember admiring her, in a way. Joanna was tiny and plump, redheaded and pretty, her freckled knees flashing below the hem of her cheer skirt on game days. *Plucky* was a word I might have used to describe her. An optimist, an overachiever.

Of course I believed I was more the type of girl the boys we knew were really interested in. But it was Joanna who ended up marrying one of them.

Away at college in Madison, I found myself endowed with new freedoms, new powers. I'm not just referring to sex, though I'm referring to that as well. I didn't burn any bras, but I did replace a few of the full, pearlescent, matronly designs my mother favored with bright, filmy things that crumpled as easily as afterthoughts. I did see draft tickets burned, and I sang songs for racial equality and an end to the war, and I conducted a series of what I called liaisons with young men whose gauzy ideals masqueraded, sometimes charmingly, as real ideas.

I had a job shelving books at the university library, where I spent a long autumn leaning on my cart in the stacks, living through *War and Peace*. (Years later, reading Adrienne Rich, I'd suffer a pang of recognition. Neutered thing, she calls Natasha. Natasha, in whom I thought I recognized my mother, once a dark, mischievous girl, still grinning like a wood sprite in old photographs.) In a Russian literature class, I read Turgenev's "Bezhin Lea," with its ring of firelight, its haunting cries echoing over the river. I appreciated these things, I decided, in a way my classmates did not. This may have been true; the bar was low. I developed a vertiginous sense of my own possibilities.

Meanwhile, there was Joanna, back in my old hometown, living my shadow life.

At eighteen, she'd married Kyle Bohannon, a lanky, sweet-faced varsity hurdler who'd kissed me once, suddenly, at a party after a football game. Like that kiss, the wedding arrived without warning, seemingly without prelude or courtship, without even a period of engagement. When I heard about it, I remembered the glow from his flushed face and the beer on his breath, his lips pressed together as if to hum into my mouth. Their first child, a boy, arrived that winter—a scandalously brief interval.

My mother said, "There's a story there, you know."

She called every Sunday, the dormitory payphone ringing, one girl or another knocking on my door to let me know. This

mortified me, as though having a mother were my unique disfig-
urement. She would be standing in the kitchen, I knew, looped
in the cord. I hated her swooping, loaded tone. She was afraid
I wouldn't catch her implication.

She said, "It could have been you, Carol."

My mother meant this one way—I had *applied myself*, she'd
say; I'd been *a good girl*—but I took it differently. After Kyle had
kissed me, I had laughed and shaken his hands from my elbows.
Telling my friends the story, I'd made a joke of it. Joanna had
done something else. She'd done the thing that separated us.

Two more children followed, one after another. "You
wouldn't even recognize her," said my mother, who attended
YWCA reducing classes every Thursday. "Some women—they
simply surrender themselves to motherhood."

My mother believed in a feminine duty to appear pleasant.
This didn't strike her as submissive, merely proper. There existed
a slatternly sort of motherhood that belonged, in her eyes, to
the undesirable classes, vaguely defined. Yet I sensed a new
note creeping into her voice, a peculiar emphasis to the word
surrender. As if there were, in fact, romance there: the heroic
acceptance of duty, the glorious laying down of one's most intimate possession, the body itself. If you could not be pleasant,
you could at least be destroyed.

What my mother valued, I was determined to pity and hate.
Poor Joanna; she had surrendered. She'd even been saddled with
a ridiculous, cumbersome name: Joanna Bohannon.

I valued the hush and crackle of old pages turning, the way
paper slipped across paper like skin. I valued skin. I wrote my
honors thesis on romantic dominance and submission in *Eugene
Onegin*, won entry to the University of Chicago, and used the
phrase *taking a lover* with less irony than it deserved. For years,
I never actually saw Joanna. She was a presence in my life, but
not a real person—just a shadow on a wall against which I meas-
ured myself.

Now I was home again, waking each morning in my starched

little childhood bed. I recalled the skimmed cream of the linguistics professor's pillowcases and convinced myself, finally, that I'd sleep better once I owned a set that felt the same. Which was how, in the parking lot of the Ben Franklin store, I encountered a small woman carrying a grocery sack, round yet spritely, tiny-footed yet wide at the hips, with a quick, mobile, resiliently childlike face. Nothing at all like my mother's depictions. But I knew right away who it was.

As for Joanna, she might have seen me only yesterday.

"Oh," she said, "Carol. Hello, there. I heard you were back."

There was more to Joanna's story, a reason that running into her felt like more than luck.

While I'd busied myself with my studies in Chicago, Joanna had met a man named Travis Snell. My mother knew his name; the story had achieved a brief notoriety. He was a park ranger who worked in the marsh outside of town, a wildlife refuge. How had it begun? My mother didn't know. In any case, things became public. In one version of the story, Kyle threw her out of the house; in another, she packed and left to live with Travis Snell in his little cabin out in the weeds. After just a few weeks, though, she came back—or was taken back, my mother said— for the children's sake.

"It just goes to show" was her assessment.

"Cheaters never prosper?" I suggested, determined to resist any lesson. My mother was a housewife (like others, she rejected the term *homemaker*: "It sounds like a construction worker"), and my father was a salesman for the local dairy cooperative. He traveled the state, peddling cheese. He'd done his duty—my mother's phrase—in the Second World War, and now he tied his tie each morning with big, clumsy swipes. I remembered Jeremy Kite's perfect Windsors, silken gems. My parents seemed bound by unwavering, passionless devotion. Jeremy and I had been different. I lay awake at night, remembering how selfishly I'd been torn at.

"It could have been worse," my mother said.

Meaning I hadn't risked a family, as Joanna had. I had not abrogated my duties to anyone but myself, had sacrificed nothing but a semester of school. My spectacle was much smaller, less sordid, less shameful. I agreed. I found myself respecting Joanna in a way I hadn't before.

My heart, those days, was waterlogged. The slightest prod could set it leaking. In the parking lot, I must have looked bleary and amazed, blinking in the sun.

"I can't get away today," Joanna said. "Maybe this weekend. I'll call."

I heard you were back. So the word was out about me, too.

Arriving early to the restaurant we'd chosen, I sat outside, pulling root beer through a straw. It was the edge of July. Light lay sheeted across hoods and windshields. Down the street, workers were draping the courthouse with bunting. At last, Joanna appeared, pushing a stroller—a pram, I suppose, the kind where the child faces the mother, leaving the two to stare helplessly, fixedly, at one another. It might have been the same one in which her parents had once pushed her.

"My daughter, Gail."

"She looks like her father."

It was true. Gail had what I remembered of Kyle Bohannon's plump mouth and embarrassed, nearly aggrieved expression. So this was what Joanna had done to seal her return. She'd fashioned a gift in her husband's image.

Joanna may have sensed this thought; she may have raised her defenses. That would explain how lunch began, a tightrope of empty pleasantries and false cheer. We were both doing well, we agreed; it was such a treat to have run into one another. I praised the unhappy infant; Joanna praised my color, my hair.

"You were in school," she said.

I registered the past tense.

"I'm going back."

Immediately, I recoiled at my own bristling tone. At the same time, I meant what I'd said. Or, more precisely, I understood that I would have to mean it, or else own the statement for a lie and own every pitiful thing that lie said about me.

Joanna leaned forward, brushing a strand of hair behind her ear and then—she seemed to hesitate for a moment, considering; beneath the hood of the carriage, the baby stared out at us from its little cave—lowering her hand to mine atop the table.

This was it, the slip that sent us tumbling.

"God," I said, "it's been terrible."

"Tell me everything," she said.

I told her everything.

The April before last, Joanna and Kyle and their two sons, four-year-old Todd and infant Collie, had taken a walking tour of the marsh. ("A walking tour," Joanna repeated, making a face that said she knew how pretentious this sounded. I was glad to see this. It impressed and relieved me, confirming my trust.) This was one of their first outings since Collie's birth, the four of them going somewhere other than church or to visit parents. The outing was Joanna's idea; the marsh was Kyle's. Migrating north, Canada geese were descending into the marsh in long lines, crowding the waters. Kyle wanted the boys to see this. An idea had fixed itself in his mind, Joanna said. He wanted his sons to be *outdoorsmen*.

There was another family on the tour, parents with a trio of hulking teenage boys, as well as an older couple in matching flannel who photographed everything. Their guide, a wiry man in his thirties with a neat brown beard, discussed the migratory patterns of geese and the various native plants along the trail. He often had to wait while the older couple attempted the perfect shot: "Oh, look, he was beating his wings and you missed it! Wait, wait, he'll do it again!" Or else he had to speak over the three teens, who jostled and swore and pelted one another with fistfuls of mud. They seemed identically sullen and hairy, differing only in size; they could have nested one inside the other like dolls. The parents made no attempt to impose order but instead marched shoulder to shoulder, wearing the expressionless masks of prisoners of war.

At one point, as the guide described a species of native wildflower, his eyes met Joanna's, and his face changed. It was hard to describe. He hadn't really noticed her before; now he did.

"He looked unhappy, almost. Apprehensive."

The tour looped several miles through the marsh. Cattails and bulrushes sprouted in thick clumps. Redwing blackbirds rode the wavering stalks. Poplars and spindly willows linked fingers over the trail, casting scents of mildew and mud, and then the view opened up. The trees gave out, there was a break in the rushes, and Joanna stood before a silver expanse of water, dark clusters of geese drifting this way and that, and in the distance low hummocks of land, untrodden islands. The marsh covered several thousand acres, the guide explained. Much had been left undeveloped, a migratory waypoint for ducks, geese, and cranes.

It was fascinating, in a way. The sudden shifts in scale, from the intimate flecking of moss on bark to the miles of cold, shallow water. The ceaseless braying of geese wove over the world like a roof. But the path had only begun curling back toward the parking lot when Todd started to complain. Earlier, one of the teens had jostled him, knocking him down and muddying his jeans; now his legs were cold and his feet hurt. "I'm *tired*," he said, investing the word with a four-year-old's keen sense of cosmic suffering.

Be a big boy, his father chided. Couldn't Todd walk on his own like a big boy?

Perhaps it was his choice of words that stirred Joanna. How ugly those *big boys* were—beyond love, invulnerable to hate. She handed Collie to her husband and held out her arms for Todd, though she knew Kyle would have something to say about this later, in private.

Joanna carried Todd the rest of the way, shifting him from

one hip to another, her shoulders and elbows turning warm and watery and beginning to ache. Todd hung limp, doing nothing to help, like a wet piece of herself that threatened to tear loose in a clump. Kyle, peeved, barely looked her way.

He must have felt bad, though. After they'd returned to the parking lot, he offered to change Collie's diaper—a rare kindness—and to accompany Todd to the chemical toilet. Alone for a moment, she wandered down to the split-rail fence that divided the lot from the marsh. Her body tingled with exhaustion, as though it were giving off a flickering aura, smoking at the edges.

"A night heron."

It was the guide, who'd approached without her noticing. He pointed to a tree that had collapsed into the reeds across a strip of shining mud. Joanna, squinting, saw nothing.

"Your eyes must be better than mine," she said.

True. He looked at her, and she saw that his irises were two shades brighter than his beard—tawny, owlish. His sharp, narrow face could have been carved from wood. He studied her in the same hard way as before, like a man reaching an unhappy decision. He offered his hand, and she took it.

"Joanna."

"Travis."

I know this moment. Not the beginning of anything, you think at the time. You don't invest it with special significance until later, at which point you hardly remember it anymore. Not the way you want to, at least, marking the weight of the light, the scent of the wind, the breath before words are spoken, and the words etched in stone. You re-create what you've lost: owlish eyes, shining mud. Your particulars take on the too-bright tint of invention.

It's hopeless. Here you are, years later, trying to crack your life open with *words*.

I might say, for example, that from across the fronded expanse of a hotel bar—this was my first foray into professional life, an academic conference on languages and literature in a gray inland city at the nadir of winter: three days of cocktails, panel discussions, and delicate internecine stabbings—I watched Jeremy Kite approach in the backbar mirror, boiling up like a storm cloud that settled over the stool beside mine. Dark longish hair swept back to conceal how it had thinned, combed through, faintly slicked, with a feminine cream whose indescribable scent would soon become so familiar to me. Dark eyes, dark woolen coat. And his black scarf was, I want to say, banded with green, minutely fuzzy, and faintly iridescent, like a bird's throat.

Something like that, surely. He was always careful about his clothes and hair. A dandy, I might have called him in other circumstances, a snob. Instead, I wound up wanting, more desperately than I'd ever wanted anything in my life, to meet and maintain his persnickety approval.

In truth, though, it's not the initial meeting I typically find myself trying to remember as much as the moments that soon followed—sweeping apperceptions of opportunity and risk, and then choices made so suddenly and completely they seemed like they could never be unchosen.

My mother had gone to Milwaukee to learn nursing at the outset of the war. She met my father there, a few years older, an Enlisted Reserves corpsman stationed at the port facilities. Later he spent a year abroad in Bristol, guarding American freight at a switchyard against rumors of German saboteurs and the very real depredations of black marketers. But these were not details my mother chose to dwell upon; instead, he "shipped out to Europe."

As she grew older, she seemed to me to become more and more a liar. Telling the tale, she began remembering things she couldn't possibly remember: the pattern on plates at a hotel restaurant, the names of freighters at anchor. Sometimes she grew fanciful. My father strode forth to meet her in polished boots, a garrison cap folded beneath his arm and brassy stitching gleaming down his sleeves. Once, she described barrage balloons tethered over the city—as though Milwaukee had been subject to the Blitz. "The spring of '42," she'd say, her voice riding the syllables.

And when she was very old, my mother believed my father sometimes visited. He'd died years before, following several strokes and an era of sad decline. My mother conjured him young and vital. "Your father put a fence around the garden today," she might call to tell me. "He had that big hammer, the sledge. All afternoon, I heard him driving stakes."

At the assisted living facility, he became a constant presence; it was almost a joke among the staff. "Never lonely," the attendants said when I asked how she was doing.

Her window overlooked the parking lot, a strip of grass, the highway. "Oh, wonderful!" she cried from her bed, blankly cheerful at my arrival, as if I were a neighbor dropping in. "My husband's in the kitchen." She tossed a gesture over my shoulder. "He'll put on some tea."

No one was there, of course. There wasn't a kitchen. Our family never drank tea. Still, the words had power. In spite of everything, I turned to look.

"I knew you before we met," Travis Snell said.

He and Joanna were in bed. The one happy interval of their affair: a few weeks between consummation and discovery, when it seemed to Joanna a delicate balance had been struck. She could have her family; she could have Travis. She could arrange things just so, sacrificing nothing. It was midday. Kyle was at work, and Todd was being watched by neighbors. Collie slept in Travis's front room. The baby had a doctor's appointment, Joanna had told the wife next door. Travis had called in sick.

"Tell me," she said.

He had light brown hair all over his body, coppery freckles beneath. His bones were solid and thick. Atop her, he was heavier than he looked, driving her into the mattress. Afterward, she lay with her head on his chest. Under the hair, he was warm and hard as a heel of bread. She heard his words through his ribs.

One summer, years ago, when Travis had first arrived at the marsh, there'd been a series of sightings. That was the word he used, the one Joanna passed to me. It slides down the thread of the story, clicking up against the next, inevitable question. Sightings of what?

"A person," he said. "Someone in the marsh."

The marsh drew trespassers of all stripes, of course. Amorous couples and mushroom hunters, poachers with frog gigs and fishing rods. This one was different. She made no attempt to avoid detection. In fact, she took no notice of anyone at all. Caught by a flashlight, she simply kept moving, picking her way across uneven ground. Pursued, she vanished.

She was barefoot, people said. She left no prints.

She?

A woman. One of Travis's coworkers claimed to have encountered her. He'd been driving a service road when she parted the cattails a hundred yards ahead and crossed in front of him, a white shape in the headlights. By the time he reached the place she'd been, she was gone. The frogs belched as normal. The cattails didn't stir.

She had red hair, the friend insisted.

Had Travis ever seen her?

"Just the once. Years ago."

Kids had been sneaking into the park that summer, scattering cigarette butts and bottles at one of the scenic overlooks, so one night Travis returned a few hours after the gates were locked to walk the tour trail. Just a hunch: it was a warm, starry night, the sort he thought might lure the kids out. He kept his flashlight off, trusting his feet to remember the trail, stepping softly, in ambush. But the overlook was deserted.

Travis stood beside the bench, trying to decide whether he was disappointed or relieved. He was twenty-two, hardly older than the kids he was hunting. The night prickled like droplets in the hair of his forearms. The overlook occupied a low knoll of heaped manna grass and sedge, offering a view of a broad expanse of marsh, the water divided into pools and channels, tangles of box elders and dogwoods, the black domes of swamp oaks and birch. Something sluiced through the rushes below, a big pike or a carp. A night heron croaked from a nearby thicket.

Gradually, he became aware he wasn't alone.

What had changed? Impossible to say; the feeling stole over him like sleep. Not a dramatic transition, electricity at the back of his neck, but a certainty that grew in stealth until it had simply arrived. Someone stood behind him.

He turned around. There she was, her feet white as wax in the dirt.

When he turned on his flashlight, she disappeared, flung backward into shadow. He paced the overlook, calling a few times, sifting the tall grass with the flashlight. Again, though, he was certain: he was alone. Walking back to the gate, he felt unsettled, but not afraid. There'd been no threat in the encounter, only a sense of focused attention, a keen yet neutral interest. In nighttime hikes since, he'd often felt something similar: an owl peering from a branch, a coyote glancing over its shoulder as it padded unhurriedly through the brush.

And he had, for just an instant, glimpsed her in the light.

"What did she look like?" Joanna asked.

Travis rolled onto his side, displacing her. He slid down her body, trim and intent, to cup her foot in his hands. He ran his tongue over her the branched bones of her instep, pressed her toes to the fur of his cheek. He did not smile.

"It was you."

I laughed. "No!"

"Well, that's what he told me."

By now, the table was a mess: braided napkins, ketchupped plates, sandwich crusts. Joanna glanced over her shoulder. Across from the courthouse, a cannon topped a pedestal inscribed with the names of the county's war dead. Had we climbed the monument steps, we would have seen, over the barrel of the cannon and the roof of the public library, a gleaming corner of the marsh.

I return sometimes to Travis Snell's story, turning it over in my mind. Surely he didn't expect Joanna's belief. Why tell the story at all, then, something so outrageously false?

Jeremy Kite could speak and read German, Frisian, and Scots, a historian of that clade of languages that rose from the Elbe to overspread the north and west of pagan Europe. Had I asked, he surely could have informed me that *ghost* comes from the Old English *gast*, meaning "soul, spirit, breath, life," a word itself derived from the proto-Indo-European *ghois*: "to be excited, frightened." The etymology is revealing, embracing as it does both our dread and our desire for the things that quicken us. (*Quicken*, he might have said, his fingers at my thighs, ready to twist me open as easily as separating a mussel at its hinge.)

This was the usual West Germanic word for "supernatural being," the dictionary informs me, *and the primary sense seems to have been connected to the idea of "to wound, to tear, to pull to pieces."*

At the beginning of the third and final year of my second marriage, I took a maternity leave to care for my younger daughter, Cat. It was early afternoon, winter. David was working, and I had gotten it into my head that I'd cook a shoulder roast.

Rubbing the Dutch oven with trimmings, browning the beef, chopping vegetables—I must have been delusional, courting that extra labor. There was something I wanted to prove, or some failure I wanted to make visible, spectacularly. Cat had been difficult all week, blasting us awake every ninety minutes, night after night. I'd begun sleeping in the nursery so that I could calm her quickly: David was teaching an eight o'clock class and had grown prickly about his sleep schedule. Cat was not hungry, it seemed; she didn't need to be changed; she simply demanded a witness. To what? Her life, I suppose. "Here I am," I'd say, lifting her from the crib. "Yes, yes." And she would hush against my body—craving, it seemed, these little affirmations and reinforcements.

This day, too, she'd been cranky and irrepressible, shaking with rage if I set her down for even a moment. She was on my hip as I covered the roast at last and left it to simmer.

I'd never envisioned this for myself. Not motherhood at all, not at first—and then, after my first marriage, after Natalie, not motherhood again. Yet here I was, reliving everything. The aches and exhaustion, the tenderness pressed down like a lid over frustration, the savage little tug of a mouth at my nipple. Entire days with an infant are lived underground, down in the biological basement of your life. It's a type of soured passion, the face you look into an echo of *his* face, asking always more and more. What you thought you were about—a university career, the classes and meetings and delicious, petty dramas; the busy comings and goings of students and colleagues, books and ideas; the endless pleasant stoking of your various indignations— seems very far away.

Dinner was cooking. The bus bearing Natalie home from school would not lumber up the block for another half-hour and, for the moment, at least, Cat was quiet. I didn't dare put her down, but I could, by resting my elbows on the countertop, take some of her weight off my shoulders. I stood like that, letting sweat track down my back and between my breasts, fantasizing about a shower before David and Natalie came home. If I could just get Cat to sleep, even for a few minutes, it might be possible. I closed my eyes.

Someone walked into my kitchen.

Just like that—just like Travis Snell said. I heard nothing. I simply knew.

"Mom?" I said.

And when I opened my eyes, the air around me stilled and she was gone.

A few years earlier, between my two marriages, my mother had died like a tree—at the edges first, leaves curling. Her fingernails turned blue the night her heart gave out. Her toes softened and purpled like fruits. Her hand swelled in mine, knuckles sinking in a tide of cool flesh. The nurse receded into the wallpaper, leaving the two of us alone.

Could I convince you that I felt it, the exact moment it happened? A brief shadow over the sun, the swift winging of a diaphanous form upward and outward, trailing stillness behind. A silent interval passed, and then the nurse stepped forward, and stillness—along with the knowledge of what I'd felt just before—gave way to brisk, logical bustle.

She'd been lucid, more or less, until quite near the end, when the morphine took her under. We talked about my father. She knew he'd died; she remembered that much. She wanted to know how long it had been.

"Eleven years."

"My," she said. So simple and mild, so unlike her. She fell quiet for a minute. Then she said, "Was I alone all that time?"

Meaning, *Where were you?* This was more familiar: the little barb, the quick pluck at my skin. I was grateful and pained, as I would have been at any small, temporary recovery.

I'd once thought it impossible to reconcile myself to my parents' bloodless marriage. How could I, after my mornings spent before the mirror in Jeremy Kite's bathroom, dreamily touching the toothmarks that darkened my thighs? Over lunch, this was what I'd complained about to Joanna. Yet it seems to me now that I hadn't been sincere. What had really bothered me was the impenetrable intimacy of the home I'd returned to. Little touches: his absent fingering of a hair of hers that had entangled itself in his sweater. Her fingers at the soft, crumpled lining of his hat, inspecting the stitches of a previous repair. Such details were irreducible. They exposed my romance for the airy, porous thing it was. "Tying the knot," we say. My parents lived in a tangle whose loops I'll never be able to follow to their ends.

"Eleven years," my mother said. "I never thought it would take so long."

After my mother died, Joanna was the first person I called.

We've kept in touch, fitfully but vitally. For months, nothing. Then a letter arrives in a familiar hand, a long e-mail appears with no subject, the phone rings an hour after dinner on a quiet evening. (Neither of us is comfortable with texts, which seem too easy, too flippant somehow, for whatever this is we have.) We open with apologies. *Dear Joanna,* I will have written, *Where does the time go?* "Oh," Joanna's voice on the line will say, "I've been meaning to call forever!" But in truth, I suspect we choose our silences, our distance. Our lives are too different to bear a daily bond. After all the early drama, she remains Joanna Bohannon. Meanwhile, with two marriages well behind me, with middle age more or less behind me, I still manage my occasional adventures and setbacks. For me, I've learned, there must always be that initial astonishment, the whole world electric with assent, and always, afterward, the same sad shriveling, the return of my life as it otherwise must be lived. Daylight seeps through the curtains.

"I felt it. I felt *her.* I felt her leave the room."

"I know you did, honey. I know."

Not a lie, I've come to believe. Something gentler if just as false, a construction absorbed into the landscape. The fence the tree has grown through, drawing the wire into its trunk.

My mother was a big, boisterous woman, with a creased face that had been round and beautiful in girlhood but sprawled and softened with age. A remarkable storyteller, a casual fabulist, too fiercely opinionated to remain beholden to facts. I hated this about her. I mistook it for faith, for desiccated Puritanism. I told myself this was what I was escaping when I left for Madison and then Chicago. I did not think that, along with her height and vigor, her hair that frizzed without mercy and had to be pulled and pinned or else accepted, I'd also inherited my mother's habits of mind. We were idealists, given to the same leaps and justifications, the same slips and excuses. My mother had strung barrage balloons over Milwaukee. I'd loved Jeremy Kite.

I recognized this eventually, but not in time.

Out of grief and regret, then, I sensed her presence leaving. Years later, exhausted and alone, trapped by the very things she'd embraced, I called her back.

As for Travis Snell, there are swamp gases and fogs and all the little scientific tricks played by starlight. It was dark. Expecting to see a person, you might think you saw a person. Remembering what you'd seen, you might grant the memory a face you loved. You might shape certain details to fit your fetish. Does that make you a liar? You've found the ghost you need.

"Maybe my heart's broken," Joanna said as we rose from the table together. "Maybe that's the fitting end. I'm supposed to go drown myself in the marsh." Stepping to the pram, though, she gave a small, pliant shrug—an unburdening, a dismissal. When Gail began to fuss, Joanna leaned forward, dangling her hand as a plaything. Her daughter latched onto a finger. She had her mother's red hair.

These days, Natalie and Cat call mostly for practical advice: bank loans, dental work, wedding registries, insurance policies, how to grow ever more pregnant with grace. This is Natalie's first time. She was late to marry. Graduate school came first, and then a career. Tonight, she calls to say her ankles are swollen. Her hips ache. Sleep with a rolled towel under the small of your back, I tell her. Don't be embarrassed to sit down to pull on your pants.

Hausfrau, Jeremy Kite might say. His smile would be unkind. ("She gave up," Tolstoy writes; "she let go." Lovely Natasha becomes, in the end, a happy broodmare.) But on my kitchen table tonight, fresh from the press, sits an advanced reader copy of my next book, reappraising the life and poetry of Elizaveta Polonskaya. We need the old Russians more than ever these days, to keep refreshing our hope for the new. A celebratory bottle of Barolo breathes atop the butcher block, beside a ripe heirloom tomato and a hunk of Grana Padano. I sink a knife into the purple fruit, flaying it open with swift, immaculate strokes. At some point, I must have been taught this—how to cut without pressure through skin and flesh, not to damage but to transform. The little blade in my fist turns wet, glazed with golden seeds.

PELICAN

The young parents swore they had nothing to fear. The moment they'd thought they'd been waiting for: back porch, summer stars, sleeping toddler, the river slapping at the bottom of the yard. Case numbers statewide dropping for weeks, an e-mail from the cottage's owner detailing disinfection protocols between each set of guests. A getaway, they'd called it: getting away from the world. Still came this giddy sense of exposure, nearly naughtiness. Only natural, both agreed. There wasn't a time that wouldn't have felt like too soon. Still, they had nothing to fear.

He sat up in a strange bed, panicked. "What is it?" his wife asked, drowsing. Out the window, early light twitched off the crimped and sliding river. Their daughter stood poised at the edge of the pier.

He went over the back porch railing. He wouldn't remember the drop to the grass; his wife would have to tell him, later. To him it seemed he simply appeared in the yard, not sprinting but clawing his way to the pier, the way one moves in dreams, never in time to prevent the worst. Their daughter would do it, he knew: pour herself in with hardly a splash. He'd awakened with the thought.

Pelican. Along the length of the pier they faced one another. Larger than he'd have guessed, almost precisely the size of a toddler. With colorless eyes it regarded him; briefly he registered its majesty, stupidity, and contempt. The white wings unfurled. With crabbed steps it turned, launching from the pier, feet splatting the surface until it lifted into a glide, crossing a hundred yards of river in seconds and swooping up into the oaks on the opposite shore.

A story they'd tell: how skittish they were, how ready for disaster to curl back and strike. "Daddy thought you were a bird," his wife said, lowering the girl to his lap in the cottage kitchen while coffee brewed. Still, he was proud of himself. He thought she was, too. The way she caught his eye, saying this: a test they'd passed, their vigilance affirmed.

"Bird!" the girl whispered, secretly, naughtily, to the heat of the afternoon, to the white flocks winging overhead. With her head tipped back in the backyard and her arms thrown wide, spinning circles, she rose to her toes to fly.

A DOG'S TOOTH

A family joke: why did Melody name her son Early?

"Well," Melody says, "it's not like I thought I'd never have one."

Her sister calls this cruel. "Might as well have named him *Accident*," Jeannie has said, in one of her implacable moods. "He'll be explaining all his life."

Jeannie's own children: Esther, Ezekiel, Zechariah, Elisha, Ruth Anne. The oldest is eight years old. The next will be Jonah or Moriah, depending. "As many as God plans," she says, answering the question that is sometimes asked, and although she typically smiles, saying this, there's something unsmiling in her manner. Something stern, judgmental, and proud—even hateful, Melody sometimes thinks. The reflected hate of the God who invented eternal damnation. Her little sister's flush of pleasure at the thought of such rough justice, and herself on the winning side.

His middle name: Andrew Early. It's what he goes by. Melody refuses to regret the decision. The name, the admission it contains, is a covenant. She'll keep nothing from him.

Nineteen and pregnant, she found herself back in Cadillac, Michigan, where she'd grown up. Her mother and her mother's second husband, Hardy, accepted this—what Hardy called "the state of your affairs, pun intended"—with surprising kindness, even grace. Though they must also have found it gratifying, in a way. Vindicating. A comeuppance.

"I always gave the two of you free rein," her mother, Sylvie, says this afternoon, firmly valedictory after a third glass of wine.

"As much as I felt I could—I made that decision. And look how things turned out."

Saturday, Memorial Day weekend. The war is over, the statue toppled, the banner hung: *Mission Accomplished.* Everyone—Melody and her boyfriend, Ron, and Early; Sylvie and her third husband, Claude, and Harpo, their dog, a pit-bull mix—is up in Petoskey, visiting Jeannie and Christopher and their brood. Though the day is cloudy and unseasonably cold, Christopher, Claude, and Ron have taken the children to the harbor, with its gritty strip of sand and municipal signage warning of swimmer's itch, while Melody, Jeannie, and Sylvie have gone out to dinner. The restaurant offers a view of Lake Michigan. White spray fans over the breakwater. White waves spread like cream across the open bay.

Only Harpo has been left out, back at the motel where Sylvie and Claude are staying. Jeannie says she doesn't trust him around her children.

After dinner, Melody and Jeannie drive their mother back to the motel, waiting together in the idling minivan until Sylvie and the big blockheaded mutt emerge from their room. Harpo drags Sylvie by a length of leash across the parking lot toward a retention pond. Stumbling only a little, like a child being dragged by her parent through an airport or mall, Sylvie waves them away: all is well.

"I hate when she's like that," Jeannie says.

"Like what?"

"You know."

Melody knows: their mother's flighty confidence and too-bright blouses, her fingers weighted with rings, her grand pronouncements and copper-rinsed curls, her glasses bruising purple whenever she steps outside. Her drunkenness. As children, Melody and Jeannie learned when to unite against her, defending themselves and one another. Though Melody thinks she hears, in her sister's voice now, a harsher note, not just pity or derision but disgust.

Melody, who has matched her mother glass for glass, slaps for the handle that will recline her seat another notch while Jeannie drives; she allows these apperceptions of trouble to flow over her the way the blurred world flows by outside—flowing and departing, as she and Ron and Early will, too, if they can just make it through the weekend.

Dizzy, dulled, she flops down on the sofa. Elisha and Zechariah have been allowed a DVD before bathtime and bed. Anthropomorphic vegetables reenact the story of Noah's ark. Muzzy air circulates through the house, bearing snippets of talk from other rooms. At the kitchen table, Early is showing Ezekiel how to play flash videos on Ron's laptop. "I don't know . . . ," Jeannie begins to say. *If that's a good idea,* drowsing Melody supplies, while Ron offers something that sounds like reassurance.

    On television, the rain has begun in earnest. The pious vegetables huddle within the safety of their ark, and Zechariah, who of all her nieces and nephews is the one Melody can't bring herself to like, turns to her and says, "Maybe that's what we need. A good flood."

Zechariah is five. This can't be something he came up with on his own. The boy isn't particularly bright, Melody thinks, only alert, permanently aggrieved, with overlarge eyes and mousy strands of hair as finely separated as the teeth of a comb, his scalp glowing through like candle wax, his voice habitually pitched to a whine. His pale skin is sensitive; something at the beach today made him break out. Shirtless, shoulders pinkly crusted with calamine, smelling of that and of the syrupy sauce of SpaghettiOs, a scent that seems always to cling to him whether he's recently eaten or not, he has turned to Melody to test out this statement. Something he's overheard. Something Jeannie or Christopher must have said.

Yesterday, driving up from Cadillac to Petoskey on 131, Melody, Early, and Ron crested a hill and saw the whole town spread before them, and beyond it the sweeping blue arc of the bay. Ron whistled—"Would you look at that?"—while Early leaned forward in the back seat. White sails on the water, white plumes of wake, shattered strip of evening sun: for Melody, a flash of optimism, not unusual for these visits. She was going to see her sister. Her *sister*. Aside from Early, who could be said to have a stronger claim on her? And who in all the world could be better positioned to understand Melody—where she's come from and the choices she's made, this life she's managed to scrape together for herself?

As they descended the hill, the bay edged behind the boxy brown bulk of the hospital where Jeannie works as a nurse's aide. Jeannie nearly lost her job last year, when she was found to be the one seeding waiting rooms with religious tracts. *Pray, and you shall be well!* Directions to an evangelical church printed inside. Melody learned this from Sylvie; Jeannie has never mentioned it.

"Turn it off!"

Melody shudders awake. It's Jeannie, crying out in the kitchen.

"Turn that garbage off. That—that trash."

What has happened, apparently, is that Ron has shown the boys a video. An educational video, he insists, one he uses in his classroom, but Jeannie is adamant. "I know what some people mean by *educational*."

Christopher is summoned. "I know it must seem a little strange to you," he begins.

Ron says, "It seems like—"

But before he can finish, before he can land the punch he intends—the word Melody, watching from the doorway, grits her teeth against—Christopher interrupts. "We're not asking you to feel the way we do about this. We're just asking you to respect our way of living while you're under our roof."

A big man, Christopher, bulky in a way that seems somehow babyish, with little pointed breasts beneath the fabric of his polo tee and a rounded, downy, blushing face. Over the years, he's never been anything but polite to Melody and Early, always accommodating, never quite warm. She's wary of him. She suspects another Christopher lurks beneath that doughy surface, someone she'd be wise to fear. Like an infant's, his face seems to communicate, even at its sweetest, the possibility of sudden changes, unpredictable curdlings of emotion. There's a force he'd call faith moving through him in ways unguessable to someone like Melody. Lending him strength.

He has saved Jeannie, after all—that's the word they'd both use. And he is talking over Ron, who's not an easy man to talk over.

But Melody's eyes, as this is happening, remain mostly on Early, still seated at the kitchen table, his empty face turned to his limply curled hands. He's retreated to that place he goes sometimes, some secret redoubt of the mind, outside clamor silenced by high inner walls.

Go to him, she orders herself. But in the end she doesn't move; she can't seem to force herself through the doorway and into the kitchen, into the middle of things. She stands frozen in a bloom of guilt. She's still a little drunk.

Later, as he brushes his teeth in the upstairs bathroom, she catches his gaze in the mirror. "Did it scare you? Aunt Jeannie yelling like that?"

"Nuh-uh," he mumbles around the brush. His reflected face offers her nothing. He'll be ten before the end of the summer. Gentle, thoughtful, rib-skinny boy.

"She wasn't mad at you. It's just that she has certain beliefs. Uncle Christopher, too. And they're not the same as what I believe, or Ron. And sometimes those differences lead to—well, to surprises. And when people are surprised, sometimes they get upset."

The sort of speech she's had to make before, in one form or another, for Early's benefit. Her voice sounds cheery and false, a tinkling bell.

"Okay," Early says.

He may have more to say tomorrow, or the day after, or next week. This has always been Early's way: a dam of silence failing, crumbling all at once in a complex torrent of emotions. When he was four and Sylvie and Hardy decided to separate—"to drink at different establishments" was how Hardy put it—Melody was surprised at how little the news seemed to affect her son. He was too young to understand, she thought, though Hardy had been like a grandfather to the boy.

One day, she and Early met Hardy at a playground in Cadillac—the sort of arrangement she'd promised to make, thinking it was what everyone wanted—and when the time came to say goodbye, Early tore off his sneaker and hurled it at her. She caught the little blue-and-orange Nike against her chest. Small as it was, it still shocked the breath from her. Getting him back to the car became a tearful, shrieking struggle, his bony weight thrashing about in her arms. Hardy stood aside, helplessly grinning: "Hey, there. Hey."

That night, still shaken by the outburst, she showed Early her welted forearm, raked by his nails. *You hurt me.* She made him look. *You see? You see what you did? You did this to me.* Early touched the marks he'd raised on her skin and cried, scrambling up against her chest and clinging there until she hugged him back. She thought maybe that would be the end of it, though it has turned out to be just the way things are between them sometimes. Just life.

Fade in: the night sky clotted with stars. A violin trills an arpeggio of solemn wonder. The voiceover begins. A man's voice, deep and mellifluous, expressing with great poetic delicacy an idea that ultimately boils down to the view that life is—as Melody has read elsewhere, stated plainly—a side-effect of the tendency of complex organic molecules to form within stars. Over the course of eons, these compounds have been caught up in the slow accretion of solar systems, planets, Earth. They have come to constitute, among other things, human bodies.

A symphony swells over a rapid montage: the sun flaring off telescope lenses, unblinking human and animal eyes, Hubble images of spiral galaxies, purple mountains' majesty, amber waves of grain, pedestrians pouring down a crowded city side-walk, time-lapses of the night sky wheeling over desert plains. The camera pans to the horizon, where a distant city casts its nebular glow upward. The stars float above a teeming grid of suburban constellations.

"We come from the stars."

"Horseshit," Ron says, spitting the word he would've spat ear-lier, had Christopher not cut him off. "But I suppose you think I should be used to dealing with that sort of thing by now."

Ron has shown Melody the video as they lie together in bed, upstairs in Jeannie's house. But her reaction, apparently, her defense of its pedagogical value and Ron's good sense in sharing it with Early and Ezekiel, has underwhelmed.

"Certain students. Certain parents. It's Jesus this, Jesus that."

A practiced complaint: if you work in public education in this part of the country, Ron sometimes says, it's hard not to end up feeling about Jesus the way the principal in *Ferris Bueller's Day Off* feels about Ferris Bueller. Ron was raised Christian himself.

She doesn't know the details. He's not quite estranged from his parents; he just doesn't like them. He's rejected them, and that act of rejection, Melody suspects, has itself become almost parental—a tender wellspring of aspirational self-image, an original exemplar of the man he wants to be. Freethinker. Gadfly.

But Melody isn't interested in getting into it with Ron right now. She rolls onto her side, away from him.

"They're not *certain* anything," she says. "They're family."

Melody's a paralegal, Ron a vice principal and debate coach at the high school in Cadillac, the same school she and Jeannie once attended. Eleven years older than Melody, he was already teaching when she and Jeannie were in high school, though he never taught them; back then, he was working over in Muskegon. He moved to Cadillac later, when he "needed a fresh start." He's the sort of person who needs fresh starts, Melody understands, the sort who can wear out a welcome: a fierce little terrier of a man, wiry and balding, with a quick, aggressive smile, big hands, hairy wrists, skinny legs hard as rails.

They met through a dating site. On their first date, when the subject of their age difference came up, he flashed her that smile of his, an icy mouthful of small, bright teeth.

"Bet you were trouble," he said.

As simple as that, laying out certain possibilities between them.

This should have struck Melody as a seedy thing to say, and rather sad: a teacher imagining a student. It did, in fact, strike her as seedy. But he'd said it easily, happily, without the almost subaudible tinge of shame she'd learned to expect from such lines. As if he really were inviting her to condense whole chapters of her history down to a word, *trouble*, from which they both might wring at least a few stupid drops of pleasure.

He lies in what he probably hopes she'll take as chastened silence for a while. And then, under the covers, his hand finds her hip.

A touch of apology at first. But slowly it grows—as she allows it, relaxes into it—into something more confident, more insistent.

Sylvie and Claude's motel room stinks of cat. The window unit is to blame, its wash of cool air acrid, faintly urinous. "Drives the mutt crazy," Claude says, untroubled, reclining on one of the beds. He's watching a news recap edited like sports highlights, a game begun with burning Manhattan towers and finished with burning Iraqi tanks. Harpo occupies the other bed, the covers twisted into a nest of his own making, the mattress exposed. He doesn't look crazy to Melody, only put-upon, his nose turned to the air conditioner, his tormentor. In the six months since Sylvie and Claude adopted Harpo, Melody's only ever known the dog to be sweetly stupid, galumphing about after morsels of food or affection. Still, when Early—who seems to have decided from the start to love this dog wholeheartedly, like a brother—dives onto the bed to embrace Harpo, she watches the muscles ripple across the broad, brindled back, the piggish ears flick. "Those are your good clothes," she says warningly, though she knows what she really means is *Careful, careful.*

Some cosmic wires must be crossed somewhere: it's a fear that belongs to Jeannie, who has banished the dog from her house. To make up for it, Melody scratches Harpo's neck, iron muscle bunched beneath heavy folds of skin. The dog grins up at her, innocent and grateful.

Sylvie leans into the bathroom mirror, curling her eyelashes. She likes to complain that her eyes are too small—apologizing, too, for passing the trait on to her daughters.

"You should demand a new room," Melody says.

"Tried," Sylvie chimes. "No vacancy: the holiday." She blinks rapidly and receives her reflection's approving smile.

"Well, I don't know how you stand it."

"Patience, honey. 'All Things Must Pass.' What's that, the Bible?"

"George Harrison."

"Close, then." Sylvie laughs. "Close enough."

Where does it come from, this urge to fix things? No one wants Melody to fix things. Only Melody seems to want this, though most of the time she doesn't know what needs fixing, exactly, nor how to fix it, nor how to make the feeling go away.

Jeannie and her family attend an evangelical church on the outskirts of Petoskey, a prefabricated steel shed that shares a graveled lot with a rental-truck company. Nondenominational, they call themselves, as if staking a proud and lonely claim. Inside, folding chairs have been arranged in rows facing a lectern. Felted office partitions divide the space. What could be back there? *The holy of holies,* Ron might wryly speculate. But Ron, like Claude, isn't here. "I think I know better," he told her this morning, as if his absence were his own recent decision, and not something they'd planned all along. "And I think you should, too."

"Don't start."

Claude was more easygoing: "Just an old sinner," he said from the bed in the motel room. "If God wants me, I'm easy to find."

"Look," Ron said. "You want to support your sister, show your respect, apologize on my behalf, I get it. But just think a minute: this guy Jesus, he knows the centurions are looking for him, and he camps out in Gethsemane anyway. That's not heroic—not in my book. That's suicide by cop."

But it's not so different, really, from any church service, from the services to which Sylvie, in her occasional fits of sobriety and self-flagellation, used to drag Melody and Jeannie. A hymn is sung, handwritten lyrics flashed onto a whiteboard by an overhead projector:

> Judge eternal, throned in splendor,
> Lord of lords and king of kings,

> With your living fire of judgment
> Purge this land of bitter things.

And if these gently murderous lyrics are accompanied by the young, mustachioed pastor on a twelve-string guitar and a woman in a flowing blue dress who dances beside him, slapping a tambourine, and if certain phrases seem to inspire her to shake the thing over her head as if raining words down upon herself—*Cleave our darkness with your sword*—well, so what? Who is Melody to deny these people whatever joy their singing brings them, simply because she can't share in it?

It's Ron she's thinking of, Ron she's silently arguing with. That stupid video. It bothers Melody in a way she can't quite articulate, a ticklish dissatisfaction she hasn't gotten to the bottom of yet.

Another feeling is stealing over her as well—a tentative sort of seduction. It has to do with the woman in the flowing blue dress and the way she beats and shivers the tambourine, the way she turns to the young pastor as he strums and sings, matching her movements to his.

Cleave our darkness with your sword, indeed.

Next comes a prayer like a tunnel to be ducked through, eyes squeezed shut while the young pastor croons. Memorial Day blessings are conjured: thanksgiving for a swift victory, divine protection for troops overseas, divine wisdom for the country's leaders. Nothing is said that Melody couldn't bite her tongue and bring herself to endorse, if she could only ignore specifics. Who doesn't want safe soldiers, wise leaders? Still, her bowed neck stiffens.

An *amen* is offered, the children released to Sunday school. All her nephews and nieces rise, and Early along with them. "Honey," she says. The look her boy turns upon her is studiously blank: what does she want from him?

To remain by her side, under the umbrella of her protection. To allow her to protect him. Her mission in life. Her sole purpose.

A hand on her arm—Jeannie's.

"It's okay," her sister says. To her and to Early both.

Off he goes, led by Christopher and the woman in the blue dress, shuffling along with the other children into the hidden space behind the office partitions.

Motherhood as a series of ambushes: the thought has occurred to Melody, in certain moods.

The other week, for instance, she stood in the hall with a basket of folded laundry, watching through the bedroom door as Early played with his Legos, part of a *Star Wars* set she'd gotten him for Christmas. He never knew she was there. *Skew-skew-skew*: his sound for lasers. And then he flicked one of the little figures from his desk. She couldn't tell whether it was a good guy or a bad guy. The figure skittered under the bed. Early made no move to pick it up. He just kept playing.

Jericho, the young pastor is saying. Faith brought down those walls. Faith spared the Israelite troops, who seized the city without a battle. Worship was their weapon, the blowing of their horns, their joyful noise.

And aren't they all on the front lines here, as well—here, in this church?

The caching of awful tracts in hospital waiting rooms. Such joyful noise.

No mention is made of the sacking of the city, as must have happened once the walls came down. Were the Israelites simply welcomed in at that point? Surely not. There must have been fighting in the streets. Burning and looting and pillaging and rape, partisan potshots from streetcorners and rooftops. Forced pacification. Mass executions, survivors sold into bondage. From beyond the office partitions comes the sound of children singing.

"What did you learn about?" Melody asks Early, out in the parking lot.

"Jericho," he says.

She and Ron have reservations at a restaurant across the bay in Harbor Springs, but something in Melody rebels at the thought of leaving Early at Jeannie's house all evening. Upstairs, Ron shows Early how to tie the tie Ron has lent him, while Melody, down in the kitchen, announces the change. One less thing for Jeannie to worry about, Melody suggests.

Busy with dinner, Jeannie keeps her back turned. "Mmm-hmm." A tone that says she's not so easily fooled; she knows Melody's motives. It's not SpaghettiOs tonight but Prego micro-waved in the jar, a box of macaroni shucked into boiling water, presliced pepperoni from a resealable bag, Bunny Bread slathered with Country Crock. Jeannie's shoulders are narrow, soft, and sloping, her hips broadened by this pregnancy and pregnancies past, her small feet planted in a soldierly stance. In a crowd, say, would Melody even recognize this person from behind?

Jeannie half-turns. "One thing I've been meaning to say, though."

In her voice, a buried wire vibrates with happy rage.

"We heard you last night. You and Ron. Everyone *heard*."

There is typically, during these visits, a moment at which this happens, or at which Melody realizes it's already happened: some emotional tipping-point surpassed, the initial hopeful pleasure of seeing her sister again replaced by a leaden, bricked-in feeling. The visit becomes—or reveals itself to have been all along—something merely to survive.

Lies, Ron informs them, stabbing his salad with relish. The Jericho story, he means. Sacked by the Egyptians a thousand years before Joshua and the Judeans arrived on the scene. Of course Ron would know this. He carries ammunition for every battle, keeps his powder dry. "It's just more rotten Manifest Destiny myth making. Know what that means, kiddo?"

"Sure." Early pinches a soft bite from the innards of his dinner roll. "It means propaganda."

"That's it, kiddo. That's it exactly."

Melody ought to agree. But something is wrong, wrongness like a heat against her skin. It has to do with this restaurant in Harbor Springs, not quite prohibitively expensive but close, the white linen napkins and crystal stemware, the golden lamplight softly diffused, blue evening dusting the windows, a manicured street of shops outside, and the big waterfront mansions anchored behind wrought iron, their soaring wings outspread to either side of heavy oak doors, while across the bay in her underinsulated house with its water-stained ceilings and useless, snarled antenna bolted to the chimney like the remnants of a broken umbrella, pregnant Jeannie limps about on swollen feet, sustained by sodium and preservatives, putting too many children to bed—all this, together with the word *propaganda* in her sweet son's voice, a word gnashed out with angry, superior satisfaction because it's what he's heard so often from Ron.

"Let's change the subject," Melody suggests. She's nearing the bottom of a second cocktail, sweet with simple syrup and muddled basil.

At the door to the bedroom in the upstairs hall where he'll sleep in a bag on the floor at the foot of a bed shared by Zechariah and Ezekiel, she catches Early by the shoulder—more roughly than she intends, spinning him around. "I don't want you repeating what Ron told you tonight around your cousins, okay?"

"Why not?"

"Because I'm the one who has to hold everything together."

This is the truth. Suddenly she feels it plainly—her life scattered about her in fragments, everything pulled farther and farther apart, scratched into separate piles by the grasping hands of all the people she wants to love and needs to please. Peace, she thinks. Please. If only for one weekend, let there be peace.

"Can you help me?" she asks.

Early shrugs her away.

"I just don't like liars," he says.

"Ron," she says, for the second time, "*no*," and after that he leaves her alone.

The boy piloting the pontoon swings past Hardy's pier and Jeannie and Melody, fourteen and sixteen, throw themselves overboard together. Someone, another boy from downstate, another boy with money, a family cottage on Lake Cadillac, reaches out and smacks Jeannie's leg as she leaps, a hard flat sound Melody just has time to register before the lake shuts over her head. She sinks, blowing strands of pearls through her nose, down almost into the grasp of weeds before kicking and rising, clambering at last onto the burning, splintery boards of Hardy's pier. The pontoon is chugging away.

Jeannie comes next, dragging herself from the water as if her body weighs a million pounds, though in fact there's nothing to her: sliver of girl in a neon green bikini, blonde hair streaming down over bones and goosebumped skin, a hot welt spreading in the shape of a hand across the back of one thin thigh.

Up the brushy hill to Hardy's house, one of a line of nearly identical board-and-batten cottages, vacation rentals mostly, incompletely winterized. The second floor, an attic beneath the eaves that Melody and Jeannie share as a bedroom, is barely insulated, so that in a few months they'll be waking to darkness and clouds of breath each morning, frost on the insides of the windows. A screen door on the back deck opens into the kitchen, where heavy smoke-dimmed curtains winnow the sun to a greasy twilight. They stand together a minute, dripping onto the linoleum, shivering as if in presentiment.

The television burbles in the next room. An empty can,

dropped, clinks down into a crowd of empties on the coffee table, and Hardy laughs.

Sylvie calls, "Are those my girls? My little mermaids?"

Jeannie says, "Jesus Christ."

Melody wakes with the memory at the front of her mind—as if, while she slept, some part of her remained wakeful, parsing the past, sorting and snipping and bringing to the front this scrap of something useful.

Useful how?

The feeling it gives her. A reminder.

When they were wild and lonely together. When all they had was their empty hands, their empty bodies, whatever they could fill these things with, and whatever they could glean from each other.

Christopher splits open the pack of hotdogs with his thumbs. The franks spill out, scattering across the hot grate of the grill, sizzling. Harpo sits nearby, grinning expectantly.

Everyone is here for the holiday cookout, even the dog. Perhaps Jeannie, too, occasionally feels the need to make weekends like this into *something*—or perhaps she has her own regrets, openly acknowledged or not, after their encounter over the bubbling Prego last night—because she's relented there. Still, Harpo remains leashed to the picnic table, and in the swirl of children Jeannie often seems to place herself between them and the dog, making of herself a sullen, lumped, protective presence, like a musk ox at the edge of the herd in one of Ron's videos, eyeing the wolves. Stardust, Melody thinks. Horseshit, she thinks. The thought's slowly coming together, her reasons for hating that whole line of scientific wonderment. She gulps her rum and Faygo Redpop, iceless, from a Ball jar. Claude's supplying the rum: Flor de Caña, he's told her, what he calls the good stuff. "Keep 'em coming," she's said. It's so easy to make Claude smile. She feels she ought to accomplish that much, at least.

"I mean, look around," Sylvie's saying, beside her at the picnic table, continuing the victory lap begun at dinner the other night. "My girls, my grandchildren." Mission accomplished, Melody thinks. You never protected us, she thinks. She sees the president in his flight suit like a boy playing war, remembers Ron jabbing a finger at the television, saying, "Remember this." Ron's prophecy for the future: first farce, and then tragedy.

Where *is* Ron, anyway? Off to one side, planted in the weedy sand by the chain-link fence, taking it all in. Mentally recording his bitter anthropological notes.

Early scratches Harpo's ears, rubbing the hot, soft inner lining the way the dog loves—his tiny, oily eyes squeezing shut as he pants, jowls unpeeling from black gums, crooked tartarous teeth. Nearby, pressed to the clapboards of the house like a cartoon spy, stands Zechariah. Old lotion peels pinkly from his forearms. His eyes are dark, his mouth still somehow faintly ringed with last night's orange sauce. He's watching Early, watching the dog. There's something in his hand.

A few minutes ago, having stepped into the kitchen to call Hardy, Melody saw, in the living room, where the DVD of Christian vegetables was witlessly running on repeat, Zechariah and her son locked in conversation. She couldn't tell what they were saying to one another—not with the phone to her ear, Hardy's voice coming through. But their body language made it clear: an argument, a fight. Early jabbed a finger at the television just as Ron had, the day the president hung his banner. *Propaganda.* She heard it without needing to hear it.

 "Melody?" the voice on the phone was saying. "You there, sweetheart?"

A plastic spork, she sees. That's what Zechariah is holding.

"Not sure what all there is to celebrate," Hardy said. His usual line. She could picture him clearly, his hunch of shoulders and spine, absently scratching a whiskered cheek. Thoughtfully, he added, "Grilled meat." He had a story of watching Skyhawks streak low overhead, smearing napalm over the face of a jungle ridge and rolling over in the sun. And then he'd moved forward with the rest of them on the ground, Marines, into the smoke, to see what was left of who had been there and who was still there, waiting. Each Fourth of July, he'd put in earplugs and take himself to bed with a bottle of whatever was handy as soon as the sky pinkened.

"Thank you, though," he said. "For calling, I mean."

"Of course."

Melody calls on holidays, tries to keep in touch—once a month or so. She remembered how she used to look back, across the lake, from whatever boat or beach she'd found to watch the fireworks, from whatever boy's arms, to the cabin where Hardy was suffering. She'd felt so guilty, always, and so relieved. She'd never wanted to go home. She'd found reasons to stay out with whoever was around to stay out with.

"Jeannie there?" he asked.

"She wants to say hi, but she's busy getting circles run round her by all these kids."

In fact, when Melody asked to place the call, Jeannie had rolled her eyes heavenward: a private glance between her and her God. "Sheesh. When's the last time I talked to *him*?"

"She doing good, though?" Hardy wanted to know. He was sober these days, supposedly.

"Sure," Melody said, though at this point she was not much listening. She'd just watched Early and Zechariah head out to the backyard, still locked in some state of disagreement, and Claude's drinks, mixed strong, were beginning to hit. She had to go, she told him. She said, "I love you."

"Love you, too, sweetheart."

Always a disappointment, those words—saying them, hearing them. Words like that ought to *do* something, she thought.

Zechariah creeps forward, spork in fist—creeping up behind Harpo and Early.

Rising, Melody spills her mother's drink with her elbow.

But her lunge comes too late. Zechariah is closer; he'll do what he pleases. He buries the plastic spork in Harpo's muscled haunch.

Everything happens at once. The cooler's kicked aside, the grill goes over, and the poor dog, yowling, pours himself around in a liquid curve toward the source of the pain. Melody arrives. It's Early she's trying to save, Early she wants to sweep away from it all, but it's Zechariah who falls through her hands, to be caught in the crook of her left arm. Her right hand slips into the dog's mouth, a fit so perfect and so immediately socketed in place it's as if this were the whole point of her lunge: to lock her bones between those teeth.

Poor Harpo seems as shocked as anyone. After only a moment, he lets go.

Christopher lifts her. She feels her head cradled against his wide, pillowy breasts. And it *is*, in fact, like being cradled: the closest she'll ever come, perhaps, to understanding what her sister has found in this man and his faith. But shortly hereafter, trying to explain all this to Jeannie while her sister rinses and scrutinizes Melody's hand beneath the kitchen tap, Melody begins to babble. "What I mean," she says, or hears herself saying, "is we were never really held like that, were we? Never cradled. I mean, probably literally we were, of course. But never in the ways that really mattered, never really, never, never heavenly—"

Jeannie looks at her, alarmed.

At the urgent care they X-ray her hand and tell her how lucky she is: no discernible damage to joint, ligament, or tendon. Just a series of punctures, a bleeding constellation, each star a dog's tooth. They bandage her hand and write a scrip for Tylenol with codeine.

"What about scars?" Ron asks.

"Does it hurt?" Early wants to know.
"A little," she replies, as close to the truth as she can manage.

Ron drives. Early, in the backseat, drowses. Melody rests her head against the cool passenger glass, allowing the road to thrum through her skull, mixing with the codeine. Back to Cadillac. Back to her own bed. Her own life, such as it is. This isn't so different, really, from the end of any visit to Petoskey: relief and sad deflation, a painful throb growing slowly more distant.

At the same time, however, a new thought is occurring to her, or several soupy thoughts are stirring at once, coagulating, as if she's been working all this time on some continuation of the argument she was imagining with Ron during the church service, the argument she's been imagining ever since he showed her the video. Organic compounds from the furnaces of stars: so what? Don't those same compounds form the stinking fertilizers that are sprayed over farm fields and rinsed away by rain, running to the rivers to burn away the fish? Aren't they also found in the warheads of the Hellfire missile, the IED, the laser-guided bomb?

She straggles forward, grasping for words—mumbling vaguely.
"Babe? What is it?"

She pretends to sleep.

But every so often, Early stirs, too, shifting in his seat, emitting wordless vowels of complaint, denial, and fear. As if he can hear, somehow, her thoughts. And Melody is suddenly sorry to be thinking such things. She's sorry for everything. "It's okay, baby," she manages to murmur the next time he moans, because it turns out there really are some truths she wants to conceal from him, secrets she'll keep for as long as she can. Though of course he'll find them all out for himself one day, when he inherits the Earth.

BREEDERS' CUP

Now that he lives alone, Doc works every day. On Christmas morning, he's in the birthing pen of Harlan Trimble's dairy barn, squinting through his fogged breath as he sutures the hindquarters of a Holstein. "Cast her goddamn wethers again," Harlan said over the phone, which means that for the second time in three days the cow, shivering and straining, has rolled her uterus inside-out and spilled it into the open air. Three days after a stillbirth, she can't seem to stop pushing.

For the second time, Doc washes and replaces what she's spilled. Barehanded, he eases the red folds back into the body. The exposed tissue hasn't necrotized yet, but it has grown cool. Harlan's been up at the farmhouse for half the morning, watching his children tear open presents he can't afford. Back in the barn now, he stands back, packing tobacco behind his lip with his thumb. For him, it's just another story in a book of bad news. He's already confided to Doc that, barring a miracle, he'll have to sell off before the end of the coming year. Leaning on the gate to the pen, he drops a red ball of spittle between his toes.

The mattress suture is designed to anchor skin to muscle and draw the muscles tight, but Doc's seen surgical tape pop like floss. Certain animals persist in their suffering, refusing to relent. Again and again, they pour their steaming insides out, until shock and exhaustion finally bring them to the ground. They lie on their sides, panting heavily until they stop, stubborn until death. The cow shudders—nervous, hurting. "Hey, now," Doc says. "Hey, there, dearie." Sometimes he hums snippets of songs. Finished, he steps back, wiping his hands on his coveralls.

"Laced her up like an old boot," Harlan says.

Doc pours the bucket of Betadine suds into the frozen barn-yard. For breakfast, he had a banana, three aspirin, and two cups of coffee; the idea of conversation exhausts him.

Besides, what's there to say? Three nights ago, Doc hauled the calf out by the forelegs—a baby bull, perfectly formed, so freshly suffocated he could barely believe it wasn't alive. He took the soft muzzle between his hands and blew into one wet nostril and then the other. His mouth filled with salt, but this changed nothing. Harlan fired up the backhoe to dig a shallow grave. Doc found an old stool in the milkhouse at the end of the barn, lingering a moment in the humid warmth of the holding tanks and condensers, popping his icy knuckles. As the cow nosed the dead thing, lapping the afterbirth, he sat down to offer what comfort he could, emptying her heavy udder, milk steaming in the straw.

Late that night, home again, alone, he watched without any particular interest a meaningless West Coast bowl game between two directional schools and caught himself, as he reached for the beer on the end table, humming. As if to soothe a hurting ani-mal. But there was no animal around to be soothed except him.

Little Star, his terrier mutt, was up in Dani's room, asleep.

Christmas, a cold Appalachian morning, air like a blade at the leading edge of winter. Harlan scribbles a check and asks Doc not to cash it right away. The cow groans and pushes, passing a bit of urine. The sutures hold for now.

The squirrel lies in a looped nest of entrails, tail flung back like a tattered cape, forelegs outstretched in a dream of flight. Margaret's breath catches. It's shocking, how much can spill from one small body. Still, when the dog trotted up to the house, bloody-muzzled, she'd known what she'd find.

He watches from the screened-in porch, fluting thin whines through his nose like a kettle. The dog. Prichard's Flying Aureliano.

Boxes clutter the detached garage. Six months here, and still she's unpacking, or still not unpacking. "Goodness," her friend Alice said, mildly exasperated, when she and Win visited on Thanksgiving. "Boxed up to leave already?"

Margaret locates the shovel, together with a rake, a weed cutter, a pitchfork, and a posthole digger, all stacked inside a corroded fifty-five-gallon drum—equipment and décor courtesy of the house's previous owner, an elderly widower who'd sold the property for a song after his lung cancer went into remission. He was moving to Hatteras, he told Margaret at the closing. He was going to spend whatever miraculous days remained to him beside the sea.

She slips the shovel beneath the squirrel, using a stick to drag a stray coil of viscera onto the blade. Real country living, the thing she's left Asheville to find. This, at least, is how she has explained the decision to Dennis and Ryan, her sons.

Christmas morning, and she's burying an eviscerated rodent in her backyard.

"What you need here," Alice said on Thanksgiving, patting Win's knuckles expectantly, "is a dog."

Prichard's Flying Aureliano won't leave the porch while Margaret's standing by the door. She has to step into the kitchen, out of sight, before he'll slink in. He's a brindled greyhound, an old racer. His long face carries all the marks of his breed's hemophiliac nobility, its brittle intelligence.

Win manages a local animal shelter. "Fresh out of sweet little things," she said when Margaret visited. "They go fast, this time of year." She regarded Margaret with what Margaret decided to call a gimlet eye. "If that's what you're looking for."

Margaret worries that Win is unkind to Alice, whom Margaret has known forever. She has no actual grounds for suspicion. There's just something pushy and judgmental about Win, a self-righteousness that suggests the capacity for cruelty. It's easy to imagine her indignant, fanatical.

Sometimes, though—particularly at night, when sleep is

slow to come—a cold charity descends, transforming Margaret's assessments. Win is ten years younger than Margaret and Alice. Like an animal's, her life seems unidirectional; she suffers no doubts. She's found her calling. She's found Alice. Alice, for whom Margaret nursed an impossible crush through much of junior high, when they shared the kind of terrifyingly intimate friendship that must only exist, she thinks, between girls of a certain age.

Margaret may only be jealous, after all, only bitter. Only damaged: a divorcée.

Trying to impress Win, or else to challenge her, she asked about the old greyhound, abandoned by a previous owner.

In the kitchen, she wets a washcloth to clean the greyhound's muzzle. Dennis, Ryan, and Ryan's wife will be arriving any moment. There can be no sign of blood.

"Kind of quiet," Ryan said, the first time he and Stephanie visited.

Dennis, customarily, was less cautious. "Is this some sort of midlife thing?"

"I like the quiet life," Margaret told Ryan. With Dennis, meanwhile, she adopted a tone of bluff dismissal: "You don't think your old mother can take care of herself out here?" Her sons have long divided her; catering to them means splitting into separate selves. Now she's become a homesteading pioneer for Dennis, and for Ryan a cloistered nun. In truth, she's not sure what she's doing out here, twenty minutes from the nearest supermarket. If this is a response to her first year after the divorce—gathering loose ends in a West Asheville rental, a neighborhood too hip for her and too young by half—it's an overcorrection. She's skidding now; in some small yet fundamental way, she's lost her grip on the road.

But her sons—and their father, for she's sure Dennis, at least, tells Parker everything—don't need to know this.

Over the past several days, Margaret and the greyhound have reached an uneasy détente: he'll stand rigid beneath her hand, allowing her to trace his spine. Now, though, he retreats, nails ticking through the den, past the pitiful plastic spruce and down the hall. She follows, washcloth trailing droplets—her foolish, dotted path—and corners him in the back bathroom, where the toilet works but the faucet sputters rust and the claw-footed tub is cracked beyond repair, a beached whale. The greyhound cowers, gazing up at her with bleak, soulful eyes.

No. Not at her. At the washcloth in her hand.

The torn and emptied squirrel. The mechanical rabbit, that whole past life.

"Oh, honey," she says, dropping the washcloth into the tub. She settles herself cross-legged on the linoleum's scuffed, gritty roses and offers an empty hand.

This is what her life has come to, eighteen months divorced: holding her breath while a dog named Prichard's Flying Aureliano edges forward with his bloody, uncertain snout, both of them waiting to see whether he means to sniff, lick, or sink his teeth into the delicate net of bones she's extended. Carefully, as if her touch carries a heat he must ease into, the dog slips his head beneath her hand. The ridged dome of his skull fills her palm. After a minute, she takes his felted ear between her thumb and forefinger and begins, gently, to rub. And from Prichard's Flying Aureliano comes a noise she's never heard before: a moan, a door swinging open in his chest. All at once, he melts into her.

Why now, after days of fruitless overtures? A gentler dialect of body language she's stumbled upon, a scent she gives off when she's feeling sympathetic, or simply the final slow erosion of his defenses. She loops an arm over his muscular shoulders. His panting fogs the space around them with the coppery scent of a small, terrified death.

They're still sitting together, his bloody muzzle cradled in her hands, when she hears the crunch of tires on the gravel drive.

Doc's daughter calls at lunchtime. Dani's nineteen, a sophomore at Tulane. This is her first Christmas away from home; she's spending the holiday with her boyfriend's family in Raceland, a bayou town southwest of the New Orleans. Josh is twenty-three, a roofer and a house painter. Once, Dani sent a picture of the two of them to Doc's computer. She's a pretty girl, lanky and freckled with a quick, aggressive smile. In the picture, Josh looks fat. He has round pink cheeks and a sad, fuzzy beard. "Merry Christmas, honey," Doc says. "How are you? How's Louisiana?"

"Warm," she says. "The sun down here, even in winter— you'd barely believe it."

Out the window, Doc can see his front yard, crisp grass beneath a gray sky, blackberry brambles snarled at the fringe of the woods. The sun's a powdery disc. He lives at the end of a dead-end road, a house he and his wife chose for its seclusion.

"Dad, I want you to ask me something. Ask me why I'm so happy."

In spite of himself, Doc smiles. "Okay. Why?"

"Oh," she says, "no. I shouldn't say. Let it be a surprise."

Dani and Josh are flying up for New Year's. That evening, readying her bedroom for their arrival—the terrier, who has adopted the space as her own in Dani's absence, yawns and stretches on the floor—Doc flips the light switch off and on, studying the space in darkness and in light. It's full of things she's left behind. A plush menagerie atop the dresser, a prom-night Polaroid of her with some friends—parrot-colored dresses and beaming, embarrassed faces—taped to the corner of the mirror. A lump in the middle of the made bed turns out to be one of her tee-shirts. At first, the shirt seems to feature the Coca-Cola logo—an odd choice for Dani—but spreading the wrinkled thing smooth reveals the word *Cthulhu* in the iconic cola font.

The eldritch mysteries of teenage girlhood: he's never pretended to understand her.

Still, the thought that he's paying $30,000 a year to send his child hundreds of miles away for months at a stretch sometimes makes Doc's chest ache. Her absence is an egg he's swallowed whole.

Susan, Doc's wife, died in a single-car accident when Dani was fourteen. No rhyme or reason to it, no explanation. She left Dani and Doc alone together. Somehow, they survived. They performed the hard labor of little gestures, day after day. He browned hamburger in a skillet and collected her laundry from the floor. She did her homework beside him at the desk in his office. "You're crying," she said, her voice buoyant with wonder. He hung his coveralls out to dry, and the next morning the sun soaked and rebounded from the gold-stitched rod of Asclepius over the breast.

He's still trying to figure out what to do without her.

He sits in her room with her shirt in his hands and the dog between his feet, replaying the music of their conversation. *Ask me why I'm so happy.*

At the Asheville airport, she throws her arms around his neck and he kisses her hair. "Darling," he says. She smiles and steps back, one hand on his shoulder, swinging aside to allow Josh in. He's taller than Doc expected. Not fat, either, but broad through the chest and shoulders. Still, despite all this bulk stuffed into a sweater and corduroys, he seems young. Perhaps it's the way he moves—gingerly, as if a tiny Josh sits deep within his body, pulling levers whose signals take a moment to reach his hands and feet. His eyes are bright behind black-framed glasses. "Dr. Jeffries. So great to finally meet you."

"People call me Doc."

"Okay—Doc." He actually blushes. But his grip is strong, his palm roughened by work.

They eat at the steakhouse near Dani's old high school. In a foothill town of 4,000 or so, this counts as fine dining. Dani and Doc sometimes ate here on nights he was too exhausted or heartsick to cook. Filled with halting conversation, charged silences, and shocking moments of eye contact, those nights out together felt more than anything like dates. Later, finally home, his daughter twists on the couch, fingers knotting in terrier fur as Little Star lays her chin across Dani's knees.

"This is harder to say," she confesses, "than I thought it would be."

Doc looks up from the fireplace and the little house of kindling he's built. Outside, Josh gathers split logs from the pile. Evening clings to the windows like lint.

"I was going to say on the phone the other day. But then I couldn't."

"It's about Josh?"

Dani nods.

His chest billows with purpose. "You're home now. Whatever it is, we'll deal with it."

"Dad, we're engaged."

She works a ring from her hip pocket and slips it on: a silver band, a little pearl.

Josh, Doc thinks. Little boy in a man suit. Josh, who has been nothing but pleasant, socking away sirloin and mashed potatoes, asking questions about Doc's job, answering questions about his own, speaking in a husky voice that stammers sometimes, as though certain sentences must be primed before they can be drawn up from his belly. Josh, who pushes his glasses up his nose after speaking and looks to Dani for approval, watching her with a tiny, hopeful smile. Josh the painter, Josh the roofer. Silly Josh. Josh the husband.

"You're so young," he says.

"I know."

It's difficult to read her expression.

Josh returns, depositing an armload of firewood beside Doc. Dani shows Josh the hand that wears the ring.

"Oh," Josh says. For some reason, he offers his own hand for Doc to shake. Doc stares. Josh frowns: he, too, seems confused by the gesture. He sits with Dani on the couch, their knees touching. "Let's, let's . . ." He squints, struggling to recall a line he's spent hours rehearsing. "Let's talk about this."

"Excuse me," Doc says.

Outside, night doesn't fall but rather sweeps up from the

earth into the branches, the sky. Doc sits on the front steps, blowing into his palms. Once, Susan told him about a Sunday when she was eight or ten weeks old. She claimed to remember, though she knew this was impossible. Her parents carried her to the altar of their church to have her baptized. The pastor dipped his hands into a bowl of water and washed her scalp. He spoke her name before the hushed congregation and pronounced her beloved in the eyes of God.

Dani sits beside him. "Cold out here, Dad."

"'Ask me why I'm so happy.'"

"What? Oh. That's right." She doesn't sound like a child. "I am, yes."

"Okay," he says.

"Dad, there's something else."

In the dark, it's easy to mistake her for Susan: the same sharp chin and nose, the same sharp smile hooking her mouth to one side. But in sunlight, he knows, her green eyes reveal honeyed rings around the pupils, a perfection entirely her own.

"Something else," he says.

She lifts his hand from his knee and places it on her stomach.

On New Year's Eve, Dennis and his friends drink beer on the porch, laughing and roughhousing on the other side of the cold glass while Margaret sits with Ryan and Stephanie, watching the ball drop in New York. Afterward, she falls asleep on the sofa and wakes in darkness. Ryan and Stephanie are gone, but a few of the boys are still outside. A tiny orange coal travels in a circle, lighting bits of faces. She recognizes Dennis's lips, the whiskered curve of his jaw. The next morning, the boys are gone. Dennis snores beneath a quilt on the living-room floor.

In the kitchen, Ryan pours water into the coffeemaker. "You're the first up," he says, discounting himself, so resolutely in character that, despite the new surroundings, she almost expects to hear Parker's heavy morning tread on the stairs.

She takes the dog for a walk.

The woods are bare, shot through with sun. The dog slides along, drawing the world in through his nose. Margaret, huffing, follows at the length of a leash, the pace of a dogtrot. She would've thought she'd have stopped loving Parker long before they opened divorce proceedings. But her dumb love is robust; new longing sprouts unbidden from old habit like shoots coppicing from a stump.

Dennis is sitting up when she returns, holding a mug, his back to the sofa. "I like this," he says, rocking from side to side, making the floorboards creak. "Totally primitive."

That night, they caravan into town for a dinner at the steakhouse. As always, an atmosphere of casual indulgence pervades the place. Steaks come ringed with opalescent fat, chicken and fish encased in batter. Salads are iceberg wedges with shreds of carrot, soaked in mayonnaise and oil. The buttermilk mashed potatoes are wonderful. MADE FRESH DAILY, the menu notes, providing another reason to suspect the salads, for which no such claim is made. Margaret resists speculating on the ratio of buttermilk to potato. Ryan orders a third beer and offers a rambling, good-natured, pointless anecdote about the congressional office where he works. Dennis leans back, studying his sister-in-law's sweatered breasts. Stephanie ignores the glances, feigning enthrallment with her husband's story—or else she really doesn't notice and really is enthralled. She's a sweet girl; anything's possible.

After dinner, Ryan hands his keys to Margaret without embarrassment or apology. Dennis kisses Margaret's cheek, shakes his brother's hand, and enfolds Stephanie in a lingering hug. He's continuing up the mountain to Asheville—where, since his return from Hawaii a few months back, he's been living on Parker's dime. Ryan and Stephanie will spend one more night before driving back to D.C., where Ryan aides the local House rep and Stephanie studies international law at George Mason. Dennis's rattletrap Cherokee turns left, shoots through a stale yellow, and disappears.

"I'm worried about him," Ryan says from the back seat. "This morning, there were marijuana butts all over the porch."

Beside Margaret, Stephanie fidgets. Margaret understands. Ryan would have told her this already; they would have agreed not to worry Margaret with it. But now his tongue's been loosened. Her elder boy: sweetheart, do-gooder, snitch. *Marijuana butts.* "They're called roaches, honey."

Silence. But it's too late to worry about Ryan and Stephanie's opinions. She lost them, Margaret imagines, upon their arrival, when they met the dog with the bloody muzzle and the mother with the bloody hands. "Oh, he likes to kill squirrels," she said, affecting breeziness. Stephanie stiffened. A portcullis of bland concern descended over Ryan's features.

She imagines Dennis recounting the past week to Parker, back in Asheville. *Have you talked to Mom lately? She's primitive!* The fantasy is darkly satisfying.

"You think he's happy?" Ryan asks at last.

Who can know such a thing about themselves, Margaret wonders, let alone about anyone else?

"He's different," Ryan insists. "Than before Hawaii, I mean."

In the passenger seat, Stephanie reaches back without turning around, her fingers finding Ryan's wrist. Ryan is thin, with slender, girlish forearms; his wrists are braceleted with coarse black hair—Parker's contribution—and knobbed by porcelain bone. Margaret knows them well.

Having planned to leave by eight, Ryan and Stephanie are out the door next morning at 7:55. Margaret waves as the Subaru slides through the trees. Winter engulfs the fading motor, the cold air between one ridgeline and the next faintly tympanic, like the hollow inside a shell. Rubbing goosebumps from her arms, she turns and goes inside. She's depleted; her sons' lives have thundered past like semis on the interstate, and some vital wisp of herself has lifted in their wake and followed. A pleasant anhedonia settles. Ryan's wrists are Stephanie's to touch, and as long as he's up in Asheville, Dennis remains Parker's priority, not hers. And Parker, now that her sons are gone, is less than a ghost.

The dog curls between toilet and tub. Throughout the past week's bustle, this has been his sanctuary.

"Out?" she asks.

They pass the silvered barn with its rotten roof, its weary southpaw tilt. Margaret is afraid to enter, lest it choose that moment to collapse. From out here, though, the house seems equally suspect: the peeling clapboards, the screened-in porch with its sheepish, smiling sag. Beyond the barn, the wooded ridge rises. The dog trots along, sniffing. Day by day, she shows him the bounds of her land—how to run free, how to return. One of Win's recommendations, actually. Win speaks through Alice: "Win thinks . . ." "Win mentioned . . ."

Truth be told, Margaret has grown fond of these explorations herself. She, too, is learning the topography of the ridgeline, its crenels and outcrops, its deadfalls and thickets. She has begun to lay claim to this place. Here it is, she thinks, jogging along, sneakers chuffing through dead leaves. Her primitive new life.

A livestock veterinarian by trade, Doc spends several days a year with dogs, offering discount vaccinations for rabies, distemper, adenovirus, parvo. This blustery afternoon, he's in the parking lot of the local shelter, combing his fingers through fur and jabbing needles home. A line has formed. January's a popular time for vaccinations: most of these dogs were gifts.

Win, the shelter's manager, supervises the volunteers, collects payments, fills out paperwork, and offers customers cocoa from a thermos. She's a big capable young woman with the faintest shadow of a mustache. "Margaret and John Quick," she says, as if introducing a couple. And the pair does, in fact, seem well matched: a woman and a greyhound, both fine-boned and slim, with long noses and large, slightly protuberant eyes.

"John Quick," Doc says.

"His racing name was ridiculous," the owner replies. "So, 'John.'"

"And 'Quick'?"

"Oh, that name's mine. But appropriate, right?"

Doc pinches a fold atop the brindled neck, slips the needle into the tented skin, and thumbs the plunger. "Good boy." Palming the syringe, he knuckles the muscled trench between the bladed shoulders while the dog pants into his other hand. He's always liked greyhounds—their streamlined faces and wicker-basket chests. A volatile marriage of power and frailty, like thoroughbreds. Last fall, Doc watched the Breeders' Cup on television. As the horses paraded to the starting gate, tossing their heads and dancing, his eyes prickled with tears. The poor things: attach those muscles to such matchstick legs and of course bones were going to break. Everyone knew where it would lead, but still they went on. The horses fired themselves down the track to the clamor of bells, their bodies elongating, clinging jockeys blurring to blots. He rubbed his eyes, furious and embarrassed. In two minutes, it was over.

The woman is smiling. "You went somewhere a moment."

"Guess I did."

She thanks him; he nods. She's ushered to a nearby table, where a volunteer places the label from the vial Doc used in a logbook and delivers a pitch about charitable donations. Across the lot, Little Star rests her chin on the open window of Doc's truck. Other dogs typically fail to interest her—an indifference not unusual in rescues—but she likes to keep an eye on them. Do she and Doc appear well matched, too, with their whiskered jaws, furry brows, and the absent rasp of breathing that accompanies an inward cast of mind? Already Win is calling new names, moving things along: no time for such questions. The world's no mystery to her, as it so often is to Doc.

Alice plows a chunk of porterhouse into her mashed potatoes. Margaret smiles, picturing Win's consternation: Win, evangelical vegan. Margaret can't dispute her on the facts—who could?— but she's repulsed by Win's certainty, as she is by certainty in general. In the face of such righteousness, it feels good to sin. It feels good to corrupt Alice with the occasional steakhouse dinner. With blatant disregard for personal and global health, they breathe the air of their shared history.

They've been talking about Dennis. Parker left a voice message yesterday: their son has been fired again. Or else he quit—the details are unclear. Parker was angry, chewing his words. "Enunciate, please," Margaret used to say when he shouted at her, which only made him angrier, more garbled.

"Just call me," he said at last—taking a breath, gathering himself. "We've got to figure what to do with this kid."

Is it really so bad, Margaret wants to know, that she hasn't called back?

"Probably." Alice has a plump, comic face that scrunches with mirth or distaste, a little upturned dollop of a nose, a milkmaid's complexion: creamy brow, ruddy cheeks, faded blue eyes. She's a high school English teacher, an optimist, someone for whom "the children are our future" serves as a heartfelt creed. She regards the problems of youth as knowable, solvable, or at least survivable, at least susceptible to wisdom and advice.

Margaret regards youth as a muddle, her own most of all. For a time when she was thirteen, fourteen, and fifteen, she knew Alice's skin nearly as well as her own. They staged giddy raids on one another's bodies. Margaret was what her mother, mortifyingly, called a late bloomer, Alice just the opposite. Margaret studied the moles on Alice's left hip, her rosy downturned nipples, the firm roll of flesh pinched above the waist of her jeans, with a fascination that left her slightly ill. Memories of one encounter—as innocent as their toes knocking beneath the cafeteria table or as terrifying as slipping a hand inside the waistband of Alice's underwear to touch that shocking hair—bred thoughts of the next. The steakhouse, with its buffet lines and sneeze guards, its joyous din, is pleasantly reminiscent of a school cafeteria. It was with Alice that Margaret first glimpsed the various intimacies and revelations of sex. Alice was her first love, her first heartbreak.

All this lies between them now—on the table, beside the bloody steaks.

"I *will* call," Margaret promises. "Eventually."

The possibility that this might be a lie settles between them as well.

Parker is all burly confidence, his russet hair expertly graying at the temples, a signet ring embossed with the Citadel palmetto decorating one enormous, hairy, manicured hand. He heads a private security firm—a booming business, Asheville in recent decades a magnet for wealth from the Research Triangle, from Atlanta and D.C., from as far away as Hollywood, its hills a hive of vacation homes and gated communities—and reads philosophy in his spare time. He invokes Hobbes on the state of nature and the creation of property, Rawls on the veil of ignorance and the moral constructivism. He has a child's faith in the power of fairness and a soldier's focused intensity on concretely defined goals. When he says *Rawls*, it sounds like he's growling. Arguing with him makes Margaret feels vicious and doomed, a dog bred to attack a grizzly.

During the divorce, Dennis—a mechanic by training if not always by trade—left for Maui to service tractors and combines at a Monsanto seed farm. The announcement shocked Margaret: not only the distance, but the employer. Parker, in the midst of their other negotiations, mocked her concern. "Folks raise such a stink about GMOs. But really, Margaret, can you tell me what's wrong with it?" He affected an exaggerated drawl, a send-up of shrill mountain ignorance: "Ah ain't eating nothin' with *genetics* in it!"

Margaret has a southern accent. Parker, raised with money, hardly does. This was how she sounded to him, she understood.

Worse, she had no ready response; she didn't know enough about the science behind her position. She'd been too lax in her beliefs, too complacent—too unlike Win, perhaps. Lazy. A characteristic flaw, Parker would probably attest. In any case, there would be no voice of reason in this debate over Dennis's future. All she could do was retreat into herself, concentrating on escaping the marriage intact.

Dennis returned a year later, sunburned and broke. Parker paid for his ticket home, for the lease on his Jeep, for his Asheville apartment. This was in part because Parker could afford it—she'd made no grab for his income in the settlement; she has her own accounting work, which is enough. But it was also because Parker, in winning the Monsanto argument, seems to have won Dennis. The jobs their son quits, the jobs from which he's fired—his bosses have all been "control freaks," his coworkers "blowhards"—the drugs he puts into his body: these are Parker's problems now. Margaret has learned to let go.

Alice knows all this. In moments, and without speaking—with their eyes, the shifting of their bodies, an adjustment made to the weight of the air over the table—they pore over old grievances together before moving on to new topics. Dessert arrives. Margaret hands her phone across the table to show Alice a photo of John Quick, his paws and snout muddy from digging in the woods, the kitchen linoleum stitched with wet prints. He gazes up from the center of the mess. To Margaret's eye, there is something regal, imperious, in his expression: *Behold!*

"Getting fat," Alice says.

"So what? He's retired."

Alice squints at Margaret over a wedge of cheesecake, her nose wrinkling, a familiar expression of fond judgment.

"What?" Margaret asks.

But she already knows. She's become the kind of person who shows people pictures of her pet. Last night, John Quick curled at the foot of her bed—she'd tried lifting him onto it, but he'd only sat shaking, peering mournfully over the edge, until she helped him back down—sighing endlessly through sleep, a steam engine. She thinks about him when they're apart, worrying he'll be lonely or bored. This never happened with the fish, lizards, and rodents her sons had had when they were growing up, or with Karpov, Parker's ancient, incontinent Russian blue cat.

John Quick is different. She considers him often.

A pining schoolgirl.

"You look happy," Alice says.

Late winter is the season for equine infectious anemia testing. Doc's all over the western third of the state, pulling blood. As he gathers vials and ships them in batches to a laboratory in Knoxville, his refrigerator fills and empties, a cold heart. From the top of Del Carroll's sloping pasture, he can see for thirty miles: rows of gray mountains daubed onto gray sky. A cellular tower winks atop the nearest ridge, red lights afloat over a sifting of February snow.

His phone buzzes: a message from Dani.

The horse snorts, braided muscles stiffening, as Doc pushes the needle into a vein as thick as his thumb. "Hush, now," Doc whispers into the large triangular ear. The syringe draws full of blood, a hue between chocolate and wine, which he injects through a rubber stopper into a vial. The glass fogs. Beneath that film, the dark cells are aligned, still waiting to be pulled into the lungs.

"My little girl had an ultrasound this morning," he says in the farmhouse kitchen.

Del Carroll, who has twin sons and a daughter—a toddler whose voice rings through the rooms, refusing some request made by Kim, Del's wife—raises a mug of instant coffee in salute. "Grandpa Doc."

Home in the evening, Doc pulls a beer from behind the vials and opens Dani's message once again. A Rorschach test fills the phone's screen. It could be a map of ocean currents, solar winds, a nebula thousands of light years across. But amid the chaotic swirls Doc spots a long, orderly curve, the dome of a skull. His finger leaves a smudge on the screen.

"I know it's impossible," Susan said. Still, she remembered. The hand that cupped her head, the chilling water. A finger lay across her brow, shielding her eyes. Faces floated in the middle distance. Beyond them hung a vaulted roof, carved from clouds.

A sea of voices. Everything was strange. Water curled mysteriously in her ears.

She told him this during their engagement, when she spent her days off riding with Doc from farm to farm. She was a registered nurse, fearless. She slipped a hemostat into a surgical incision in a Hanoverian's flank, clamping off an artery while Doc worked. If anyone could remember something that had happened when they were two months old, it was Susan. Her perceptions arrived with fiery clarity.

Doc envies that fire. His early memories are a muddle, shapeless days under a distant, scattered sun. He knows his father ran a framing crew and had small white calluses across the pads of his palms. He knows his mother had a false canine she removed before eating, placing it in a glass of water beside her plate, and that sometimes she grinned, gap-toothed, across the table to make him laugh. But as soon as he tries to remember a specific instance—a time his father touched his face, a meal when his mother smiled—this knowledge dissolves into mere information.

The present is little different. His business ledger contains busy months of appointments and emergencies, supplies ordered and received, mileage numbers for his truck. He remembers these things in the thinnest possible way, recollections as flimsy as the pages the ink bleeds through. His days flow together, undifferentiated, as if he's lost the ability to make new memories entirely.

He remembers his daughter. He remembers his wife.

As for the rest of it, the time without them, the whole before and after of his life?

He is forty-seven years old.

John Quick is dying.

Margaret finds him sprawled in the bathroom one night toward the end of March, his feet twitching between the feet of the tub. His tongue dangles; his chest squeezes through endless rapid, shallow breaths. His eyes are wide, the gluey whites revealed, turned to the ceiling in an expression approaching religious ecstasy.

It's Sunday. The automated message at the nearest veterinary clinic lists their weekday hours but no emergency contact. Or was there? Too late; Margaret's already hung up. She's an accountant. She loves the slow lives of numbers, combining and dividing as they make their long migrations down and across the columns of a spreadsheet. She's no good in a crisis, as Parker was always quick to point out. "Oh, for crying out loud," he said as they drove Ryan to the emergency room for an appendectomy. Then he laughed, because that was what she was doing—crying out loud, far more loudly and tearfully than their son.

"Calm down," Alice says when Margaret calls. "I'm going to put Win on, all right?"

"Win? No, I don't want to talk to—"

"Listen," Win says. "Here's what you're going to do."

Win calls to warn him: "Surprise." A few minutes later, a battered Volvo station wagon rattles up the washboard drive he's long meant to have packed and graded. A woman springs from the car, takes a few running steps toward the house, and turns back, stricken. Spotting him in the kitchen window, she waves with both hands.

It would be a lie to say he doesn't recognize her.

When he asks if the dog has ingested anything unusual, Margaret Quick touches the base of her throat. "Unusual? What?" Nothing to do but—in the absence of better ideas, without time even to determine what a better idea might look like— what comes to mind. The dog lies on a carpet remnant in the laundry room. Margaret sits on the floor, her fingers hesitating an inch from his ears, as if fearing the damage a touch might do. In a drinking glass, Doc mixes water and hydrogen peroxide. He draws the solution into a plastic syringe, draws back the wet curtain of John Quick's jowl with a hooked finger, and slips the syringe between two clenched teeth. Action comforts him: warm fur beneath his fingers, swift rote motions. He gives himself over to the knowledge stored in his hands. In the other room, his half-finished beer scores a cold zero into the coffee table. He hears himself humming low, involuntary notes, an old song.

At the door to the laundry room Little Star waits, watching like she's seen it all before.

Margaret watches, too. Her eyes are round, gull-gray.

The long body clenches. The veterinarian straddles and lifts John Quick, tipping the dog's head toward the floor. Without moving, Margaret feels herself receding into a corner, tucked away beneath the sink like a bottle of bleach. Or else they are receding from her, man and dog. She thinks again of Ryan, awaiting surgery, twelve years old—just beginning his long retreat into adulthood, transforming himself from a warm, quiet, gently effeminate boychild into the man he's become, a permanent stranger, circumspect and decorous, a self-described fiscal conservative. He peered up at her mournfully as the orderly arrived to wheel him away. "You'll be fine, honey," she said. "You'll be so good." She was powerless; it was less than a promise.

The dog heaves, bringing up a brown slurry with a rich, fishy odor.

Fur and flesh. Small, crushed bones. The rotted carcass of a squirrel.

After rolling the soiled carpet and stuffing it into the garbage bin behind the garage, Doc stands for a minute, leaning against the house. The evening is cool but muggy, hinting at spring. The stars look blurry. He dials Win.

"Where else was I going to send her?" Win asks. "It sounded like an emergency, and you're not far. Besides, what other vet's going to open his doors Sunday night without charging an arm and a leg?"

"Okay, sure. But I think she wants to camp here."

"She's had a scare, Doc. My God, her dog." Win laughs. "Give her a minute. Does it make you so uncomfortable?"

As long as Doc's known her, this has been her response to the cruelty, stinginess, and reticence of the world. She dismisses it, coldly laughing; she, for one, will have none of it. Around Win, it's impossible to be less than your most generous self without feeling like a joke. Inside, he offers Margaret coffee, and Margaret, despite the hour, agrees.

The coffeemaker burbles. He returns to the laundry room, uncertain. The woman and her dog seem superimposed here, their colors too bright, their edges too distinct. It is Little Star who makes them seem real—Little Star, who has wandered over to sit beside them, gazing up at the woman and twitching her mustache, having decided, it seems, to be jealous of the attention the greyhound is getting. Doc can think of nothing to say. "He kills squirrels," she offers. "I keep burying them, but I guess he digs them up." Is this an explanation, an apology? He falls back on professional talk. Take the dog to his usual vet tomorrow, if anything seems amiss. Most likely, though, everything's fine. He had a meal that didn't agree with him, simple as that. "Simple as that," she repeats. He glances at the coffeemaker. Still burbling.

"You know what my son said to me after his appendectomy?"

He shakes his head.

"He said, 'You had me all concerned.' *Concerned.* Twelve years old. But that's him, that's Ryan."

A son. He wouldn't have guessed her to be a mother. Her skittish, erratic energy recalls the spinster women he sometimes meets through his work. They live alone, sharing trailers or ramshackle cottages with cats and dogs. A she-goat to keep the kudzu out of the vegetable plot, a mule for good conversation.

They're proud of their loneliness, these women. They pay with wadded bills loose from a shoebox or stripped from a roll buried in the flour tin. Doc's a cloud across the face of their day. They eye him like they're waiting for the thunderbolt.

Maybe Margaret senses this line of thought, or maybe she's just filling his silence. She leaps ahead, talking rapidly. She and her ex-husband unmarried one another—that's the word she uses. They took back the vows; they didn't mean them anymore. "But we waited until our youngest was out of the house. At least we did that much."

"I'm sorry."

She flicks the apology away. "I mean, a part of me felt—oh, not relieved, exactly. Unburdened. Parker, the kids: I was done being *concerned*. Let them care for themselves. Goodbye to all that. Goodbye. Goodbye to that whole, whole . . . that whole . . ."

She looks up at him, flushed, flyaway hairs glued to her cheeks.

"That whole cup of trembling," Doc supplies.

"Oh—*that*."

The coffeemaker beeps, rescuing them both.

By the time he returns with her mug, she's wiped her eyes and run her fingers through her hair. One hand strokes the dog's ribs. The dog blinks with every touch.

Doc lowers himself to the floor, too. Little Star pads over to his side and nudges his free hand. *The cup* . . . Susan's words, the old-time religion of her childhood. Without mentioning her, he feels as if he's revealed everything.

"I should apologize." Margaret studies her coffee. "That was what Parker would have called an outburst."

"I have a daughter myself." This, too, feels enormous, a confession. "Sent her off to college the other year."

She makes a noise of acknowledgment, still embarrassed, not looking at him.

"She's pregnant now."

"What?" It takes a moment. Then she laughs. "Oh, no." She

covers her mouth, but it's no use. She laughs and laughs. A rich, dark sound—it must leave stains, coloring any conversation it touches. Finally, she gathers herself. "No shit," she says, panting.

Nothing for a time. Four sets of breath running along at different speeds, overlapping, humans and dogs.

"I *am* sorry," Margaret says.

"For what?"

She giggles. Her cheeks are wet again.

A hand-addressed envelope arrives in the mail, quaintly out of place amid advertising circulars and bills. Inside is a photograph of Margaret and John Quick—a self-portrait, the phone held at arm's length. Where can you print photos anymore, these days? Her other arm is around the dog, their heads drawn together, the resemblance clear. Folded around the photo is a brief thank-you note on a sheet of letterhead. Her cursive is large, swooping, the product of a swift pen. *Margaret Quick*, CPA.

If you need a hand with your taxes, she writes. But Doc's already filed.

Still, he feeds her number to his phone, asking it to remember.

Often, that spring and into the summer, Parker calls to complain about Dennis. "He won't listen," Parker says. "I talk to him and it's like I'm not even there."

"Sure," Dennis replies when Margaret calls. "Dad's just *full* of advice."

She hangs up, a warm sense of solidarity overspreading her. Parker's a bully: it's no mystery why someone wouldn't want to talk to him.

"He doesn't look for work anymore," Parker says. "Just smokes pot and plays videogames all day."

"And cashes your checks," Margaret says. Because that's Parker's real concern, isn't it? She hangs up in the middle of his ensuing tirade. Dennis is twenty-two. She doesn't blame him for lacking Parker's preternatural drive, his suffocating sense of duty.

"Yes," she tells Dennis, "he's full of it."

But she wakes, one July night, to a call from county lockup. Dennis talks fast, slurring: something about a fight at a bar. "Arrested?" she asks, hoarse with sleep. From the floor, John Quick raises his head, doubtful.

"Spring me, Ma? Bake a key in a cake?"

He grins when he sees her, one eye puffy and dark. Blood rims his teeth.

"Don't freak out," he says. "Jeez."

Drunk? Perhaps. But the slurred speech has more to do with his split and swollen lip.

"What happened?"

They're in her car, heading to his apartment. "You know," he says. "Stupid shit. Somebody says something, somebody else says something back."

"Mmm-hmm. Where do you come in?"

"I was the somebody else."

Always that capering edge to his conversation. Even now, prodding the swollen half of his face, he remains hidden, the damage simply another mask. During his months in Maui, she'd heard almost nothing from him. He posted just a handful of photos to his Instagram. No gorgeous sunsets, green mountains, blue waves. Instead, farming equipment. A service pit grimed with oil. The dim interior of a bar, mostly empty, front window blank with sunlight. The green rows of a soybean field converging toward a line of low trees. The closest thing to a scenic shot was a single-lane bridge over a stream, the abutments and guardrails hairy with vines. *This is my bridge,* Dennis had written.

"And who was the first somebody?" she asks.

For a little while he's quiet. Then he turns away, looking out the window. "Donner and Jess."

"Wait. Your *friends* did this to you?"

He says nothing. She studies his reflected face in the window, blurred as if by water. Climbing the steps to his building, he stumbles into her, his warm shoulder clubbing her breast, a whiff of sweat and beer. She helps him up, and he lets her help him. Fishing his keys from his pocket, he says, "Let's not tell Dad, please."

And this mollifies her a little. *Let's. Let us.* He's chosen her tonight, not his father. He's chosen her again, as he did at the very beginning. Through a difficult labor he cleaved to her, refusing to be moved. He twisted himself between her hips, a knot drawn tighter and tighter, excruciating. In the end, he had to be cut from her, extracted like a pit from an olive.

The hall smells of cigarettes. Overhead fluorescents buzz. Not a cheap place, exactly, but institutional, the kind of place that creates the illusion of cheapness by shunning character. Though it's nearly two in the morning, Margaret hears a television burbling through one of the doors they pass. From another comes a strange, rhythmic clinking, like a spoon inside a bowl. "Oh, what a night," Dennis sings in his cracked voice. The shadow has passed; it's all a joke again. He opens his door. She glimpses a corner of the darkened apartment: a poster of a lingerie model, the taut ligament of her inner thigh disappearing into her bikini briefs; an ashtray on the carpet; a spindled chair lumped with clothes.

"Honey," she says.

Dennis slips inside. "Yeah?"

"What happened in Hawaii?"

"Don't tell Dad," he repeats, closing the door.

Night in Louisiana is a liquid. Above the hospital parking lot, bats cut like frenzied fish; moths foam the streetlights. It's cooler inside, but Doc's passage down the hall still feels delayed, the air resisting his limbs. The elevator rises like a diving bell. In her room, Dani's hair spreads across the pillow in a weightless burst.

Josh and his parents—Burt and Marianne, a big, pleasant, ruddy couple Doc met during a previous visit, just as plump and drawling and warmly bashful as their son—are there already. They step outside, giving Doc and Dani a minute alone. His hand goes to her forehead.

"It's not a fever, Dad."

He tries a smile. But the sight of her, sunk in bed with pale cheeks and a confused expression that masks her pain, reminds him of the little girl to whom he would read winding fantasies of travel and danger—*The Lost World, The Hobbit, Watership Down*—until she slept.

He received the call this morning: she'd entered labor a week ahead of schedule and three days ahead of the flight he'd booked. At the tiny airport in Asheville, he was told he wouldn't be able to leave before tomorrow. Waiting there or driving to Charlotte and hoping for a standby seat seemed impossibly passive. So he got into his truck and drove first to Win's, to drop off Little Star, and then to Atlanta and turning southwest, angling across the piney desolation of central Alabama and the casino glare of the Mississippi coast, stopping only for gas. And here she is at last, another contraction arriving, hooding her face, cranking pulleys in her neck.

So he presses his hand to her forehead.

"I was sure I wouldn't get here in time."

"Well," she says, her expression turning inward, so that even with his hand on her forehead she seems hopelessly distant, "welcome to the party."

Not twenty minutes later, even as a doctor discusses the decision to suppress or induce, the process begins in earnest. Doc and Josh's parents are ushered to a waiting room. Plastic plants and vinyl chairs. On the wall, a sailboat in oils, tacking into the wind.

"Never gets easier," Burt says. His huge, soft hands lie in his lap like a pair of kittens. "Wasn't easy the first two times, with Tank."

"Tank?"

"Thomas," Burt says. "Thomas the Tank."

Josh's older brother. He lives in Albuquerque now with his wife, a Russian woman.

"Belorussian," Marianne clarifies.

"Same thing." Burt grins. "But you should see the two of them together. This tiny little thing, this doll. And Tank? Well. He's like us." He gives Doc a shy glance, almost coy. "I'll tell you, it's hard to imagine. That part of it."

They're both watching him carefully—taking his measure, Doc thinks, in a way they haven't until now. Down the hall, something is happening that will cement the three of them far more permanently than before.

"What do you call Josh?"

"Boomer," she says. "Tank and Boomer."

They share a laugh, awkward and tense.

"Do you have a name for Dani?" Marianne asks. "Something you call her?"

Doc considers the sailboat. Motel art, the painter's one trick a curling, waxy buildup to the waves, an added layer of paint imbuing the water with motion and force that the sailboat lacks. Compared to the ocean that resists it, the hull's an eggshell, the sail a cloud.

"Darling," he says.

When Dani was small, Doc used to tease her about her dolls. Dry fluffs of hair, smooth pink skin, molded expressions of contented placidity—these weren't babies. "You know what you looked like?" he'd ask. "You know the look on your face?"

This one's the same. Waterlogged white skin scalded into scarlet patches of stress and fright, a mandrill's cinnamon mane, scrunched features shifting between righteous indignation, anxious inquiry, and walled-off refusal. And yet the body fills the crook of Doc's arm just so, like an ingeniously carpentered joint. He cradles the child to his chest.

Josh, who has been taking pictures of everything, takes another.

Here is Doc's grandson. His name is Ezra.

John Quick woofs once. Parker appears, crossing the lawn with
a military stride, double-time. He kicks at a branch torn from
a maple by last night's storm, but it tangles his feet. He grabs
it, snaps it over his knee, and whips the pieces from his path.

"Parker," Margaret calls. "Good morning."

She could be wrong. It must be nearly noon. At four in the
morning she sprang awake to thunder over the valley, rain sheeting down, and the timorous shifting of John Quick beneath the
bed. It was as though she were waiting for something: she'd
opened her eyes in a state of electric dread. And then, following
a gust that set the porch screens buzzing like hornets, she heard
it: a tremendous wet splintering, the *whump* of an enormous
body throwing itself to the ground. The whole house shivered.
She rose. On the porch, rain slithered through the screens in a
mist. Lightning revealed the yard, shrunk to the size of a room
by the storm—and there, in a corner of the room, a fallen body.
The barn.

The screens buzzed. The room went dark. John Quick buried
his nose in her hand.

She returned to bed, dripping, and slept as if drugged, waking
late to suffocating Sunday heat, pollen-colored sunlight, and
her phone ringing one last time. She ate breakfast, paused to
consider the iridescence of a June bug that had found its way to
the table—its tiny, wet-wood scent—and made her way outside
to survey the damage.

"I've been calling," Parker says. "Where the hell have you
been?"

"My barn fell down." Margaret hasn't seen him in many
weeks, and she's pleased to discover that the interval has diminished him. Or perhaps it's simply that he's here, on her land,
where she can name the flowers, where the rustle beneath her
feet when she reads on the porch is the resident black snake
dreaming of rats as he sleeps in a coil, where her dog stands loyal
by her side. Parker was always big, but now he seems excessive,

the body beneath the clothes slackening, dripping from the bones. Only his face remains firm, an expression of concern laced with disapproval—Parker has never managed to summon the former without the latter—that suggests she's to blame for the shingles and boards strewn about the yard.

"Dennis is gone," he says.

"Gone?"

"I thought he might have come here." Parker bends to pick a loose nail from the grass. He says, "Margaret."

They walk back to the kitchen. Dennis hasn't been returning his texts or calls, Parker says, not for the past several days. This morning, Parker visited his apartment. When his knock went unanswered, he let himself in. "The place was a sty."

This much doesn't disturb Margaret. Without bothering to ask, Parker grabs a Mason jar from the drainboard and fills it at the sink. His throat bobs as he drinks. Margaret watches him consider his surroundings. A cobweb puffs in a cornice. He sets the emptied jar on the counter and worries the point of the nail with his thumb. He's wearing pleated khakis and a wine-colored golf tee damp at the armpits, bulging in a humid roll above his braided leather belt. He aims his paunch at her. "He hasn't called, e-mailed, anything?"

"Not for a week or two."

"A week or two." He flinches at the imprecision.

"Just tell me what it is, Parker."

"Beer cans everywhere, dirty clothes. The whole place stank like yeast. Marijuana, too, I think." He eyes her. "Not that you'd probably care about that."

Toward the end of their marriage, there was a bad evening when Alice, hearing something in Margaret's voice on the phone, came over with a swirled glass pipe and a plastic baggie, an indulgence Margaret hadn't allowed herself since college. When Parker came home, he stood in the doorway of the den where Margaret and Alice had sprawled across the furniture, sniffed the air, and said, "You two ought to be ashamed." And Margaret, to her horror, found that she was. The weight of his gaze could shame her.

Now she says, "Fuck you, Parker."

He actually recoils.

But her triumph is short-lived. He passes the nail from one hand to the other before bulling ahead. "So I shake some clothes off a chair and sit down, and I call Ryan. 'Heard from your brother lately?' And he says, yeah, he has. Just last night Dennis calls, sounds like he's in a bar. 'Are you good? Are you happy?' Dennis keeps asking. 'How about Stephanie?' And then he laughs—real slow, Ryan says, like water pouring from a jug. 'What's she wearing?' he asks. And when Ryan asks what the hell, Dennis hangs up."

"So he was out at a bar last night," she says. "Maybe he stayed over at a friend's place."

Though of course things between Dennis and his friends haven't been so good lately.

"Maybe," Parker allows. "Could you just try calling him? He's not answering for me."

Seven rings, then voicemail. "It's Dennis," Dennis's voice says. "Leave one."

What can she leave besides her number in his MISSED CALLS list? Margaret hangs up.

"What do you think?" Parker asks.

His uncertainty troubles her more than anything: Parker is actually worried. As long as she's known him, Parker has had his *concerns*, his burdens, his bothers—but he does not, as a rule, worry.

"I'll keep trying," she promises. "Meanwhile, Parker, I'd appreciate if you got out of here."

Just like that, she banishes him—as simply as a dark thought.

Something has changed, though. She leans back, breathing deeply, but the house is too hot for comfort. John Quick, no fan of houseguests, is probably panting on the bathroom linoleum. Stuck to the refrigerator, twitching in a draft, is the card that arrived in the mail a few weeks ago: a birth announcement, the veterinarian and his daughter and the in-laws. The pretty daughter and her husband, baby-faced beneath his beard, hold a fat little newborn between them. *Ezra Arthur.* The veterinarian smiles like his chest will burst. Dennis will call if he needs her— won't he? The nail lies on the table where Parker left it, glinting.

Doc falls from his truck into the barnyard, into the wet heat of the day. Harlan Trimble stands in a haze of exhaust and flying splinters. The chainsaw severs the trunk of the fallen crabapple. The broken tree shifts, the severed section rolling a few feet through the grass. Harlan kills the saw and grins around his tobacco. "Good firewood," he says, shoving sweat across his brow. "Was going to cut it anyway."

Last night's storm has strewn the barnyard with branches, black shingles from the house and dark green ones from the barn, torn leaves, bits of trash. "Hell with it," Harlan says, leading Doc into the barn. He's in a vicious good humor. "Someone else's problem, now."

They are cataloguing Harlan's animals for sale. It's a small herd, the work of an afternoon. Body condition scores, general health checklists, records collected in an accordion file that Harlan will present to his accountant and to the clearinghouse that sells the cattle at public auction. In the barn, Holsteins stand submerged in the heat and their own dull, inoffensive stink. Tails switch; flies circle and descend. An orange cat with a tattered ear leaps the gutter to accompany Harlan and Doc as they work. Harlan aims a lazy kick, but the cat springs aside with the nimbleness of a seasoned mouser and continues along with them untroubled.

Harlan spits. "I'm mean as a bastard lately. Don't pay it any mind."

It's the land sale, he explains. A developer wants to purchase his acreage for a subdivision. They're close enough to Asheville; the price is fair. But the developer refuses to purchase the land at the bottom of the pasture, down by the creek, zoned as a separate lot. "A *floodplain*," Harlan says. "You believe it? Trickle of piss like that? Tell me how it floods."

He'll never sell it, he fears. He'll die paying taxes on a useless strip of land he could piss across. And somehow, of course, the value of the land will still manage to rise as the subdivision grows; somehow, this will end up costing him a fortune.

"That's how it works. That's how they get you. You think you've given it all, everything you've got, but they always find a way to take a little more."

Afterward, Doc leans in the door of the barn, under the drape of muggy shadow. The small of his back aches. At one point, he had to leap away from a Holstein's kick. Less spry than the cat, he may have pulled something. The tufted pasture rolls down to the creek, a wandering line of high grass and dogwoods that by summer's end will be all Harlan holds of this place. It was Noah Trimble's farm before it passed to his son; Doc remembers the old man from years back, when he was fresh out of vet school and hustling to establish his practice, when Susan was his ride-along. Exhausted and sore, he suffers a premonition of himself dry-swallowing aspirin on this evening's cramped flight to Louisiana. But what else can he do?

Starlings foot about in the barnyard dirt. The cat rubs Doc's knee, purring.

"How much you think I can get for this crabapple?" Harlan calls. "Twenty a cord?"

Three days have passed since Parker's visit, and still Margaret can't get Dennis on the line. Time and again: seven rings, voicemail, *Leave one.* Nothing, according to Parker, has changed at Dennis's apartment. Wherever their son is sleeping, it's not at home. "I *knew* something was wrong," Ryan has called to say, more chidingly than perhaps he intends. But he hasn't heard anything more from Dennis either.

Crisscrossing Asheville, Parker has spoken with people who know their son, friends and former coworkers. "No leads yet," he says. "My guess is he's out of town."

No leads. The hard-boiled language of the beat detective. Some part of Parker is relishing this, no doubt. Still, Margaret has to be impressed by his efforts. He's always been rigorous, energetic, willing to exert himself in pursuit of whatever meets his narrow definition of a worthy cause. He can be almost admirable, really, when he's not shaming others for doing differently—for doing, he would assert, less.

"We're his parents," he intones, harumphing, professorial. "We have a duty, a moral obligation . . ."

And what, meanwhile, has Margaret been doing? Calling. Five times today between dinner and bed, she dials Dennis's number, hanging up each time before the beep. It's all she seems to know how to do.

Parker, being Parker, says it's time to go to the police. He will, as he puts it, work his connections there. Margaret prays it doesn't come to that, though prayer isn't something she's ever been very good at or, in better times, particularly interested in. *My son, my boy, my son, dear God*—a constant drumming. She pictures Dennis as he appeared at county lockup, bruised and vulnerable, burning the last of his defenses to make a few small jokes. She missed a chance that night, she thinks. A chance to say something, do something.

"I've fallen behind," she confesses to Alice.

"Behind who?" Alice asks. "Honey, behind what?"

Margaret doesn't know. A cold certainty has descended, incontrovertible, as sometimes happens in dreams: it is late and she is losing. How can she ever catch up?

Parker's fault, she thinks. His visit activated something, flipping a switch she'd very deliberately turned off. She can almost feel the chemical commands circulating in her brain now, the biological imperatives taking over once more, transfiguring her desires. A flickering cascade, old wires sparking after a long dormancy.

My boy, please God, my son—

Tonight, John Quick dozes beside the bed while Margaret ponders the net of shadows falling from window to floor. Around midnight, she calls twice more, five minutes apart. Twice she hears her youngest son's recorded voice. *Leave one.* She leaves nothing. Whatever she needs to say, it seems, she needs to say it to a warm ear. His phone rings and rings, unanswered. Margaret dials and dials.

The dog dies. It's not dramatic. The head lowers across folded paws. The breath trails away, and the eyes close like a doll's. A relief: no empty stare for Win to face as she disposes of the needle and, together with a volunteer, bags the heavy body and hefts it to the chest freezer, where it will await transport to the state incinerator, to be reduced a single plume of ash, lighter and softer than feathers, adrift above the Smoky Mountains.

It's nearly eight in the evening. Thirteen hours ago, she arrived at the shelter knowing what would have to be done today. Cancer: Doc Jeffries provided the verdict last month. A mobile ultrasound unit revealed tumors strung like panicles of milky flowers over the liver. Still, Win waited as long as she could— until the dog's eyes began to yellow, until the skin beneath his fur began flaking away. Old mutt, problem animal—part Carolina dog, part Plott hound, and who knows what else?—he'd lived at the shelter for nearly two years. No one would take him. He dragged his locked, arthritic hips around his kennel to keep his teeth pointed at visitors, emitting a low diesel rumble at anyone who made eye contact. He'd suffered all his life, and suffering had turned him fearful and wretched. It was too late for him to find another way. Win didn't mourn the diagnosis when it came, only what it meant she'd have to do.

Still, she wanted to give him what time he had left. For weeks, she braved those teeth. The dog had an uncanny ability to detect pills hidden in hot dogs and marshmallows and pieces of cheese; he couldn't be coaxed or coerced into swallowing. So Win slipped into his kennel day after day with soft words and treats, settling to the cement floor and awaiting her chance. She sank needles so expertly he never noticed. He allowed her in for a minute at a time, long enough to accept her offerings, but he never came to trust even her; each day she entered the kennel to fresh threats rasping like a saw in that bristling chest. She avoided eye contact, scattering little treats. "Who hurt you?" she whispered. "What did they do?" She pictured the old fractures tracing those hips, the tumors sinking roots from organ to bone. The dog moaned, lapping a treat from the floor and offering her daily opportunity with the needle.

Today, it wasn't carprofen.

"Let the vet do it," Win's wife implored her this morning. But of course Alice must have known the request would do no good. Win did not have to say it had to be her; they both knew it. "I'm on the front lines," she remembers telling Alice years ago, back when they were first getting to know one another. It was what she'd chosen for herself. She was a soldier.

Saying things like that, making her grand pronouncements, Win has sometimes felt herself rise, shining and tall. But of course it's different, deflating, down in the muck of the day-to-day. The late-summer sun saddles a cleft between hills. Trees crowd the road, but their long shadows all seem to bend away from the car, which fills with a heat the air conditioner can't dispel. She's not watching the road; she's watching the dog die. Again and again it happens behind her eyes. A mile from home, she rolls through a stop sign at the juncture of two country roads and a squad car materializes, the world cascading with light.

"Officer," she says, "please. I live up the road. I'm almost home."

A pale young face leans down, innocent as a flower springing from the black uniform shirt. Despite a badge thick as a slice of bread, the fat heel of a pistol at his hip, and the little canister of pepper spray's waspish gleam, his expression strikes her as somehow childlike: a child's perpetual surprise, a child's simple faith in right and wrong.

"Deputy," he corrects her. "And what you did was against the law."

"The law!" Win hears herself cry. Who can live among people so inflexible and true? "Please," she says. "I just want to go home. Just up the road. Home."

He stares—and then, miraculously, shakes his head and shrugs.

"Drive carefully, ma'am."

Let off with a warning: the evening's first blessing.

Awaiting her at home are others.

The outside dogs come tearing around the corner of the house or down from the porch or out from beneath the shaggy hazels, thumping alongside the car as it rolls up the drive. As soon as she opens the door they're upon her, all paws and hot breath, weaving around her legs as if to guide her away from the front door, to sustain her presence in their world just a little longer. They press to her thighs, waiting for her hands. Behind the house, bells are ringing: two she-goats will be tripping along the fence, craning their necks to see. The potbellied pigs will be blissed out in their wallow, the booted bantams scuttling for roly-polies in the dirt nearby. Win makes her way to the house. A bickering clutch of guinea fowl roll through the yard like speckled balls.

Inside, a cat springs away from the swinging door and ripples down the shadowed hall, where another peers through the crack of an open door like an elderly neighbor. Tetras swirl in their tank above a little catfish who meditates atop a log. In the den, a pair of canaries interlock arpeggios, and from beyond the curtain of evening light that leads to the back porch comes the pure, piercing scream of a macaw.

"Sit," Alice says, setting a plate in front of her. The kitchen window's stained-glass upper sash is as full of dancing colors as the fish tank. The plate holds a stir-fry of tofu, garden vegetables, and rice noodles—as well as a fat scoop of buttermilk mashed potatoes.

Win's guiltiest, most secret pleasure.

"Stopped by the steakhouse on my way home," Alice says, sitting beside her. "I know what kind of day this was."

From her bed by the pantry, Bella, a wizened old Lab-husky mix, raises her head to watch them eat. Years ago, she leaped from a car as it sped down the interstate—or, more likely, was shoved, unwanted, out the wind-filled door. One forepaw is missing, one eye white-webbed and blind. But when she catches Win looking back, her tongue flops out. She smiles.

Little Star is here, too, Doc Jeffries's terrier—they're watching her while he visits his daughter in Louisiana—sitting beneath the table, between Win's feet, gazing up at her with a steady, gnomic intensity that tells Win handouts are usually forthcoming at the veterinarian's meals. He spoils her.

Win offers the dog a small swipe of potatoes from her thumb.

After dinner, she walks the property, checking on the animals in a dusk the wavering gray of moth wings. The outside dogs escort her, a smelly phalanx. The goats lip halved apples from her hands. These are her rescues, come to her either through the shelter or through Doc Jeffries. Haphazardly, almost at random, she has managed to save some lives; she's done that much, at least. Behind the back porch screens, she offers a shoulder to the macaw, who accepts it with sharp, articulate feet. During the day he likes to preside over the backyard and pasture, screeching orders and rebukes. Now, as she carries him to his cage for the night, he seizes her ear gently in his powerful beak and presses his firm tongue to the lobe like a secret.

In the den, Alice takes a bottle of Bulleit from the sideboard and splashes a finger's worth into a pair of glasses. And as Win accepts her cup and sees, above it, the face of this woman who wants to share a drink with her at the end of a difficult day, it occurs to her that she has heard humans called "the commemorating animal." This may not be strictly true—she thinks of dolphins nosing their dead through the sea—but there is something awful and intimate about this moment that may, in fact, be uniquely human, a blend of emotion that she loves but would wish on no other creature.

Alice raises her glass. "My dear," she says. "My life."

"*Prost!*" Win answers, a benediction and a plea, meaning *May it be good.* She's forever turning to the future in this way, imagining perfect possibilities even as the present grows worse and worse. In a few months it will be 2020, a year that sounds like clear vision. An election year, a fresh start. But does Win really believe this—that the world can yet be redeemed? Or does she just want to close her eyes and drink?

The clink of glasses startles the canaries, who sing.

Later, as Win and Alice pull back the light summer counterpane on the bed, Bella comes wobbling into the room. Pursuing her own uniquely canine calculations, she has chosen to sleep with them tonight. Win gathers the dog into her arms. Her body is exactly the weight of the body in the freezer. The old dog curls, nose beneath tail, and Win turns to bury her face against Alice's neck. "I know," Alice says. "I know." They both have work in the morning. One hand strokes circles into Win's jerking shoulders. The other sets the alarm for tomorrow.

All night, Doc's tossed and turned, trying to arrange himself around the glinting anxiety in his gut. No good reason for it. He's in Burt and Marianne's guestroom—Tank's room, once. There's a Saints poster over the bed, an inexpertly glued model of a Plymouth Barracuda and a thicket of wrestling trophies atop the dresser, a bookshelf of Matt Christopher paperbacks and back issues of *Bassmaster*. Doc recognizes the peculiar fond dereliction of objects abandoned by a grown child, beloved but unmissed. The bed's comfortable enough. Several times, he's drifted off—lulled, oddly, as if by a presence, as if he were not alone in the bed—but something always wakes him, a sudden pain.

It's early morning now, the end of his stay. His flight departs at noon.

Across the hall sleep Dani, Josh, and baby Ezra. They always sleep like that, it seems—the three of them together, all in one room, despite Tank's perfectly good bedroom sitting empty. Dani's insistence, Burt suggested the other afternoon, as they sipped sweet tea at a park bisected by a backwater canal of the Bayou Lafourche. "That little boy's all *hers*, I'll tell you."

Dani and Josh are living with Josh's parents. In a few months, they say, a year at most, they'll move back to New Orleans. The city has a hold on their imaginations; when they speak its name, Doc senses the outlines of a dream they've constructed for themselves. What can be done? Josh's parents call Doc with their concerns, Marianne and Burt on FaceTime, their round faces filling his phone. "It's a big damn city," says Burt. "If it's just the two of them, sure, but what about the baby?"

"It's their life," sighs Marianne, "not ours."

Doc closes his eyes, trying one last time. He sees the backwater canal of the bayou, utterly unrippled, blue where the sun strikes it and brown in the shade. His sweet tea is cold. Marianne packs the remains of lunch into a cooler while Burt sits beside him at the picnic table, his t-shirt darkened by a round patch of sweat like a bullet hole over his heart. Their children stand together on the shore, the infant's head poised perfectly between their own. Beyond, the vertebral curve of a highway bridge curls over the water and descends over farm fields and distant petrochemical tanks, white as stones. Silhouetted against the tanks, tiny figures cross back and forth. Some of them stop, turning to look. And it is here that the part of Doc that remembers he is lying in bed registers the soft descent of a familiar weight beside him, and this part of him cries out, *Almost, almost!* The water prickles, a sudden wind lifts his daughter's hair, and a gull wheels overhead on black-tipped wings, tilting to consider him with its feral, red-rimmed eye.

He springs awake, his heart wrung out by some terrible anticipation.

He is alone, and the baby is crying.

Voices whisper. A light turns on, then off. Across the hall, the door creaks open, and the cries drift away from the bedrooms, toward the front of the house.

Doc rises and steps into yesterday's jeans, following a sudden, encompassing desire: Dani. Perhaps it's the dawn, poised at that delicate, ashy hour when time hardly seems to pass, but he thinks that if he could only stand with her for a few private minutes in this strange place—just him, his child, and her child—that would be enough. It could sustain until the next time, whenever that might be.

But Dani is asleep. From the hall, through her half-open door, he recognizes the form in the bed, just as immediately and automatically as he's always been able to recognize it, through all its incarnations over the years. He hovers at the door a moment. She doesn't stir.

For the rest of his life, Doc will never see his daughter often enough again.

He floats to the front of the house. Not a floorboard creaks beneath him. In the living-room recliner rest Josh and the baby, slowly rocking. Captured in the archway as though beneath the dome of a bell jar, Doc lingers unseen. The young man wears only a pair of basketball shorts; the baby wears only a diaper. They press chest to chest. The young man's head is bowed, his lips moving against the baby's hair. In a soft, husky, quavering voice, he sings wordlessly, tunelessly—almost moaning.

It's like being a ghost: unmoored, drifting through time, witnessing an unremembered morning from his own early fatherhood.

He slips outside, across the yard, into the street. It's an open neighborhood of modest clapboard houses, spindly trees, aboveground pools. The streetlights are powerless against the brightening sky—a larger sky than he's used to, one that hints at the vastness of the American West. During veterinary school, Doc spent a yearlong externship in Missoula. On days off, he'd hike the hills surrounding the small brown-and-white city. The shadows of clouds poured across the valley, the Bitterroots marched away in echelons, and Doc, who was not yet Doc, doubled over, gasping, his hands on his knees, his lungs seared by thin air and the impossible scale of his inheritance.

He is doubled again, gasping again.

His phone still sits in his pocket from yesterday, and it's the simplest thing in the world—reflex, really—to reach for it now and call Margaret Quick. For months, he's found himself returning off and on to their conversation, that story about her boy's appendectomy, the understanding between them. *Goodbye to that whole cup of trembling.*

The phone is ringing.

First she says hello. Then she says his name. Finally, she asks if he's all right.

"No," Doc says, "I'm not. I'm not."

"What is it?"

There's too much to explain—his whole life. He stands there, panting into the phone, on some level aware he must sound ridiculous, even disturbing. He awaits the click of the severed connection.

"Shhh," she says. "Hush, now, hush."

The strangest thing: bit by bit, this actually helps. Small words, fond noises, the little humming sounds he himself makes, at work with needle or scalpel. Like an animal, he absorbs these with a bare understanding; afterward, it's impossible to recall what, exactly, was said. But it must count for something. Slowly, the weight of his grief shifts, until he can stand straight once more. The world reasserts itself, refusing to be long forgotten by any living thing. Light comes streaming over the rooftops; the sun rests on the same low branch of a loblolly as a red squirrel, carelessly perched, twitching its tail. A white pickup rolls by—Doc has to step out of the way—and the bearded driver turns to stare. Doc waves, suddenly sheepish. He registers his own relief, yes, but also and perhaps more durably a sort of wry resignation, the embarrassment of being, after all, only human—wandering down a street of unfamiliar homes, asking a blessing from a stranger.

"Hello?" she says. "Are you still there?"

"I'm sorry for calling."

"No—don't be."

"I'm sorry," he says and hangs up.

Almost immediately, his phone vibrates. But it's not Margaret, calling back—it's a text from Win, who has apparently forgotten the hour's difference between them. A photo. His dog, Little Star, rests in a posture of glum alertness in Win's kitchen, her mustachioed nose aimed at the front door. *Waiting for you*, Win's written. The stubborn, silent patience of small terriers, their minds fixed on the only thing they want.

Doc texts back: *Tell her I'm on my way.*

Nothing to do now but go back to the house and pack. He'll be home by midafternoon, home with his dog. There will be farms to visit in the evening, appointments to keep. He's no braver than he ever was, no wiser or more accepting. Just tired. But simply to step through a door, to commence the responsibilities of the day, may be itself a kind of rest.

"I'm sorry," he says again, this time to the world.

Everywhere, the thoughtless morning forgives.

Margaret collapses into a chair on the back porch, trying to tamp down the beating of her heart. She has to be at work in an hour, which means she'll need to shower, dress, apply makeup, try to eat something. But when John Quick nudges her dangling palm, it's all she can do to make her way to the screen door to let him out. She falls back into her chair, dead to all birdsong and the wind in the leaves.

This morning marks a week since Parker's visit. Last night

she slept fitfully, waking every hour or so to dial her son. In the
dark, she could admit to herself this was getting out of hand.
She was ridiculous, aflame with anxiety, the light from the phone
blazing against her cheek. Around four in the morning, her phone
finally chirped in response.

ill call today

Just that. Already, her relief is shading into apprehension.
Whatever comes next, it will mean the end of this new life, this
period of blissful drift. Dennis has seen to that. An *ill call*, indeed.

She spent the night on the back porch, listening to crickets
and occasionally the radio, sipping tea. John Quick lay at her
feet. The phone, finally ringing, flung her from a doze.

But it was the veterinarian, Dr. Jeffries.

She thinks his name once, firmly, as if to test it. His real
name: *Arthur.*

It's not an easy thought to have. The man's a usurper; he has
no claim on her. He intercepted the comfort meant for her son.

No, worse. Something in Margaret, traitorous and uncon-
trollable, welcomed him.

She can guess his motives. She has, through Alice, gleaned
few things about his history, his situation, what Parker might
term his particulars. And it's true that, in one or two moments
of perilously unguarded mulling, she's compared him favorably
enough to that other man at least—her ex-husband, the second
great love of her life after Alice, the one against whom it seems
she still helplessly measures any man she meets.

Which is only to say, finally, that Arthur Jeffries has been in
her thoughts, off and on, in a way that at least begins to explain
why, when she heard pain in his voice and the supplication that
accompanies pain, her whole body lifted in response.

Now, when Dennis does finally call, she'll have to summon
it all afresh—the ridiculous tenderness that always leaves her,
as now, shaken and spent, faintly humiliated, as if publicly toppled by a wave she should have seen and avoided. The prospect
wearies her.

She'll do it, of course. Within an hour, she'll be guiding numbers safely through their spreadsheets while her phone waits to fill with Dennis's voice.

And then?

No climax, she's sure, no sudden turn, no miraculous new life for anyone—just, at best, a resumption. She'll gather the burdens she scattered, coming here. They'll be just as heavy as before. Heavier, in fact, freighted with new additions.

"Quick! John Quick!"

Margaret leans at the open door, calling.

John Quick emerges from behind the ruined barn as if bursting from it. Here is a greyhound in furious motion, his body abandoned with reckless joy to its purpose. If he's not as swift as he once was, if there's rust in the load and spring of his spine, a limp in one paw that renders jagged what was once smooth, these things are simply reminders of the morning at the shelter when he became hers. When she became his.

"He only has a few years left," Win said. "He deserves good ones."

The dog arrives, leaning against her thigh and gazing up with all the devotion a greyhound's heart can hold. She praises and pets him, and when she goes in, he trots alongside her as if this is where he belongs. A few good years. That morning in the shelter, seeking mostly to upset that other woman's expectations—Win, her impossible rival, whom she'll never catch—Margaret placed a bet on herself whose stakes she's just now realizing.

She said, "I can give him that."

NOT FOR NOTHING

The last hinge of heartwood splintered and the tree, a hundred-year-old chestnut cankered with blight, groaned over into the arms of its neighbors, where it was caught and cradled and lifted. The whole thing rotated in a way he hadn't expected, and he barely had time to toss the chainsaw aside before the trunk rolled from the stump and came down across his lap. It drove him once firmly into the earth and bounded back, shivering on the elbows of its broken branches.

He was sixty-four that spring, arthritis in one shoulder, a widower. He owned twenty acres off Pinnebog Road, boarded horses, sat up some evenings with a handle of Canadian Club. Last week he'd called the brother he still kept in touch with and made an unusual comment about his life—how it had long been a matter of settling for less and settling for less, making his peace with each settlement until finally, recently, he'd made his peace with settling for nothing, as everyone had to in the end.

A long silence from the brother. They were not philosophical men.

"Should I worry about you?" his brother had asked at last.

He dragged himself as far as he could. Halfway across the pasture, his shoulder locked up, the pain far brighter and more immediate than the distant dull throb from his ruined legs. He'd glanced at them once before beginning to crawl; what he'd seen had put the taste of metal in his mouth. He closed his eyes now, cheek to grass. One of the horses approached eventually, curious, stepping all around, an old bay warmblood with a sweetly pinkened nose. He could feel the soft earth, pressed down by her hooves, rising beneath him in response.

A young couple out for a drive found him: glorious spring morning, the black bogs shining, a lone horse poised in its pasture—keeping watch, it seemed, over something in the grass. "Not yet," he'd told his brother, and later, much later, learning to walk again on legs braced and caged, he caught himself by his armpits between the parallel bars at the physical therapist's office and felt the urge to rise suffuse him as though forced on his body from a place beyond the pain—but from where, he wondered, and why, if not for nothing?—and shook himself to tears with laughter.

ACKNOWLEDGMENTS

Because I seem to know no other way to write, these stories were written slowly, as though groping forward through a series of dark and unfamiliar rooms, over the course of more than fifteen years. Rereading them means, for me, also reading the hidden history of mistakes and wrong turns I made in the process of discovering, story by story, just what I was doing. So it seems fitting to begin with gratitude for the teachers on whose lessons I relied to right myself as often as I could: Peter Cooley, Josh Russell, Paula Morris, Ellen Gilchrist, Elizabeth McCracken, Peter Ho Davies, Julie Orringer, Fred Busch, Eileen Pollack, and Joanna Scott.

With special thanks to Nami Mun, Sara Schaff, and Jennifer Metsker for their friendship, wise counsel, and inspiration. And to Dave Karczynski, Mike Hinken, Catherine Calabro-Cavin, Michael Shilling, Brad Wetherell, Tiana Kahakauwila, Delia Decourcy, Kodi Scheer, Becky Adams, Jane Martin, and Andrea Lochen, who read some of these stories in their earliest forms.

To the Helen Zell Writers' Program at the University of Michigan, the Fine Arts Work Center in Provincetown, the Kimmel Harding Nelson Center for the Arts, and the Bread Loaf Writers' Conference for their generous support.

To Mary Dougherty and the team at the University of Massachusetts Press, and to Sabina Murray, for believing in this collection and shepherding it into the world.

To Michael Burke and Jordan Backstrom, who offered compassion, perspective, and guidance when I needed them most.

To my parents, Jeff and Janie, and to my siblings, Danielle,

Steph, Kelly, Tim, and Steve, for the love, laughter, and unwavering support. As well as to the Labries, Masons, and Belangers up north for embracing me as one of their own. And to Cerah, who has done the same.

To Georgie, my little terrier, whose long life has nearly spanned the long writing of these stories, for occasionally resting her chin on my toes while I wrote.

And—most of all, for everything, always—to Nicole.

JUNIPER
JUNIPER PRIZE FOR FICTION

This volume is the twenty-ninth recipient
of the Juniper Prize for Fiction,
established in 2004 by the
University of Massachusetts Press
in collaboration with the
UMass Amherst MFA Program
for Poets and Writers, to be
presented annually for an outstanding
work of literary fiction. Like its sister award,
the Juniper Prize for Poetry established
in 1976, the prize is named in honor
of Robert Francis (1901–1987),
who lived for many years at
Fort Juniper, Amherst, Massachusetts.